Cassy tried to ignore the seductive heat he effortlessly generated with mere words. She was not about to answer his provocative questions. She would have liked nothing better than to yell at him, "I don't want you in that way—not anymore." But they both would have known it was a lie.

"It doesn't matter anymore, Gordan. None of it matters. You can't have everything you want. I'm not part of the million-dollar corporation you are used to controlling. You can't have me."

Gordan's muscles went taut as he fought the urge to prove his point by pulling her against him and grinding his mouth against hers. Instead, he lowered his head until he was nearly eye-level with her. "I know how to go after what I want. Make no mistake, lady. I want you back."

PROJECT FLIGHT

BOOK YOUR PLACE ON OUR WEBSITE AND MAKE THE ARABESQUE ROMANCE CONNECTION!

We've created a customized website just for our very special Arabesque readers, where you can get the inside scoop on everything that's going on with Arabesque romance novels.

When you come online, you'll have the exciting opportunity to:

- View covers of upcoming books

- Learn about our future publishing schedule (listed by publication month and author)

- Find out when your favorite authors will be visiting a city near you

- Search for and order backlist books

- Check out author bios and background information

- Send e-mail to your favorite authors

- Join us in weekly chats with authors, readers and other guests

- Get writing guidelines

- AND MUCH MORE!

Visit our website at
http://www.arabesquebooks.com

ISLAND MAGIC

Bette Ford

ARABESQUE

BET BOOKS

BET Publications, LLC
www.msbet.com
www.arabesquebooks.com

ARABESQUE BOOKS are published by

BET Publications, LLC
c/o BET BOOKS
One BET Plaza
1900 W Place NE
Washington, D.C. 20018-1211

First Printing: July, 2000
10 9 8 7 6 5 4 3

Printed in the United States of America

To my nieces and nephew with all my love,
Cassandra Beverly-Goffin, S. Joyce Drake, Samuel Beverly Jr.,
Sabrina Beverly, Ethel (De-De) Lofton, Cheryl Ford,
and Deborah Ford

Chapter One

The soft knock on the open bedroom door pulled Cassandra Mosley's gaze away from the clothes she had been piling on the bed, beside her open suitcase.

"Need any help?" Sarah Mosley-Rogers asked, bouncing her six-month-old son, Kurt, Jr., on her hip.

Cassy's apartment was situated in the rear of the old, sprawling rooming house that the two sisters had skillfully converted into a country inn in the heart of the Bay area. Their grandmother had retired to North Carolina and left the property to them.

In the two years that the Parkside Garden Inn had been open, it had been very successful. The inn was bordered on one side by Oakland, California's Lakeside Park. The sisters maintained their grandmother's extensive gardens and prize-winning roses. Both girls had inherited their love of flowers from the wonderful woman who had raised them after their mother's death. Their brokenhearted father remained in Washington, D.C., where he later remarried and fathered twin boys.

"Cassy?"

"No, I'm fine. Just trying to decide how much to take. Three weeks' worth of clothes is a challenge, even for me. The weather in Martinique is always perfect," she chattered absently, her smile not quite reaching her dark-brown eyes.

The two women looked remarkably alike, from their slim, curvy frames and smooth caramel-brown skin tone to their thick, black hair. Sarah wore hers cut close in a natural style, while Cassy's was cut into chin-length wavy curls that framed her features.

"Cassy, you don't have to go. It won't hurt our feelings if you decide against it."

"But, I want to go. This trip was a wonderful birthday gift," Cassy said, unable to meet her sister's troubled eyes as she automatically took her nephew and kissed his sweet, dimpled, brown cheeks. "He's getting bigger every day," she said, before handing the baby back.

Sarah and her husband, Kurt, had thought of everything—round-trip tickets and a reservation at the exclusive Kramer House and Resort Complex on the Caribbean island of Martinique. They wanted to show her how grateful they were for her taking over the running of the inn during Sarah's difficult pregnancy and slow recovery after the baby was born. The couple was also raising their grand-daughter, Mandy.

Sarah wasn't fooled by her sister's false cheer. Cassy was terribly hurt. Her recent break up with her long-time boyfriend had taken its toll.

"When we arranged this vacation, things were different. We thought you would enjoy going back to the place where you and Gordan met and fell in love. Cassy, as badly as you need a vacation, I don't want you tormented by painful reminders. The more I think about it, the more it sounds like a really bad idea."

The Kramer House was only one of the hotels owned by Gordan Kramer, Cassy's ex-boyfriend.

Adding shorts to the pile of tops and swimsuits already inside of the suitcase, Cassy insisted, "It was a fabulous idea. How could you and Kurt know I was going to break up with the man before my trip? It just happened. But that doesn't mean I shouldn't go back to Martinique."

She folded her arms protectively around her midsection, then added, "I have to do this. It's the only way, Sis, that I'm going to be able to get on with my life." She paused before she said, "I'm sick of moping around here, trying to forget. It's not working. Going back and staying at his hotel may be the only way I can finally get him out of my system. At this point, I'm willing to try anything."

Placing the squirming baby onto the thick carpet of the lavender and ivory room, Sarah caught her sister's arm and tugged her down to sit beside her on the bed.

"Aren't you afraid you might run into Gordan while you're in Martinique?"

Her sister's laugh held little humor. "Not likely! The man is in Atlanta working on one of his projects. Why would he bother chasing after me? We broke up almost two weeks ago, and I haven't heard one word from him. Does that sound like he cares? I don't think so. This trip isn't about Gordan; it's about me. I'm doing what I feel I have to do. Besides, all he cares about is the next project," Cassy sneered. "I need this trip."

"But, Martinique? It's going to hurt being there," Sarah persisted.

"That's the point—to let it hurt and then I can go on, Sis. This whole stupid relationship started there, and I must say my final good-bye there. Then I can do what really matters. I want a home and a family of my own, someday. I'm no different from you. I want a man who can give me those things. Gordan can't give me what I need most."

Her sister squeezed her hand reassuringly.

Cassy had met the African American multimillionaire while she was working on the island as a chef in one of the hotel's numerous restaurants, nearly five years ago. Cassy had been working in Toronto when the hotel manager for the Kramer House—Martinique sampled one of her delectable desserts and hired her on the spot.

She'd been asked to prepare an elaborate meal for Gordan's dinner guests in the kitchen of his plush penthouse suite. That night had changed the course of her life.

"Are you sure about this?" Sarah asked, yet again.

"Yes! Will you stop worrying? Are you sure you can handle the inn without me?"

Sarah, a trained certified accountant, managed the business side of the inn, while Cassandra, an acclaimed chef, managed the culinary side of things. Although they had cleaning and kitchen staff, together they shared whatever housekeeping and gardening duties arose, plus managed whatever else needed to be done as well. The inn had been a dream come true for both of them.

And they had done very well, until Sarah remarried and became pregnant. She had been forced to spend the bulk of her pregnancy in bed. Sarah had almost died during the delivery, and it took months for her to regain her health. Although it was behind them, Cassandra could not help being a little overprotective toward her sister.

"You have managed the inn for more than a year alone; I think I can handle things for a few weeks without you. Besides, I have Kurt and the staff. Since you've decided to go, I want you to take this time and really try to enjoy yourself. Because of you there was no reason for me to worry about this place while I was carrying the baby."

"Speaking of the baby . . ." Cassy giggled as she watched little Kurt wiggling his way toward the open French doors. Sarah scooped him up before he got into the garden beyond.

That wonderful little boy had changed all their lives. He had certainly caused Cassy to reevaluate what was important and take a hard look at what she had yet to accomplish.

Over the years, Cassy had grown in one direction while Gordan had grown in another. And she was honest enough with herself to admit that he was not the only one to blame for the dissolution of their relationship. Things had gone downhill for them, partly due to their individual business demands and partly due to lengthy separations. They didn't see enough of each other. Until two years ago, she was doing all the traveling necessary for them to see each other. Gordan had only been to the Bay area once in all that time.

Cassy bit her lips to hold back a sob. She did not want to think about him and all that had gone wrong with them. It was hard enough to deal with the fact that she had broken up with him on her birthday—her thirty-ninth.

She did not want to remember. Yet, she knew she could not heal until she had gotten him out of her head . . . out of her heart. She told herself that her family's gift of a three-week vacation could not have come at a better time.

"Cassy, have you thought about the fact that Gordan might fly in on business? What then? You will be staying at his hotel."

She shrugged. "It doesn't matter. We've said our good-byes. We both know it is over, so his coming won't make a difference. To tell you the truth, Gordan is the least of my worries. He has obviously moved on emotionally, and so must I," she joked. "The best thing that could happen is if I meet a new man able to make a commitment. Wouldn't that be something?"

Martinique

The plush Kramer House and Resort Complex was situated on a cliff overlooking the sea outside the capital city of Fort de France. The white sandy beach and pier beyond were accessed from a set of sweeping staircases cut into the mountain. The hotel featured beautifully appointed rooms, a world-class gymnasium, five-star restaurants, tennis courts, swimming pools, hot tubs, a lush tropical garden, a casino, and a private golf course, all designed to cradle their guests in first-class luxury.

Cassy walked along the beach, gazing out at the endless blue. She had come full circle. She was back where it had all begun. And she was certain she had made the right decision in coming. It was time to stop feeling sorry over what she could not change. It was time to go on with her life. But how?

She had her share of regrets. She had wasted so many years and given too much of herself. And for what? A broken heart, plus a collection of broken dreams. She had come halfway around the world in order to let go. Was she merely running from her problems? What she felt was still lodged deep in her heart.

She dropped her head wearily as she walked on. The breeze from the balmy trade winds swept in from the sea. She spotted a cruise ship in the distance and smiled. All of it was so magical, so familiar.

A mistake? A new beginning? She hoped for relief from the inner pain that left her heart aching and nights spent tossing as she fought the memories. Perhaps that was the trouble. Maybe she should welcome them to get past them. She had done what had to be done in order to move on.

She was so busy trying not to remember that she had walked this very beach hand and hand with Gordan, that she didn't notice the passage of time. She had been in

love with him for more years than she cared to acknowledge. She'd even grown accustomed to his luxurious lifestyle, which included private planes, limousines, and expensive vacations.

It had been so romantic at first, traveling around the
world to meet him at some exotic locale and spend as
much time as she could with him. He was always so busy,
too busy to come to her—too busy to settle down.

It had taken her years to realize that his business would
always come first with him, for there would always be a
new challenge for him. The only exception was his fifteen-
year-old son, Gordan, Jr.

Well, she had finally had enough of being last on his
list. She wanted more . . . she needed more. She had no
choice but to face the truth. She was not twenty anymore.
She had done the things that were important for her
career. She had traveled and learned from the best chefs
in Paris, New York, Toronto, New Orleans, and Martinique
in order to establish a successful career in the culinary
arts. She had come a long way from that little girl having
to climb on a chair to help in her grandmother's kitchen.

It was time for her to marry and have a baby of her own.
She had wasted enough years on a man who was not willing
to share her dreams.

Yet, because of what she felt for him, it had been the
hardest decision of her life to move on. And their final
good-byes had gone badly. Thank goodness it was over.
Now all she had to do was figure out how to stop loving
the man.

Atlanta, GA

Gordan Kramer was furious. His masculine features were
hard and his jaw tight beneath the cover of a well-trimmed
mustache and beard. He stood at the floor-to-ceiling win-

dows behind his massive oak desk, staring down at the
snarled traffic far below.

"Damn it!" he muttered aloud. How could she have
done this to him—to them? He'd been asking himself that
very same question for the past two weeks and, as of yet,
had not found a satisfactory answer.

He was not a man who could be pushed into doing
something that he did not want to do. He had always been
intense and deeply motivated. He was a self-made man.
There had been no parent there to watch his high school
graduation or notice that he'd gone on to college. He had
worked his way through and hadn't stopped until he had
his MBA. He had done the same for his younger brother,
Wilham. Determined to learn the hotel business, he had
done so from the ground up.

Gordan knew he'd been fortunate. He had loved their
father and adored their mother. Their father had been a
hard-working, dedicated family man who had died too
soon, while Gordan was still a boy. And their mother had
worked herself to death to keep food in the house and
him in school and out of trouble. She had fought poverty
the only way she knew how, by encouraging her sons to
work hard toward a brighter future.

She had also taught Gordan, and he in turn had taught
Wil, how to dream. It didn't matter that Ruthie Kramer
had to scrub floors and clean other people's toilets to keep
a roof over their heads. Both of her sons were very proud
of her. But, like her husband, she had died too young. Wil
had only been eight and Gordan eighteen.

He had worked hard to fulfill his parents' faith in him.
Yes, Gordan had made mistakes along the way. His brother
had become a man he was proud of and respected. Despite
Gordan's disastrous marriage, he'd been blessed with a
wonderful son. He had few regrets.

It had taken years, but by this time in his life, he was

surrounded by the proof of his business successes. His office was situated at the top of an office complex that he owned. His hotels and resort complexes were peppered not only throughout the Caribbean, but around the world.

The two brothers were partners, working hand and hand. Currently, Wil was involved with developing and building a new complex on one of the islands off the coast of Georgia, while Gordan was close to completing negotiations on a prime piece of real estate in South Africa.

He was determined to be in a position to make a difference in the level of poverty and lack of education the indigenous people in the area faced each day. He'd worked for close to three years on this project, and he'd nearly gotten what he wanted. But Gordan didn't feel like celebrating.

His woman, his love, and his best friend for the past four and a half years had just walked out of his life and hadn't looked back. And it was tearing him apart.

His jaw ached from clenching his teeth. He rolled taut shoulders, trying to ease some of the tension in his back and neck. Nothing could ease the pain in his chest, his heart.

"Why, Cassy?" he whispered aloud, trying yet again to swallow the anguish deep inside. "Baby, why wasn't what we had enough?"

It was not as if she did not love him. They had been in love with each other for too long for there to be any doubts about their feelings. But, he would be the first to admit that things had been strained between them for quite a while. They had both suffered due to prolonged separations.

Nonetheless, he had not seen this breakup coming. He felt as if she had cut him off at the knees. She had hurled her birthday gift back at him as if it had been a guided missile meant to destroy. She didn't want it—she didn't

want him. She had packed and left while he had been
numb with shock over what had happened.

When he lifted a hand to smooth over his close cut hair,
he realized he was shaking. He'd just gotten back from
Oakland. Cassy was gone.

It had taken him some time to cool off enough to even
make the effort to go to her. He was not one to lose his
head or even show his temper. He had discovered early
on that he made his best decisions with a cool, unemotional
head. He had taken that lesson into his personal life.

When Cassy had left him, inside he had been anything
but cool. He was not much better now. He saw red whenever he recalled what she demanded of him. She knew the
hell he had lived through with his ex-wife, Evie—how she
had used their son to get back at him for divorcing her.
Evie had nearly managed to destroy his relationship with
his boy, knowing full well that she had been the one who
had ruined their marriage.

Sure it had colored his relationships with women. It had
taken him years to trust again. He had let down his defenses
with only one woman—Cassy.

He wanted her back. It did not matter what she had said
or what he had said in response. He needed her. After a
process of elimination and a few calls, he discovered her
destination. It might take a few days to clear his calendar.
If he had to go to Martinique to obtain that goal, then so
be it. He was not planning on taking no for an answer.

Martinique

"Beautiful, isn't it?"

Cassy, stretched out on a beach lounger, looked up from
the novel she'd been reading. A large straw hat and dark
glasses shaded her eyes from the late morning sun. The
tall, bronze, muscular man standing above her helped him-

self to the vacant chair alongside of her. They had met at the airport and then shared a taxicab to the resort.

"Mr. Foster," she said, trying to remember what he'd told her about himself. She'd been so absorbed in what was going on inside of her that all she could recall was that he was a lawyer from San Diego.

"Adam," he insisted.

"Adam," she smiled. "Yes, it's beautiful."

"You mentioned earlier that this wasn't your first trip to the island. Have you noticed many changes?"

"A few. Martinique is a place one can never forget."

"The sunsets might be one reason." He had striking good looks and close cut hair. His tawny, golden eyes moved leisurely over her soft, curvy length. She wore a lavender swimsuit with a brightly patterned sarong, concealing most of her long, shapely legs.

Cassy looked away. There was no doubt in her mind that he had taken an interest in her. He had clearly stated that he was single and available for romance if she so desired. He'd even gone so far as to hint that he was willing to make a commitment when the right woman came along.

Cassy knew she was not beautiful, but moderately attractive, with her smooth caramel-colored skin and thick, wind-tousled, wavy ebony hair. She was average height and weight, and her features hinted at her African roots, from her small nose to her generous mouth.

In the taxicab, she had seen him eyeing her ringless left hand before he asked her out for dinner. She had turned him down. All her energy had been used up trying to cope with her feelings.

She glanced over at him somewhat uncomfortably. The last thing she needed in her life was a new man—at least not yet. She was having enough difficulty dealing with her hurt after her breakup with Gordan. About all she could handle was friendship. She wanted her heart whole again. And she didn't want to hurt anyone else in the process.

They sat for a time, taking in the activity along the beach, neither of them talking. Adam was busy enjoying the view, which included the woman beside him. There was plenty of time, yet. He was nothing if he was not optimistic. He had climbed to the top of his profession by keeping his eyes firmly rooted on the prize.

"The people at the Kramer Corporation sure know what they're doing with these tropical surroundings, lush grounds, excellent food, and plush hotels."

Cassy made no response. She needed no reminder of the financial wizard who had crushed her heart.

"This is my first trip to the island but I've vacationed at Kramer Resorts in Paradise Island, St. Thomas, and Jamaica. I'm impressed that it was a brother who put all of this together."

Cassy's eyes burned from suppressed tears. "I think I've had enough sun." She swung her legs down.

Adam said nothing, hiding his disappointment. It was not until they were climbing the stairs from the beach toward the hotel's elaborate garden that he asked, "Cassy, could I interest you in lunch before you go to your room?"

Cassy was feeling very alone, vulnerable, and knew she was not at her best. She was tempted for no other reason than to have some company, but she was still exhausted from the time change and the flight. Plus she had not slept very well the night before. "Thank you, but no. Maybe another time. 'Bye, Adam."

Cassy did not look back but hurried along toward the side entrance. She did not breathe easy until she was inside her room on the sixth floor. She leaned against the door, wondering what she was running from. It was certainly not Adam. He seemed nice enough. He appeared to have the qualities most single women wanted in a man. He was single, attractive, friendly, and professionally very much on the ball.

The trouble was he was not Gordan. Cassy did not want to think about the man. Was her sister right? Had she made a mistake in coming back to Martinique? There were so many memories to contend with. She was still so far from being emotionally free of him.

Chapter Two

It was after midnight before Cassy climbed into bed. After tossing and turning for a couple of hours, she gave up trying to sleep, reached for the bedside telephone, and called her own number. Her family had moved into her two-bedroom apartment at the inn for the time being. Sarah and Kurt were not about to be separated.

"Parkside Garden Inn."

"Hey, brother-in-law," she teased. "Everyone tucked in for the night?"

"Just about. Mandy and the baby are asleep. How was the flight?"

"Tiring. I haven't been out of the country in a while. I'd forgotten how exhausting it can be."

"Now tell me how you really are, little sis."

A sob caught in her throat. Kurt was a wonderful man, and he treated her as if they were blood.

"Don't worry. I'm fine . . . really. Has Sarah turned in?"

"Not yet. She's right here; hold on," he said, before

passing the telephone to the woman curled beside him in the queen-size bed.

Cassy couldn't help smiling when her sister's warm voice came over the line.

"Hi, honey. Why aren't you asleep?"

"I'm a little restless. Nothing to worry about. How are things at the inn? Any problems?"

Sarah laughed. "You have only been gone a couple of days. Stop worrying. Everything is under control. You're supposed to concentrate on having fun, remember?"

"What about Susan? Was she able to handle the evening meal?"

"Just listen to you. She has been well trained, as you know, since you trained her. She has been cooking the noon meals for some time now. Shame on you."

Cassy blushed. Susan Willis had been her assistant chef for almost a year now. She knew how to handle the kitchen on her own. And Cassy herself had planned the menu for the next few weeks.

"I'm being silly. Must be jet lag."

"Relax and enjoy yourself. For three weeks you have no one to concern yourself with—no bedroom and baths to clean or meals to prepare or guests to placate or even a garden to take care of. Nothing to do but kick back and enjoy. Don't tell me you've forgotten how?"

Cassy brushed away a stray tear. It was time to stop feeling sorry for herself. Sarah was right; she was here to enjoy herself. It was time she forgot her troubles and concentrated on having a good time. Kurt and Sarah had made sacrifices to do this for her. She did not want them to think that she didn't appreciate their gift.

"You're right. The weather is fabulous. Warm and breezy. It's perfect. Thanks for everything. I picked up a copy of Beverly Jenkins's latest black historical romance."

Sarah was not fooled. "I know you feel that you did what

you had to do. Maybe being away from here will give you a chance to really think. I want you to be happy.''

The sisters had no secrets. They had always supported each other. Not that they always agreed, but love and trust were at the core of their relationship.

"I know you don't agree with me. You think Gordan and I can work it out. But Sarah, please. I had no choice. I did what was best for me. I couldn't go on with things being the way they were between us. It's over. The trouble, now, is that I can't get away from the pain,'' she whispered, around a sob.

"Cassy, if you would only just talk to him and explain how you feel. I know Gordan loves you. Honey, you know how bad things once were between Kurt and me when I moved back to California.''

"It's too late. Gordan didn't want to understand. He didn't try to see my point of view at all. Sarah, he hasn't given me any choice. The final straw was when he gave me those expensive earrings for my birthday and not an engagement ring. It hurt so much.''

"I agree it was thoughtless. But I don't want you to make the same mistakes that Kurt and I did. It took us so long to straighten things out between us.''

"I'm not you, and Gordan certainly isn't Kurt. I don't want to talk about this anymore.''

"Cassy, he flew in.''

"What?''

"Gordan came here to talk to you yesterday.''

Cassy pressed her fingertips to her temple. Her head was suddenly pounding. Finally, she said, "I'm surprised he found the time. Evidently, he was in the Bay area on business.''

"He came to see you.''

Cassy hated herself for asking, but she couldn't seem to stop the words as they flew past her lips. "What did he say?'' She was unaware of the damage to which she was subjecting her lower lip as she bit it.

"Not much. I told him you had gone away on vacation. He seemed upset."

Cassy closed her eyes against the scalding hot tears that ran down her face. "Do you mean was he was angry? It doesn't matter. It's over. Besides, he has Jillian to console him," she snapped, referring to his beautiful personal assistant, whose primary interest was her handsome boss.

"Sis, what if he follows you to the island?"

"Did you tell him where I was?"

"No! But he's not exactly stupid."

"Doesn't matter if he knows. Gordan is a busy man. He has better things to do with his time than chase after me."

"But, Cassy . . ."

"No, Sarah. When I leave here, I will have finally said good-bye to the past. I've kept you up long enough. Kiss Kurt and the kids for me."

"Okay. I'm here if you need me. Love you."

"Love you. 'Night," Cassy said, replacing the receiver.

Oakland, CA

"What is it?" Kurt Rogers asked, looking up from the television. His wife's sudden sob had scowled his handsome features. "What's wrong, baby?" He gathered her close against his chest.

"She's hurting so badly. And I can't do anything to help."

"No, you can't," he said, softly. "Cassy has to go through this alone. All we can do is support her."

They exchanged an understanding look. They had also lived through the heartache and pain that love can bring. But, in their case, they had survived a twenty-five-year separation.

"She's in love with him."

"I know. The question is: does he love her enough to put her first?" Kurt acknowledged. "If Gordan does, he has the fight of his life ahead of him."

"Yes," Sarah said, wiping away tears. "He knows where she is."

Kurt stared at her in disbelief. This woman he knew so well and loved wholeheartedly still had the ability to shock him. He grinned. "Couldn't stay out of it, could you?"

"I didn't tell him. He guessed. Honest. Now the rest is up to him. Do you think she'll be angry with me?"

He chuckled. "Maybe. If you didn't think so, you would have told her that he knows, but you conveniently left that out."

"She's going to be furious."

"I just hope he can pull this off."

"You like him, don't you?"

"Yeah, just like you do. I know what it is to lose your love. He's not the most enlightened brother when it comes to Cassy, but I believe he truly loves her."

"Well, he's known to be a financial wizard."

"In business. When it comes to his personal life, it's another matter. He is a fool if he lets her get away," Kurt said.

"Well, I'm glad you figured out what was really important," she teased, as she ran her hand over her husband's muscled chest.

He chuckled. "Took me long enough. If you and Mandy hadn't moved back to California, we might never have gotten it right."

"I was tired of running. I wanted to come home. The inn was my excuse. Are you sure you don't mind staying here at the inn rather than the ranch?"

"You're here—that means we're here. No more nights

apart for us ever again.'' Kurt dropped his head, his mouth warm and insistent over Sarah's.

She let out a soft moan as she surrendered to his masculine hunger. She loved her sister and wanted no less for Cassy than a lifetime with the man who filled her heart.

Martinique

Gordan's mood had not improved since the day Cassy had walked out on him. In fact, he was more frustrated now than he had ever been in his adult life. He detested ultimatums. That was exactly what Cassy had handed him. It was her way or the highway. He did not have time for this. He had a business to run.

He was near the end of a deal that had been several years in the making. He needed to be in Atlanta taking care of things ... needed to be able to fly to South Africa at a moment's notice, if necessary, to make this deal happen.

Yeah, he could let Wil handle it, even though his brother was up to his neck in problems. He was dealing with the construction of the new hotel and resort complex on their newly purchased Kramer Island off the coast of their home state.

Gordan was known for negotiating his own deals, not handing them over to someone else to complete. That was how he kept on top of his game. He didn't leave others to do his work—not even the younger brother he trusted with his life.

Kramer Corporation had been among the top ten companies featured in *Black Enterprises* and *Fortune* magazines. It was on its way to being number one.

Cassy had picked the worst time to start making demands. He would gladly have given her anything she wanted—except this. That was one of the things he loved most about her and hated equally; she was not interested

in what he could give her. She had made a rule early on
that if it was not Christmas or her birthday, she would not
accept gifts from him.

He had gone along with it because it seemed to mean
so much to her. It was not about money with them. It was
about what they felt for each other. And that was only one
of the reasons why he could not let her go.

"The South African group is very close to meeting our
terms. Wil is concerned that they might not accept our
last offer without you handling it personally." Jillian
Harris, his executive assistant, hesitated before she said,
"Gordan?"

He did not bother to look at the strikingly beautiful,
slim, black woman. He didn't need or appreciate the
reminder of why he should not be in Martinique.

When he spoke, his voice was deceptively soft, cool, and
in control of his temper, which was simmering just beneath
the surface. "Anything else?"

There was not a hint of his feelings. He stood by the
open patio doors leading out onto the wide balcony of his
spacious penthouse suite. The Caribbean night was clear
and balmy, with just enough of a breeze to caress his dark
skin. The sound and smell of the sea were unmistakable.
It was late and he was tired. He was also furious.

"We could be on our way to the airport in a matter of
minutes." Jillian, like all the people close to him, was highly
trained, efficient, and had developed an art form out of
anticipating his needs. What she could not understand was
why they were in Martinique.

The Martinique hotel was the crown jewel in the Kramer
Corporation hotel and resort chain. It practically ran itself,
with Kenneth Kittman at the helm. They had flown in that
evening and would be working out of the small, but fully
equipped, in-suite office.

Gordan slowly turned into the living room. He said nothing for a time, merely raising a thick black brow. His dark skin glowed from good health; his deep-set eyes were piercingly direct as he absently stroked his bearded jaw.

"That's all for tonight, Jillian. I'll see you at nine." His tone was dismissive.

As Jillian quietly let herself out of the suite, she forced herself to swallow hurt feelings along with an angry retort. She had no idea why they were in Martinique. The complex was well run and there were no problems, as far as she knew.

There was no logical reason for them to have flown in tonight with so much going on back at the head office in Atlanta, especially with the sea-island project and the South African deal pending, not to mention the Kramer Corporation everyday operations.

On top of all that, Gordan was more distant than ever. He was not a man to reveal his thoughts. But since Cassy had left this last time, he had been downright frosty.

Jillian scowled. *Cassy!* This had something to do with that country bumpkin. Jillian had never understood what he saw in the woman. She possessed none of the sophistication that Jillian prided herself on having.

What was going on between Cassy and Gordan? Had they finally broken up, as she suspected? There had been no calls from Cassy that Jillian knew of, no plans to meet. Then there had been his quick trip to the San Francisco Bay area a few days ago that had lasted only a few hours.

He'd been quietly furious since Cassy's hasty departure a few weeks ago. Something was up. His anger didn't take on the form of hot and volatile. No, Gordan had been chillingly cold and withdrawn. What if they had broken it off?

Jillian was secretly thrilled at the possibility. If so, it was finally her chance to show Gordan how perfect she was for him. This could be a golden opportunity for her. All she needed was a little leverage to take advantage of the situation.

To her keen disappointment, Jillian was not sharing the penthouse suite with him, which in itself was highly unusual. The penthouse had four bedrooms. For some unknown reason, she was being housed down the hall.

Perhaps, she should be thankful that she was on the same floor as Gordan, in one of the luxuriously appointed suites designed for his wealthy and famous clientele who demanded a certain level of privacy and security. A security guard was posted in the glass-walled office across from the private elevator. No one reached this floor unless they had special hotel clearance.

Although her suite was beautiful, she hated it—because it was not part of his suite. What was different about this trip? Other than the fact that Trudy Jones, his personal secretary, hadn't come along, nothing came to mind.

Jillian considered herself lucky that Trudy, the gray-haired witch, was recovering from a nasty bout of flu and had been confined to bed. Trudy had been with Gordan from the beginning. In fact, the only reason Jillian had gotten the job as his executive assistant was because Trudy had turned it down. She didn't enjoy the traveling and was content with her high powered job in Atlanta. Trudy did not like Jillian and made no secret of that fact.

They worked for a highly successful international corporation. Travel was a necessary part of the work. Since Jillian was a part of Gordan's personal staff, she always had a room in his suite.

Why couldn't he see that they were right for each other? Jillian understood his business dealings, while Cassy had no idea of the enormous power and responsibility he wielded day in and day out. How could Cassy possibly be an asset to him? That glorified cook could never be right for a sophisticated man like Gordan.

"Take it easy, girl," she mumbled, as she let herself inside. She had to be very careful now. She could not afford to mess up. If Cassy was stupid enough to let him go, Jillian was smart enough not to give him back.

Jillian had worked for Gordan for over five years, and as his executive assistant the last three years. And Cassy always seemed to be in Jillian's way. Jillian had quietly groomed herself into the perfect companion for a wealthy, powerful man. She anticipated Gordan's needs before he even asked. She had to work long hours just to keep abreast of his demanding schedule.

Wilham Kramer shared the same good looks and muscular physique as his brother, and he was also single. But he didn't have Gordan's charisma and sophistication. He was a bit too rough around the edges to appeal to Jillian's taste. He actually enjoyed the construction aspects of the work, not even minding getting his hands filthy. Of the two men, Gordan was the one she longed to have.

Unlike the Kramer men, she had grown up with wealth. Her father was a businessman who was a vice president for a Fortune 500 company, and her mother was a highly successful designer. Jillian had been determined to prove to her father that she was just as beautiful and just as smart as her older sister, Pamela. Unlike her sister, she had to earn his love. Jillian had graduated near the top of her class and had gone on to get her MBA. She went to work for Gordan straight out of college.

She had literally traveled the world with him, often spending weeks at a time in some beautiful tropical locale. Jillian sighed. She adored the luxurious hotel lifestyle, never having to prepare her own meals, having round-the-clock maid service.

She frequently did not see the inside of her own Atlanta

apartment for weeks at a time. And she never missed it.
She had reached her career goals; now it was time to
concentrate on a very personal goal. A wealthy husband—
more successful than her sister's stockbroker husband—
more successful than her own father—was what Jillian was
after. Gordan was perfect.

Cassy was a grade-A fool, if she thought she could walk
in and out of Gordan's life. Whatever his reasons for coming to Martinique, Jillian was ready to take advantage of
them. Martinique would be a perfect place for romance.
She smiled, suddenly very pleased with herself.

Jillian could hardly wait to soothe his broken heart. And,
in due time, she would have that sleek panther of a man
purring for only her. Yes, it was only a matter of time. She
would see to it that none of Cassy's calls made it through
to him. After all, he was a very busy man.

Gordan paced the confines of the living room. His jacket
and tie were on a nearby armchair, his shirt unbuttoned
almost to his trim waist. Brandy swirled in the snifter
clasped loosely in his large dark hand.

"Why has she done this?" he muttered, aloud.

He thought she was happy with the way things were
between them. She had given him no reason to suspect
she was unhappy with their situation.

They'd been involved for too many years for her to
spring something like this on him. All of a sudden she had
decided that they had nothing in common, that they came
from drastically different backgrounds, that they wanted
different things out of life.

From the first, she knew how he felt about marriage.
They had no secrets. He had told her about his disastrous
marriage. And they had been happy without it. Or at least,
he had been.

"Why now, baby? What made what we have stop being enough?"

But he knew the answer. It was the baby. Her nephew's arrival had caused her to evaluate her life and find it lacking. She wanted a baby and was not about to have one without the benefit of marriage.

"The only thing I can't give!" he hissed with frustration.

He would not let himself so much as think of what it would be like to have another child—a daughter as beautiful as Cassy. He carefully put down the untouched brandy rather than his preference to hurl it across the room.

He paced from one room to the next. He took no notice of the opulence and beauty of the furnished living room, the fully equipped office, the large bedrooms, elaborate kitchen, or dining room. Every one of the Kramer hotels had this same suite available for his or his brother's convenience. None of it mattered. Nothing could change the unrelenting sense of loss he had been forced to live with for weeks.

His long body was tight with tension as he walked out onto the balcony, hoping the night breeze would soothe his heated flesh. The distant palm trees, the fragrance of floral potted plants around on the balcony, nor, for that matter, the sea itself held much appeal.

"Cassy . . ."

They had been friends for a time before they became lovers. He'd broken his cardinal rule when he took her to his bed that first time. Never had he become romantically involved with one of his employees—let alone made love to one.

But there was something about Cassy that was indescribable and impossible to resist. She made him laugh. She taught him how to love again—something he didn't think would ever happen, especially after such a bitter, nasty divorce.

How was he supposed to give her up? Did Cassy have any idea what she was asking of him? She'd been distant that last weekend they shared, self-absorbed. While he had been so focused on his work, he hadn't even noticed, until it was too late, that something was wrong between them. Her birthday was on a Saturday. She had flown in on Friday evening.

Nothing had gone smoothly. They had made love that first night—unable to get enough of each other after yet another lengthy absence. It was on Saturday that the trouble began. They had an argument and said things that were designed to hurt the other one. Suddenly, everything that was wrong between them had exploded in their faces.

He kept telling himself that she could not have been thinking clearly when she issued that ultimatum or that she could not have rushed headlong into a decision that could only hurt them both. But there was no mistake.

It was true they had problems. What modern couple didn't? They did not see nearly enough of each other. He accepted his part of the blame for that. More often than not, he was away from his home office in Atlanta, while Cassy worked twenty-four/seven in the inn she and her sister ran together. It had become rare that she was able to get away, to fly to him even for a few days, since the opening of that blasted inn.

Gordan unconsciously ground his teeth in frustration. There was no real need for her to work. He would like nothing better than to take care of her—shower her with gifts. All that he'd asked was that she live with him, share his life.

A bitter growl rose from deep in his chest, as he recalled what had happened when he gave her her birthday present. Perhaps it was the size of the earring box that had set her off? She could have easily mistaken it for an engagement ring. He had given her the box and asked that she consider living with him. When she saw the earrings, she immediately went into a rage, so angry that she grabbed her things and left his house that same night. He was still reeling from the anger and bitter accusations she had thrown at him. She had walked out of his life without a backward glance. He swore beneath his breath.

The trouble was that his feelings for her had not changed. He still wanted her, as much, if not more, than when they'd first fallen in love. Despite their bitter words, he could not get enough of her.

It was shameful, yet true. Every single time he knew she was on his plane on her way to him, his body would harden with longing. Cassy had the ability to arouse him to the point of pain.

Perhaps because she reached him on so many levels? Never had he known a woman who could match his deep, sensual masculine needs to her own femininity and sweet desires. She was not afraid of his power, his potency. Her sweet body fit him like a silk-lined glove.

What had gotten into her? Certainly not him, that was for sure. They had not made love in so long that he hardly remembered the last time. No, that was not exactly true. His body remembered all too well.

Seductively sweet—she was that and more. His shaft thickened with a combination of remembered pleasure and acute longing. He wanted her—this moment. He needed to be inside her and give her the hard, thorough loving they both adored.

How could she do this to him—to them? It had taken nearly a lifetime for him to find the woman who cared about him the way he wanted to be cared about. Why did she insist that she was the only one doing the loving? How could she possibly believe that after all they had shared?

Gordan's hand was on the outside door before he realized what he was doing. He could not very well go to her room at this late hour and make demands. He certainly could not expect to receive a welcoming response. And that was exactly what he needed right now—to be welcomed into her arms, into her soft, sweet body.

Shoving his hands into his trouser pockets, he knew he was not thinking—he was feeling. He had to approach this with a clear head. He'd be better off if he waited until morning, perhaps inviting her to a leisurely lunch away from the resort—somewhere they could talk calmly without emotion.

"Yeah. Tomorrow we'll talk," he promised himself, slumping into an armchair. His long legs sprawled in front of him as he concentrated on nothing more than draining the brandy in his glass. He could wait.

It had been near dawn when Cassy had fallen asleep. And she had slept later than usual. Last night her difficulty had been in dealing with the memories of a happier time. She recalled the wonderful vacations she and Gordan had shared over the years, especially the one in New Orleans. It had been one of the very few times he had not allowed his business dealings to interrupt their time together.

They had concentrated only on each other. They had spent the evenings in a favorite jazz club on Bourbon Street. The atmosphere of the city's French Quarter had worked its magic on them. What she loved most about that special time was that it was one of the rare occasions when Gordan had indulged her, showering her with what she craved—not expensive gifts, but his undivided attention.

They had talked and made slow, sweet love, simply luxu-

riating in only each other. Cassy shivered with awareness
as she recalled what could not be denied—Gordan was a
fabulous lover. There had been nothing hurried about
their loving. It had been a special week—romantic ...
magical—one that she would always hold deep in her
heart.

"Enough of this," she whispered, impatiently. Tugging
on a robe, she stepped out onto the balcony, then filled
her lungs with the fresh fragrances of the island and the
sea. She exhaled slowly, lifting her face toward the warmth
of the sun. It was a beautiful day.

She'd always loved the island. The sky was so glorious—
endless blue, with only a few fluffy clouds floating in the
sky.

"Paradise ..."

What was she going to do to keep herself busy ... keep
the memories at bay?

The intrusion of the telephone ringing surprised her
for a moment. Cassy only hesitated a second before she
hurried inside to answer, certain she knew who was calling.

"Morning, Sis."

"Morning, Cassy." The deep male voice filled her ear.
"Sleep well?"

"Yes ..."

"It's Adam. How are you?"

"Well, thank you."

"I hope I didn't wake you."

"No. What can I do for you?" Cassy asked, her eyes
going to the clock. It was after nine.

"Have breakfast with me."

Cassy hesitated, not sure how she felt about the invitation
or what she even thought of the man. He seemed pleasant
enough, even though a new man was the very last thing
she needed in her life. Shouldn't she sort through her
feelings first before she began seeing a new man?

"You haven't eaten, have you?" Adam asked.

"No, not yet. Adam, we only just met a few days ago. I'm . . ."

He laughed. "And we're both here on vacation. I thought you told me you weren't married."

"I'm not."

"Well, since we're both on vacation, what harm is there in spending some time together? How about a swim followed by a huge brunch in the Terrace Room?"

"Adam, I have to be honest with you. I just broke up with someone. I'm not ready for anything complicated."

He teased gently, "There's nothing complicated about a swim, now is there?"

"No."

"You like the water, don't you?"

"I love to swim. I don't know, Adam."

"Why not? Only a few hours of fun."

Why not? she asked herself, then she said, "I'd like the company. I'll meet you in the lobby, in, say, half an hour?"

"Great! See you then."

Cassy did not give herself time to worry about her decision. Adam was right. This was a long overdue vacation. She needed to relax and forget.

A glance at her travel clock had her moving. After a long, hot shower, she changed into a one piece plum swimsuit, before stepping into cream beach clogs. With a sheer floral sarong tied around her waist, straw hat over her tousled, thick, wavy curls, she tossed sunglasses, a novel, sunscreen, moisturizer, a small brush, a dark pink lipstick, and a beach towel into a large straw tote bag, then looped it over her shoulder.

"It's time to get on with my life—time to make new memories," she told herself, as she walked out into the corridor and closed the door behind her.

She was halfway down the hall when she heard a telephone ringing. Uncertain if it was hers, she raced back, but when she reached her door it had stopped.

"It was probably Adam wondering what's keeping me," she mumbled aloud, then hurried toward the elevator.

Chapter Three

With her eyes closed, Cassy soaked up the soothing heat of the sun. While enjoying the ripples of the ocean caressing along the length of her body as she floated on her back, Cassy softly sang, "Steal away . . . steal away Lord."

"What are you singing?" Adam asked, close to her ear as he tread water beside her.

Cassy had been concentrating on nothing more than keeping herself afloat. "Just an old Negro spiritual. I saw a PBS special on slavery a few days ago. Our people have put down roots all over the Caribbean, and Martinique is no exception. The African influence is evident in the food and intertwined in the French Creole culture. Have you sampled any of the native dishes yet?"

"No, but I'm looking forward to it."

Cassy rolled over and began swimming slowly toward the shore. Once she could touch the sandy bottom, she looked over her shoulder and discovered Adam right beside her.

"Talk about a slice of paradise." He inhaled deeply.

"Mmm."

Cassy was conscious of the man's good looks. Adam was a tall, striking man who received his share of attention from the females on the beach. She liked that he could converse on a wide range of subjects. Yet, he was laid back and relaxed—good company. He didn't make her feel as if she had to keep her guard up, as if he were looking for more than friendship. Adam was easy to be around. It was not necessary for her to remind herself that he was not Gordan. She felt the difference.

"I think I saw that same program you mentioned. Was it hosted by Angela Bassett?

"Yes. Isn't she wonderful?"

"Beautiful." He laughed as they towel-dried themselves, then stretched out side by side on beach lounges.

"Hungry, yet?"

"Yes, but I'd like to dry off first. Adam, tell me about your city. I don't think I've ever been to that part of the state."

"No? It's a great city." Adam went on to tell her about his favorite haunts in San Diego.

Cassy was only half listening; her thoughts were on the bittersweet memories that she was struggling to come to terms with. In her mind, she could almost see herself and Gordan walking this same beach late at night. They had often walked hand in hand—that was, when they were not interrupted by his business demands. It was not often that they could relax and enjoy being together. Their early days, when they first fell in love, were filled with excitement and sweet expectations, before the passage of time brought its own realities.

"Would you consider it?" When she failed to respond, Adam asked, "Cassy? Are you listenin'?"

Embarrassed, she quickly put on her oversize sunglasses, before she said, "Sorry. What did you say?"

"Am I that much of a bore?" he teased.

"There is nothing wrong with you, Adam."

"You're just not interested, are you?"

Startled, Cassy quickly recovered herself. "The problem is mine."

"Would you care to talk about it? Sometimes it's easier to talk to someone you don't have to see again."

She shook her head. "Thank you, but I really can't see how it could help."

"Please, let me be the judge of that."

"It's personal, Adam."

"Problems generally are. Tell me about him."

She shook her head.

"How long were you involved with him?"

Cassy looked away, swallowing the sudden lump in her throat. She was grateful that he could not see her eyes, which had suddenly filled with tears.

"I'm being intrusive. I apologize."

She nodded. "It's something I'm not ready to talk about. Not yet and not here."

"Let's change the subject. How long have you been a chef?"

Cassy's smile was warm and engaging. "Officially, since culinary college, but I have been cooking since I was a little girl. My favorite thing was to help my grandmother in the kitchen. She raised both myself and my sister after our mother died. Our father was so broken up by her passing that he didn't think he could handle two equally brokenhearted little girls. It was years before my father remarried and my brothers were born."

He nodded. "I bet you're a wonderful chef. Have you traveled much due to your work?"

"Oh, yes. I believe you learn the craft by working with some of the best chefs in the world. Experience is the best

teacher, or at least it was for me." She went on to name
the cities where she had lived and worked.

"I'm impressed. Now, tell me, what is your specialty?"

"Pastries. My family is fond of my tropical pie—it's a
cream pie filled with coconut and pineapple and topped
with toasted meringue." She lost her smile when she
recalled that it was also Gordan's favorite.

"Sounds delicious."

She looked away, desperate to push away the painful
memory.

"I'm about dry. How about you?"

"Yes." She forced a smile, reaching for her tote bag.
After applying a fresh coat of lipstick, she brushed her
thick, wavy curls, trying to bring some order before she
finally gave up and placed the straw hat on her head. Once
she had the sarong knotted around her waist, wiped her
feet free of sand, and slipped into her clogs, she was ready.

Adam's smile was indulgent. Other than slipping his feet
into sandals and pulling on a colorful short-sleeve shirt
over his head, he was ready. "This place really gives me
an appetite. I'm not sure if it has something to do with
the sea air or what, but the food here is fabulous."

Cassy laughed. "You'd better be careful or you will have
to work to get the extra pounds off when you get back
home. But, yes, you're right. The food is fabulous."

Busy studying the menu from the open-terrace restaurant, Cassy looked up at the sound of a surprised masculine
voice.

"Cassy! How are you?"

"Ralph!" Cassy laughed, greeting an old friend and the
hotel's maitre d' with a warm smile. Taking his hand and
accepting a kiss on both cheeks, she said, "It's so good to
see you. How have you been? How's Renee? The children?"

He laughed heartily, a big man with a barrel chest and a winning smile on his deep brown face. Although his hair was mostly gray, he had the face of a much younger man. "Everyone is well. How about you? The years look like they have been especially good to you, *Cheri*," he teased.

She had often cooked with his wife, Renee, at the Halleys' home during her time off when she worked on the island. Like Cassy, Renee was also a chef and worked at the hotel. She was an expert on the island's local cuisine. She had taught Cassy how to prepare many of the island's specialties. It was where Cassy had developed a distinct Creole flavor to her classic French cooking.

"I'm well. I must admit I've missed the food, the people, and those beautiful sunsets. You notice I said food first," she giggled.

"We've missed you, *Cheri*. Renee gives it a good try, but you are the only one who can make those scrumptious cream pastries. I'd die for one forkful of your pies."

Cassy laughed. "Thanks. I'll see if I can do something about that while I am here," she promised. "Are André and Ria still working at the hotel?" She referred to the couple's children.

"André is working here. Ria, our oldest, has been promoted to a management position in the Kramer House— Jamaica. And Renee is still head chef in the Martinique Room."

"How exciting for Ria."

The Jamaica hotel was fabulous and Cassy was pleased by the younger woman's success. The Halleys were a very close-knit family and they had made her feel welcome in their home. They remained close friends of her and Gordan.

"Gordan Kramer is a fair man. He remains a favorite with

his employees here on the island. Our economy remains strong and we are proud to have third generation islanders working at Kramer House."

Cassy dropped her eyes. The last thing she wanted to hear was how wonderful Gordan was. She had purposefully postponed her visit with Renee because she was not ready to discuss the situation between her and Gordan. The other woman knew both of them too well. She had known Cassy since she first fell in love with Gordan Kramer.

Cassy reassured herself that all she needed was time to come to terms with the changes in her life. Time would heal the still-painful wounds of the past.

She promised herself that she would see Renee soon and renew their long-standing friendship. Coming back to the Kramer House where it all began was only the first step in her healing process. A few more days was all she needed.

Suddenly noticing the question in Ralph's eyes as he gazed at her table companion, Cassy blinked, embarrassed that she had completely forgotten about Adam.

She quickly said, "Adam Foster, please meet my good friend, Ralph Halley." She watched as Adam stood and the two men shook hands. She found herself offering an explanation. "Adam and I met at the airport and shared a taxi to the hotel."

"Are you enjoying your stay with us, *Monsieur* Foster?"

"Adam," he corrected. "Yes, very much."

"How long will you be with us?"

"I left my return date open. I have no reason to rush back." Adam smiled, but his eyes were on Cassy.

Approached by one of the waiting staff, Ralph hastily excused himself saying, *"Excusez-moi. Cheri*, we'll talk soon. *Oui?"*

"Oui," she nodded.

"I take it you worked at this hotel?" Adam asked.

Cassy chuckled. "Yes. Nearly five years ago. The hotel, as you know, has four restaurants." She went on to name the one specializing in classic French cuisine.

"Sounds like a dream job."

"In some ways. I worked under a master chef and learned so much while I was here. And I made some wonderful friends."

She decided not to mention that she was well known around the hotel, not only because she had worked there but because of her relationship with the owner.

That relationship was a huge mistake that she was paying for in spades. Even though they had been apart for weeks, she still wondered how much longer would it take before the disappointment and heartache begin to fade?

"You're not only a very talented woman, but I have a feeling you're also a fascinating one, Cassy Mosley," Adam said, studying her closely.

Cassy smiled, then picked up her menu. "Shall we see what looks good?"

"Gordan, it's getting late. Aren't you ready for lunch?" Jillian asked. They'd been working since nine, and she was more than ready for a break.

Gordan had emerged from his bedroom, dressed casually in charcoal-gray slacks and an ebony linen shirt, to find Jillian already working in the suite's office. Since she was on the telephone, she had waved her good morning to him.

"Gordan?"

He did not look up from the printout of the financial report he'd been studying. He had drained the glass of mixed tropical fruit juices left over from breakfast. His eyes did not move to his beautiful assistant but to the floor-to-ceiling windows beyond. He was having a difficult time concentrating on the work in front of him.

His thoughts had been so full of Cassy. His temper had eased somewhat. He woke this morning feeling calmer about the situation. Perhaps he had finally gotten over the shock of Cassy walking out of his life? Knowing he had a plan of action seemed to help.

Cassy had claimed that he did not have room in his life for her, that business meant more to him than she did. The trouble was she was unwilling to listen to reason. She claimed to want a commitment. Why didn't she feel that that was exactly what he had offered her? He'd asked her to move in with him. How much more committed did a man have to be to prove his feelings for a woman? Why must it only mean marriage?

What was he going to say when they saw each other again? Fighting over it would not solve anything. He had to keep his temper in check. He assured himself that he would find a way to make her listen.

He had been married before. That mistake had nearly destroyed his self-respect and his manhood. He had vowed to never again give any woman that much power over him. Now all he had to do was to convince Cassy that marriage was not their only option.

Tired of being ignored, Jillian walked over to where Gordan sat in a comfortable armchair and perched on the wide ottoman in front of his chair. She reached out to touch his arm when she said, "Gordan, I have the new figures from St. Thomas. Would you care to see them now or would you prefer to wait until after lunch? Shall we dine in the Terrace Room? It's so refreshing this time of day."

Gordan blinked, before he said, "I'm sorry. What did you say?"

Jillian's smile was beguiling as she calmly repeated what she had said.

He glanced at his gold wristwatch and then the silent telephone. Food had been the last thing on his mind. Cassy had not returned his call. He had waited until eleven, not wanting to disturb her rest. Now, suddenly, he was having difficulty dealing with his impatience.

Even though he was aware that she could be anywhere on the property, he wanted to see her now, wanted to get the entire matter settled between them. Their estrangement had gone on long enough. He did not like the idea that she might not welcome his calls, any more than he liked the possibility that she might not want his kisses and lovemaking.

"Excuse me," he said, rising and going into his bedroom. He stopped at the bedside telephone and dialed Cassy's room. He was scowling when he returned a few minutes later.

Trying not to be obvious, Jillian said, "I take it, you aren't hungry?"

"I'm ready. You?"

He was not pleased that he had no choice but to wait. Cassy would know by the messages that he was in the hotel and wanted to see her. If he did not hear from her by this evening, then . . .

"The Terrence Room?" Jillian asked, closing her compact, assured that she looked her best. She was dressed in a pale-blue linen dress that complimented her creamy pale-brown skin. Her long, deep-auburn hair had been swept up in an elaborate French roll.

"Yes." He waited politely for her to precede him out into the thickly carpeted corridor.

Gordan brooded in his private elevator, all the way down to the lobby. He was accustomed to being greeted by staff, and he normally took time to talk, but not today. He nodded but did not linger as they moved through the hotel.

"Gordan!" Ralph said, pleased to see his old friend. The two men slapped each other on the back affectionately.

"How are you, my friend?" Gordan asked, grinning.

"Good."

"How's the fishin'?" Gordan quizzed, able to relax for the first time that day.

"Great! We'll go out if you have the time." Ralph smiled politely at the lovely lady at Gordan's side, recognizing his snobbish assistant.

Aware of his duties, Ralph escorted them to the center table in the room, which had long been reserved for VIPs. Once they reached the table, he hesitated. "Would you prefer to be seated with your lady?"

Gordan lifted a brow. "Where is she?" he asked, overlooking the menu he'd just been handed and taking note that Kenneth Kittman, the hotel manager, had joined them at the table.

Ralph nodded, indicating the direction. "Straw hat in the purple top," he said, before excusing himself and motioning to the head waiter.

Gordan acknowledged the other man at the table with a nod.

Jillian was not fooled by Gordan's silence. Her gaze had followed his. She placed her hand on his arm, whispering, "What is she doing here?"

"What?" Gordan had been so absorbed in watching Cassy that he had not caught what Jillian had said.

"Nothing." Jillian smiled, reaching for a glass of ice water. She could not stop herself from quietly asking, "Did you know Cassy was here? Is she why we are not in Atlanta?"

Gordan looked at Jillian pointedly, then he rose to his feet. "Excuse me."

"Decided?"

"You go ahead and order first. I'm still making up my mind," Cassy said.

Adam smiled indulgently at her before he gave his order to the waiter. "Your turn."

"Mmm ... I think I will have the crabmeat salad and ice tea with lemon," Cassy finally said, handing over her menu.

"Good choice," Gordan said, dryly. "The seafood is always wonderful here on the island."

He did not care what she ordered, but he did resent the fact that she was clearly enjoying herself with another man.

"Gordan!"

Her eyes traveled up to his dark, arresting features. His coppery-brown skin gleamed with good health, his thick, black hair had been cut close. His nose was strong, while his mouth was wide with full masculine lips, which were framed by a well-groomed mustache and beard that followed the curve of his firm square-shaped jawline.

Unconsciously, she flared her nostrils, as she tried to capture his unique masculine scent. He was so blatantly male. Her head filled with images of the two of them together, locked in an intimate embrace. The tips of her breasts instantly hardened as she recalled the undeniable pleasure he gave her.

She knew every smooth inch of his long, hard body, from his broad shoulders to his deep hairless chest, trim mid section, lean hips, hard, muscled legs, and long, narrow feet.

Their reunions had always been hot—raw with need from long-denied desire. But it was his intense, deep-set, dark-brown eyes that claimed her attention now. She lifted her chin, forcing herself to accept the obvious. He could be ruthless. He was a man known for not stopping until he got what he wanted. Did he want her back? Was that why he was in Martinique? Or was it merely a coincidence?

"Enjoying yourself?" he asked, pointedly, his eyes leisurely exploring Cassy. He gazed into her large, velvet-brown eyes before moving onto her small features, then lingered on full, raspberry-tinted generous lips and down to her full breasts and slim waist.

She was in purple—her favorite color. Her beauty was only enhanced by the swimsuit, which didn't even come close to hiding her seductive allure. He could not see them, but he knew her legs were long and shapely, and her hips were softly rounded.

Although he detested the game she was playing with his emotions, he had memorized every one of her sweet secrets, from the way she liked to be stroked to the way she cried out when she climaxed. She was his, and he was not a man who took kindly to sharing.

"May I join you?" Gordan did not wait for a response but took the empty chair across from the other man.

Cassy glared at him, determined to forget the bitter-sweetness of their last weekend together. She told herself that the erotic things he had said and done while he had made love with her no longer mattered. None of that changed the painful way they had parted. She had to focus on the bitterness and anger he generated within her.

"What do you want?" she asked, tightly.

"You know exactly what I want." He leaned forward, offering his hand to the other man. "Gordan Kramer. And you are?"

"Adam Foster," he said, clearly shocked. "Are you the owner of Kramer Hotels and . . ."

Gordan nodded. "The same. Pardon the interruption,

but Cassy and I have not seen each other in a few weeks."
He asked smoothly, "Are you vacationing with us here at
the Kramer House, Mr. Foster?"

"Yes. Call me Adam."

"Do your accommodations meet with your approval?"

Cassy's pretty mouth tightened with temper. She would
have loved to slap the smug smile from Gordan's generous
mouth. They both knew he was not here because of hotel
business. He had followed her. But she wanted to know
why. Everything that needed to be said had been said. This
was pointless.

Adam looked from one to the other, his curiosity piqued.
"The hotel and resort complex is exceptional, but you
don't need my confirmation."

Cassy had had enough. She placed her linen napkin
beside her place-setting with care, then said quietly,
"Adam, I apologize, but I must excuse myself. I need to
speak to Gordan privately." She collected her tote before
she rose to her full height of five seven.

Both men stood. Adam was tall, but Gordan was taller.

"What about this afternoon?" Adam asked, clearly not
pleased at the change in plans.

"I'll meet you in the lobby around three."

"Good."

Cassy heard Gordan's angry release of air from his lungs.
She chose to ignore it—to ignore him. Cassy walked away,
without a backward glance. She skirted the crowded dining
area, following the pathway through the garden.

Gordan had no trouble keeping up with her. At six three,
his stride was long and purposeful. His temper simmered
as they circled the building.

Cassy was the first to speak. "What do you want? Why
did you follow me?"

Gordan caught her arm, thus halting her progress.
"Why, Cassy? Why are you taking it this far?"

Cassy stared at him. There was no mistaking the frustration and cold fury in Gordan's eyes. "You're wasting your time. I said all I had to say in Atlanta."

"Why are you doing this to us—throwing away what we have?"

"You really don't know?" She shook her head in disbelief, then snapped, "As usual, you didn't hear a word I had to say before I left." She swallowed back tears. "For such a brilliant man, you can be so dense."

Wrenching herself away from him, Cassy ran along the walkway. She had had enough—enough of his thoughtlessness. He had not even known she had been unhappy.

It was probably only after she left that he accepted that they had problems. It was testimony to how out of touch he was with her feelings. What was the use in going over it yet again? It was over.

By the time she reached the door, he was there to open it for her. "Will you stop following me!"

"You've said what you had to say. Now it's my turn."

"I won't go through it again."

She hurried past the corridor, which was lined on both sides with exclusive boutiques that offered everything from fine jewelry, designer clothes and footwear, and local artifacts, to expensive lingerie. Gordan had no difficulty keeping pace with her.

They had neared the lavishly decorated, bustling lobby when he caught and held her arm. He said, quietly, "I'd like to speak with you privately, but if you prefer it can be in the lobby."

Cassy could tell by the angle of his bearded chin that he was not backing down. Gordan intended to have his say.

"Okay," she whispered.

Cassy considered jerking away from him, but realized it

was a wasted effort. Maybe she did owe him that much consideration. Nothing more.

"Where are we going?" she asked.

"The penthouse," he said, tightly.

Cassy did not care where they had this discussion. All she wanted was to have the whole thing over and done with. She stared wordlessly ahead as Gordan escorted her to the private elevator.

Running her hands over her bare arms as goose bumps rose on her skin, she had no idea why she was suddenly cold. She tried but failed to convince herself that it had nothing to do with nerves or the man at her side.

She said nothing on the ride up to the penthouse. She was all too aware of the fact that the last time she had taken this elevator with him they had been lovers. She was also aware of how she looked, in her sun-dried swimsuit, without benefit of makeup, other than a touch of lipstick, and her hair crushed under a hat.

Cassy told herself it made no difference. She had been involved with the man for more than four years. Gordan had seen her under many different circumstances. Besides, he knew her body as well as he knew his own. No matter how ridiculous it seemed, though, she was not thrilled at the idea of having to confront him not looking her best.

Cassy refused to so much as glance at him. Yet, she was cognizant of his brooding, dark gaze. Gordan was a powerful man used to managing and controlling a large, successful corporation. He had built his business from the ground up. He handled huge sums of money on a daily basis. He was also known to be generous. She would be lying to herself if she did not admit how much she admired and respected him, not only because of his devotion to his son and his younger brother, but his fairness and generosity to those he employed.

When they had first fallen in love, Gordan had not hesitated to take time away from his work to get to know her, to win her love and trust. Unfortunately, once that had been accomplished and he had made her his lady, he turned his attention to what was really important—his work. It took her a while to grasp it, but she eventually had no choice but to acknowledge the truth. Gordan wanted her, but only on his terms.

Cassy closed her eyes, trying not to look at him or inhale the pine scent of the soap and aftershave he preferred. She would not allow herself to be vulnerable because of what they had once shared. It was best left in the past. She would not let herself dwell on how it felt to be in his arms . . . in his bed . . . with his body a part of hers.

There were other men in the world. Unfortunately for her, none of them aroused as sensuous a response in her as Gordan. But then, not one of them had claimed to love her and then hurt her as badly as he had.

That pain had not been a small thing. Yet, it had grown until it overshadowed what they had once shared. She wanted that pain to end. But she was wise enough to know it would never end until Gordan was completely out of her system.

Cassy hurried out of the elevator before he could touch her. She did not want his hands on her, not ever again. She walked ahead of him to the tall set of double doors and waited as he used his key-card to let them inside. It was not until they were in the suite, with the doors closed, that she turned around to face him.

"Gordan, I'm cold and sticky. I need a shower, so let's make this quick. I don't know why you followed me to Martinique and, quite frankly, I don't care. I told you how I felt in Atlanta. Nothing has changed."

"Would you care to come into the living room? There are soft drinks, wine—whatever you would like," he said, evenly. His taut mouth was the only clue to how tightly he worked to hang on to his temper.

She was gripping her tote bag with both hands when she said, "Just say what you have to say so I can leave."

Chapter Four

Gordan was careful to keep his hands deep in his pockets. That was the only way he had to stop himself from touching her. He ached to have Cassy back in his arms, yet, at the same time he was angry because he'd found her in the company of another man. He was infuriated by the way she had thrown his feelings back in his face as if he no longer mattered to her.

"Tell me about this Adam Foster. Does he have anything to do with why you want out of our relationship?"

Cassy took a step back as if he had struck her. She knew he was angry; it was in every line of his long, muscular body, as well as etched across his dark face.

"How can you ask me that?"

"Answer me, damn it!" He banged a fist on the hall table. They had not gotten as far as the spacious living room. He caused the crystal lamp and vase filled with flowers, which were resting on the polished surface, to shake and Cassy to jump.

She took a deep, steadying breath. She had never seen him this upset—this coldly furious. Although she did not feel physically threatened, she was uncomfortable.

Lifting her chin, she said, "I met Adam at the airport, here in Martinique. He has nothing to do with what happened between us."

Cassy could not look away from his deep-set eyes and the pain she saw in their depths. She forced herself to drop her gaze. Could it also be anguish she saw in his eyes? How could she hurt him? He would have to love her with his whole heart for him to feel hurt.

No. What she had done was hurt his pride. If he had truly loved her then he could not have let her go. He would have agreed to her terms. And that was not what happened. His refusal was why they were fighting—why she had cried herself to sleep night after night.

"We never should have become involved in the first place," she whispered. "We come from vastly different worlds. It was a mistake from start to finish. But it's over. It's time for both of us to move on."

"Wasn't it only a few weeks ago when we were together that you claimed to love me, Cassy. Or was that also mistake?" His voice was raspy with emotion, even as he inhaled her scent. "We made love over and over again. Another mistake?"

Cassy stared at him before she collected her rattled nerves enough to look away. Her cheeks were hot, when she snapped, "This is not about sex."

"You've no complaints in that department, have you?" He waited, as if he actually expected a response. When she refused to give him one, he clasped her around the waist and pulled her against him. "Have you?"

"You've made your point."

"No, I don't believe I have," he whispered, before he dropped his head in order to reach her soft throat.

He pressed his mouth there at her pulse point, then touched his lips behind her left ear, a particularly sensitive place. She trembled in response before his mouth was hot and insistent against hers, as he gathered her close—so close that her lush breasts pillowed on his chest and his shaft thickened, heavy against her.

"Gordan . . . please. Don't do this." She managed to free her lips from his.

"Why not, baby? It's the only way you'll let me have you," he said, his frustration apparent. "Cassy, you think I don't know that you want me now? Just as you wanted me the last time we made love. It's always been like that between us—hot and sweet."

He had issued a clear challenge that she could not deny. Cassy pushed against his chest and was relieved when he didn't try to hold her. Her legs were shaking, so much so that she had to lean against the table to keep from falling.

She took a deep breath before she said, "What is the use of arguing with you? You never bothered to ask what I need. But then, you've never cared, have you? I don't know why you are here. Just leave me alone. I don't want anything to do with you."

"Ready to run away again, Cassy? It's a whole lot easier than facing the truth."

"What truth, Gordan—the truth as you see it? No, thank you. I have given you more than four years of my life, hoping that you would see how much you meant to me— hoping you'd eventually realize that I'm not like your ex-wife. But it didn't happen. You won't let it. Well, I'm not wasting another day on a man who is afraid to make a commitment to the woman he claims to love." Blinking back tears, she whispered, "Gordan Kramer, I don't want your kind of love. It hurts too much."

He growled deep in his throat. "Hurt! Lady, you talk to me about hurt. I have offered you everything I have to

give and you tossed it back in my face as if it meant nothing
to you. If nothing else I think you owe me an explanation.
Make me understand why, after what we've been to each
other, it has stopped being enough!''

They glared at each other like sparring partners in a
boxing ring.

She threw a hand up in frustration. "There is no point
to all this! It's finished.''

Determined not to let his temper do his thinking for
him, he persisted, "Look, baby, can't we at least sit down
and try to talk this out? You're upset and so am I. Standing
in the foyer yelling at each other is not getting us anywhere.
Please, come inside . . .''

"Why can't you understand? I can't take any more of
this.''

"Cassy . . .''

"Excuse me,'' Jillian said. Having let herself into the
suite, she looked from one to the other.

Neither Gordan nor Cassy responded, their eyes locked
in a battle of wills. The air practically crackled with tension.
Cassy was the first to regain some measure of control. She
forced her eyes away from his, only to collide with the
deep satisfaction in the other woman's gaze.

Cassy raised her chin before she said, "Jillian. How
appropriate.'' The funny thing was she was not angry with
the woman. Why waste the energy? Gordan had always had
the power to choose.

Up until now, Cassy had had the luxury of knowing that
his choice had been her. Suddenly that had all changed
and Jillian was loving every minute of it. She looked like
a fat cat, ready to lap sweet cream. Cassy had not a single
illusion as far as Jillian was concerned. Jillian was more
than ready to soothe Gordan's wounded ego, all the way
to his king-size bed. And Cassy was furious at herself for
even caring.

Gordan said, "Jillian, do you have a reason for being here?"

"But, of course. I'm expecting a call from Trudy on the sea island project. I assumed you would need the information this afternoon. And Kenneth Kittman and his wife would like to have dinner tonight to discuss the hotel. He has quite a few interesting ideas on improving the Kramer House—Martinique. And then . . ."

Cassy had heard all she planned to listen to from either of them. She interrupted, "Don't let me intrude."

She walked past the other woman and quickly let herself out into the thickly carpeted hallway.

Gordan followed, closing the door behind him before he said her name. She had reached the gleaming elevator doors.

Ignoring the security guard in the glass-walled office across from the elevator, Gordan said, "We aren't finished."

"You are wrong," she said, quietly. "We've been finished for quite some time. The problem is that neither one of us could see it. I've stopped running from the truth. I suggest you do the same. Good-bye, Gordan."

Grateful that she did not have to wait for the elevator, Cassy pressed the floor number with a sense of relief. The door closed, as firmly as if a wall had been constructed between them. Yet, that did not explain the tears that filled her eyes and trickled down her cheeks. It was over—finally over.

Just last evening, she had wondered what it would be like to see him once more here in Martinique, where they'd met. Now she knew. It had been devastating. She was forced to wipe her face just before the elevator door opened on her floor. She not only looked a mess, she felt even worse.

As she entered her room, she acknowledged that she had made a dangerous mistake in underestimating the man. She should have known he would come after her. Why hadn't she seen it coming? Sarah had warned her, but she had not taken it seriously.

Cassy had almost convinced herself that Gordan would not care one way or the other, especially considering that she had walked out on him. Why should he? He'd always been too caught up in what was really important—Kramer Corporation.

Why had he come? Was it simply a matter of pride? It had to be, since he had been ignoring her for months, content to wait until she could travel to him. And then there was his all-important South African project that had overshadowed everything—including his love life.

The trouble was that with Gordan there was always another new deal. He thrived on challenges. Money had not been an issue for a very long time with him. He had amassed a fortune. The Kramer hotels and resorts were extremely elegant and lush and were run as flawlessly as any first-class hotel in the world.

"Let it go," she whispered, aloud.

It was time she pulled herself together. Cassy walked purposefully into the bathroom and turned on the shower. She would not waste her tears on him. He was not worth it.

So why couldn't she forget the sweet magic of being back in his arms? He'd held her against his hard length, surrounded by his masculine scent and seductive charm. Her hands balled into fists at her sides.

She should be concentrating on repairing the damage the hot sun and sea had done to her hair and skin— nothing else. After soothing her face with cleansing lotion, she eased under the warm spray of the shower, armed with a tube of shampoo and one of her favorite lilac-scented shower gels. She did not turn off the water until she was reasonably certain that the hot water had soothed not only her taut muscles, but hopefully her tumultuous emotions. Unfortunately, she could not turn her thoughts off as effortlessly as she did the water.

Why had he kissed her? More important, why had it taken her so long to stop him? She needed no reminders of what it was like to be in his bed. When it came to making love, Gordan knew how to give pleasure.

The man had a keen sexual drive and was capable of focusing his total attention on the giving and receiving of pleasure. He knew how to control his own needs until she had reached at least one climax—more often than not, several—before he sought his own release.

He had been right when he talked about their last time together. It had been hot and wild. After they had been apart for a time, they would literally spend days in bed, making love as if it were possible to make up for the lonely weeks of separation.

The extended times they were apart contributed greatly to the friction between them. And her desire for commitment was at the heart of their difficulties. They simply wanted two different things. In this instance, there was no compromise.

Besides, what chance did any woman have against his assistant, the beautiful Jillian Harris? Gordan spent more time with Jillian than he had ever spent with Cassy.

That self-satisfied smirk on Jillian's face had almost caused Cassy to forget her grandmother's home training. She would not let that woman get to her. It did not matter . . . it did not matter . . . it did not matter. Jillian was welcome to the man. Cassy had taken herself out of the race. She no longer wanted that particular prize. She wanted more.

Gordan had made a mistake when he followed her to Martinique. He could not change her mind. It seemed as if all she had done by leaving him was put a big dent in his colossal ego. She'd be making a huge error in judgment by thinking differently. What she had done was offer him a challenge—something he could not resist.

He was so wrong about her. She would fight him if she had to for the kind of future she wanted. She had made the decision that was right for her.

Gordan had placed her last on his list—a position she refused to accept. And, if by some miracle, all that changed tomorrow, it would still not be enough to make her happy. Gordan had nothing to offer her because he'd made up his mind long before they had ever met that he would never marry again. Not Cassy nor his feelings for her were strong enough to alter that decision. And she was grateful that she finally realized it.

Some day she would have a marriage brimming with mutual love and respect. And she would hold a child of her own in her arms. For years, she had not let herself even fantasize because she secretly yearned for Gordan to be her husband and the father of her child.

Deep in her heart, she knew that marriage to him was the only thing she would have sacrificed her career goals in order to achieve. As his wife, she would have gladly traveled the world at his side.

No! It could never happen. And it was long past the time to let go of fairy tales of happily ever after. From now on her dreams must be for the future—a future she must share with some other man. She had to be strong enough to go after what she wanted from life. She had wasted years on him.

All she needed was one man not afraid of commitment. "A man like Adam," she said, aloud, thoughtfully.

Well, she did have a tennis date with him. She should at the very least allow herself an opportunity to get to know the man. Adam deserved that much. Besides, she already knew that she liked him. It was a start.

* * *

As Gordan dressed for the evening ahead, he realized that he was still as aggravated as he had been the moment Cassy left. He'd practically snapped poor Jillian's head off when she'd walked in on them earlier. He could not help it. He'd been furious and had not welcomed any interruptions.

"Cassy . . ."

He'd never known her to be so unreasonable. They had to talk this through before it destroyed what they had. What they needed was time alone—time to discuss their differences.

Things could not go on much longer the way they had been. If he wasn't careful, he would lose her for good—something he was not about to let happen.

Yet, here he was preparing for a business dinner with the hotel's manager, Kenneth Kittman, and his wife, Ann Marie. Jillian naturally would be joining them since she arranged the evening. Kenneth wanted to go over a list of ideas of improvements from which he felt the hotel and their guests would benefit.

For once, Gordan was not interested. He was so caught up in what was happening between him and Cassy that he could generate interest in little else. He consoled himself with the knowledge that it was only one night.

Besides, Cassy was furious at the moment. Once she calmed down, then they would find a way to work it out. The one thing that gave him hope was that she had not said she'd stopped loving him.

He had waited too long to find a woman that suited him. She was not only lovely, but she was genuine. He was not about to give in without a fight.

At first, he had been in shock when he learned that Cassy had chosen to vacation in Martinique and stay at his hotel. Kramer House—Martinique would always be special to them. It was where they met—where it all began for them.

Maybe she did not fully recognize the significance of why she had chosen to recuperate here. Her coming to Kramer House gave him hope. It allowed him to wonder if she might be having trouble letting go. It was one puzzle he was determined to solve.

What had she meant when she said he had never bothered to ask what she needed, or that he hadn't really heard a word she said in Atlanta? He'd heard every hurt-filled word. How could he have avoided it when she had practically flung them at him as she packed?

The lady had made herself abundantly clear when she threw her birthday gift in his face and stormed out of his house without any travel arrangements. She did not care how she made it back to Oakland. All that was important at the time was getting away from him as fast as she could.

He'd been furious—so much so that he had made a huge mistake. He had sent Bradford to take her where she needed to go. But he had not gone after her himself that night—not tried to stop her from leaving until they had talked it all out. He was still paying for that mistake.

He'd let his own hurt and anger cloud his judgment. Instead of doing something about the situation, he had brooded over it for weeks.

"Where does she get off telling me that we should never have become involved in the first place?" he muttered to himself, as he groomed his beard. He had come chasing around the world to find her, something he had never even come close to doing for any other woman including his ex-wife, Evie.

Cassy was right about one thing—the business demanded a great deal of his time. Why was that suddenly such a problem? They both had demanding careers. There was nothing new about that. And theirs was hardly a new relationship.

What was her point? She had known from day one that he needed to move from one hotel to the next to oversee the company. She also knew that the business was not just for him. He had responsibilities to his brother, his son, and all the people who worked for them all over the world. She knew all this going in. Why was it such a big issue now?

It was certainly not all on him. Cassy was the one who had taken on a new demanding business. She had been the one who no longer made time to be with him. He had never thrown that in her face. He had been more than generous, eager to fly her in on his private jet any time she wanted to come and join him.

"If it were up to me, we would have spent every weekend together," he grumbled to himself. It was not his fault that she had chosen the Parkside Garden Inn over him. His lifestyle had not changed since the day they met.

"Why all of a sudden is it my fault that she's not satisfied?" Gordan asked himself, as he glared at his reflection in the mirror, trying but failing to fasten his tie.

He did not care what she said—their separation was not all his doing. She had to take some responsibility. They should have spent more time together. All she had to do was get on the blasted jet and come to him. He never once told her not to come or that he was too busy. He had been willing even to share the precious little time he spent with his son with her. The three of them had vacationed together often enough.

Nor had he ever tried to hide the fact that he needed her in his life. He wanted her with him every single day, which was why he suggested that she move in with him. That was as committed as he could get!

As he pulled on the silk-and-cashmere-blend suit coat,

he recalled the kiss he had stolen from her. Cassy had been pliable for a time, her soft body conformed to his. Her mouth had opened sweetly under his. He moaned deep in his throat. No matter what she said, he knew she still found him as desirable as he found her.

Even seeing her in the company of another man had not shaken his faith in her loyalty, which was saying a lot, considering his past. Cassy was upset with him, furious with him, yet he knew deep inside that she had never betrayed what they shared. He had no fears that she might sleep around on him. That was not her way. Just as she knew he would not cheat on her.

Although he enjoyed sex just as much as the next man and had a keen sexual appetite, he had no difficulty keeping his pants zipped while he was away from his woman. And Cassy was that—his woman.

And she took care of all his needs. Despite the passage of time and long periods of abstinence, Gordan's desire for Cassy had not lessened. If anything, he wanted her more. She kept him hard, anxious for more of the same. It was a pity that they could not spend every waking hour making love. He chuckled softly. At least then he could stop this ridiculous idea that marriage was the sole answer for them. There had to be other options.

"Gordan," the sultry feminine voice filtered in, from the other side of the bedroom door.

"Be right out, Jillian."

Gordan's forehead creased into a frown. No, this was not the way he would have liked to spend the evening. But for now it would have to do. He would be relieved when it was over. Then he could concentrate on finding a way out of this dilemma with Cassy.

* * *

After seeing the Kittmans out, Gordan's manservant, Ben Bradford, inquired, "Would you care for anything more, Ms. Harris?"

"No, thank you," Jillian said, absently, her gaze on the man seating himself in one of the armchairs. He stretched his long legs out in front of him.

"Sir?"

"Nothing for me. Good night, Bradford," Gordan said, quietly. After a time, he roused himself enough to say, "Thanks, Jillian, for acting as my hostess this evening."

"I enjoyed it," she smiled.

Gordan was thoughtful, unmoved by her dazzling smile. He was remembering how intrusive her appearance had been earlier that afternoon.

After deciding he could not afford another such interruption, he said evenly, "I prefer that you work out of the hotel's business office while we're here. Please, get whatever you need from the in-suite office tonight before you leave."

If he heard her sudden gasp, he gave no indication. "Good night, Jillian." Gordan rose and walked out onto the softly lit balcony.

He went to the wrought-iron railing and stared down at the grounds far below. He could see the lanterns along the garden walkway. Was Cassy down there tonight?

"You're upset with me," Jillian said, from the doorway.

The only thing Gordan was conscious of feeling was fatigue. He was fed up with the situation—tired of doing without. The evening had been a long and empty one. Where had Cassy spent her evening? Had she been alone? Had she even thought about what they'd discussed earlier?

"Gordan?"

"No, I'm not angry with you."

He had no emotions where Jillian was concerned. His head was overflowing with thoughts of only one woman.

Cassy should have been there tonight. She should have been his hostess and then, later, his lover for the rest of the night. He yearned to make love with her all night long.

He had to stop himself from wondering how she might have spent her evening. It was the only way he had of containing his temper. The possibility that she might be out with Foster tonight did not sit well with him. One glance had told him that the other man wanted her.

Gordan headed a corporation, but he was as possessive as the next man. Cassy was his just as he was hers. What was she up to? Did she hope to make him jealous with this other guy?

No. She had no way of knowing when or if he was going to return to the island. Besides, Cassy was not into play acting, which was only one of the things he adored about her.

That was his bottom line. Gordan quite simply adored the woman. Despite their problems, she made him happy. On the nights they were apart, he enjoyed talking to her on the telephone. It allowed him to close his eyes and imagine that Cassy was beside him in bed.

Oh, yes, he needed her tonight. He needed her with him every night. He'd had enough of sleeping alone. It didn't matter if the bed was in Atlanta, the Caribbean, or South Africa.

They had not seen each other in a few weeks, but even though this time was different, he had been thrilled to be able to just look at her. And she had looked good today.

Her amber-tone skin glowed from good health and natural beauty. She had covered her pretty curls with a hat, but he knew how her hair felt—how she felt in his arms, against his skin. She had not been wearing any perfume today, but all he had to do was close his eyes in order to fill his head with her womanly scent. That thin knit of her swimsuit could not conceal the softness of Cassy's full, pointy-tipped breasts or the voluptuous flare of her round hips. She had tied a sheer skirt around her waist to cover her firm thighs and shapely calves. She hid nothing from him, for he knew all her sweet secrets. He had no difficulty recalling how beautiful she was with or without clothes. Nor could he forget how warm and silky her skin felt against his and how she tasted.

Gordan had no trouble remembering what it was like to be deep inside Cassy's tight sheath. They fit together perfectly. She would purr deep in her throat when she was very aroused—hot, sexy little moans that told him she was close to climaxing.

He closed his eyes, forcing back a husky groan. He had wanted her when he found her sharing a meal with another man—just as he wanted her now. His shaft had hardened in preparation to make love. All he needed was her . . .

"It's a lovely night, isn't it."

The provocative feminine voice came from directly behind him. The night air was suddenly filled with her alluring perfume. Silky, smooth, slim brown arms encircled his waist from behind and small hands began to move beneath his jacket, over his silk-covered chest.

"Neither one of us has to be alone tonight," Jillian crooned, close to his ear.

Gordan had been momentarily stunned with disbelief. He clasped both her hands and pulled them away from his body. Turning to face her, he snarled, "Jillian, what in the hell do you think you are playing at?"

"It's obvious that you're no longer with Cassy. I think it's time you knew that I find you attractive. I have for a very long time. Gordan, let me help you forget her. Let me . . ."

Gordan stared down at her, not believing what he was hearing. Eventually, he folded his arms on his chest, then he said, tightly, "Stop right there. You've said enough. I

suggest you leave now and we will both forget this ever
happened.''

"Please, give me a chance. Let me show you that I'm
the woman for you. I have all the qualities that you desire
in a woman. I'm smart. I'm . . .''

"I'm glad to hear it.'' A muscle jumped beneath his
bearded jaw, before he said, evenly, "Let's assume you're
smart enough to step very cautiously. I'll tell you this once.
I don't want you, Jillian. I do not become romantically
involved with any of my employees.''

"Cassy once worked for you.''

"You're not Cassy. If you value your position, you'll get
out of my suite—now. And you will never bring this up
again. You, lady, are replaceable.''

Jillian blinked. "I apologize. I overstepped.''

Gordan said nothing. To his relief, she left, closing the
outside door firmly behind her.

Chapter Five

After her tennis match, Cassy surprised herself when she curled up on the bed for a nap and actually slept for several hours. It was after eight when she awoke, a bit disoriented. As she stretched, easing tight muscles in her shoulders, her sister came to mind.

Maybe Sarah was right—she did need the rest. Keeping the inn running smoothly had been a demanding job, but she loved every minute of it. As she grew older, Cassy realized that she was more like their grandmother in that she genuinely loved caring for others—cooking for them, putting smiles on their faces.

It had been a highly stressful time with her sister on bed rest for so many months. Cassy had certainly shared Sarah's worries for the baby. Because of Sarah's age and complications, it had not been an easy time for any of them.

Cassy had not minded the added work that her sister's pregnancy had placed on her own shoulders. But it was the preparation and presentation of the food that she truly enjoyed.

She smiled; her happiest memories were of helping her grandmother in the kitchen of their big, rambling old rooming-house when she was too young to even use a knife safely. That didn't stop Cassy. She learned how to mix and sift flour with glee, loving the warm kitchen smells and her grandmother's tender encouragement. She was lucky; she came from a long line of great cooks.

Grandma Mosley had made spectacular homemade breads and pastries. Her hand was light and her crusts were exquisitely tender and flaky. Cassy had learned the knack from a master chef. She often made her grandmother's sweet potato nut bread for the diners at the inn. It had become a local favorite, along with her four-cheese omelet and cream pies.

She had no regrets as far as her chosen career. She had been lucky to be able to travel and work under talented chefs in Toronto, Paris, San Francisco, and the Caribbean.

In fact, she had been so comfortable with her culinary skills that when their grandmother retired to live with their Aunt Rose in North Carolina, Cassy knew she could head any restaurant with ease. But the Parkside Garden Inn was a dream come true for both sisters, and it was something they had done together. Plus it had brought Sarah and Mandy back home to Oakland after years away.

It was only lately, after Sarah's marriage, that Cassy started taking a hard look at her own life. The years were passing much too quickly and she had met her career goals, but she had not met that all-important personal goal.

As she stood on the balcony staring at the stars, she wondered if it would not seem so urgent if she were not approaching her fortieth birthday in less than a year. Or if she were not so deeply in love. Or if she had not witnessed how difficult a pregnancy could be for an older woman.

Maybe none of that mattered as much as the knowledge that she'd loved Gordan with her entire heart for years. But that love had stopped being enough, and she had stopped pretending that it was.

Telling him that she longed for his name and the right to carry his baby had been particularly difficult for her. Did he even suspect how painful the process had been for her? Or had he only considered how it affected him? More than likely the latter, she decided sadly.

Brushing away a single tear, Cassy went to dress for a late dinner. She changed into a burgundy slip dress that she teamed with a velvet floral silk-lined jacket. After a quick brush-through of her hair, she applied a touch of gray shadow to her lids, highlighted her dark eyes with black mascara, and finished with a deep rose lipstick. After stepping into black patent-leather stack heels and grabbing a small, black evening bag, filled with the bare necessities, she left the room.

She decided to eat at the Martinique Room, which highlighted local cuisine. It was located on the ocean side of the hotel on the tenth floor. Even at this late hour, it was crowded. A small band played in the background and grass-green carpet was underfoot. The restaurant provided a spectacular view of the water and the marina in the distance.

"Cassy! *Bonsoir.*" Jacob Winslow greeted her at the entrance, kissing her cheek. He was a good friend of the Halleys. Cassy had even gone out with him a few times when she had worked in the hotel. That was before she had met Gordan. "It's good to have you back with us," Jacob grinned.

"It's good to be back. How have you been?"

"Busy," he laughed. "Boss-man keeps me hopping."

"Is Renee cooking tonight?"

"*Oui!* Only the best for the boss's lady. Will Mr. Kramer

be joining you tonight?'' Jacob asked, as he escorted her to a small table near the windows.

Cassy momentarily stopped before she recovered herself and continued on. When she was seated, she said, "No, I'm dining alone. Please, tell Renee hello for me."

She graciously accepted the menu, thinking that if she had to explain to one more person why she and Gordan were not together, she would start screaming and never stop.

It was her own fault for coming to this hotel—his hotel. Her sister certainly had warned her. She was the one who did not belong here. Perhaps she should be thinking about changing hotels. Running away—hadn't Gordan accused her of doing just that?

"I will send the wine steward over. And please enjoy your meal."

Cassy nodded her thanks and studied the view out of the floor-to-ceiling windows rather than the menu. It was a lovely night—a night meant for romance. Candlelight, crisp linen tablecloths, fine china, and flowers, all designed to add to the mood.

Her entire body had stiffened at the mentioned of Gordan's name. She should have expected it. Gordan was well liked and respected by his staff. Whenever she traveled with him, she'd always been proud of him, especially because of his fairness and generosity.

Tonight she didn't want to so much as think about the man. As she looked at the menu, she knew that what she was worrying about was the distinct possibility of running into Gordan again that day. She had not recovered from their earlier encounter.

Determined to push him away from her thoughts, she tried to recall the last time she had seen Jacob. Oh, yes, it had been in the Kramer House—Jamaica, where she had been spending a long weekend. If she remembered correctly, the Jamaican complex had been a promotion for Jacob and he had been very pleased with himself.

Jamaica . . . She closed her eyes and recalled romantic walks with Gordan in the moonlight, late night swims in the Caribbean. Her eyes popped open in mute frustration. Cassy's hands were unsteady as she sipped from her wine glass, swallowing too quickly and nearly choking in the process.

Her waiter smiled, *"Mademoiselle,* may I take your order?"

She nodded and placed her order, even though food no longer seemed to matter. Maybe she should go home—just pack her bags and get on the next plane back to the States.

That was bound to upset her family, given the sacrifices they had made to send Cassy to the island. She had to stay. She told herself that if seeing him had not already killed her, surely it would make her stronger—heal her aching heart.

This very minute, Gordan was probably having dinner with Jillian. The woman would gladly soothe his wounded pride and damaged ego. Cassy would be fooling herself if she thought anything else.

When her meal was placed in front of her, Cassy smiled her thanks. Although everything was excellently prepared and presented, Cassy could only pick at the meal. Her appetite had vanished.

"Don't tell me you don't like my Pithiviers, *Cheri?"*

"Renee!" Cassy quickly rose and hugged her dear friend. "It's so good to see you. You look wonderful!"

The older woman's rich pecan-colored skin was just as smooth and unblemished as it had been the last time she saw her. Her thick, wavy, black hair reached the middle of her back and had a few more strands of gray in the braid that had been twisted into a coil at her nape, but Renee's smile was still warm and engaging. She was dressed in a coral chef hat and coat.

"I couldn't believe it when Ralph told me you were back. And then Jacob tells me you are here in the restaurant tonight. I had to come out and see you. How are you, *Cheri*?" Renee's French Creole accent was as charming as she remembered.

"I'm fine. Just decided to take a few weeks off. Ralph tells me that your babies are all grown up now. You have reason to be proud of them both."

Renee laughed. "We have been blessed with both of them. You're looking wonderful. I take it running your own inn has kept you too busy to come and see us, *oui*?"

Cassy said, with a smile, "I apologize. I have missed you all so much. Tell me how you've been. Still in love with that wonderful island man of yours?"

Renee giggled like a school girl. "Can't help myself. It gets better as time goes on. I'm still as sassy as ever. Sister girl, why you not eating my food? My pastry crust not as tender as yours?"

Cassy was pleased when Renee took the empty chair across from her. "Everything is marvelous. I think I'm suffering from a bit of jet lag."

"Why you here alone?"

Cassy shrugged, deciding to change the subject. "It's so good to be back. So good to see old friends. I missed you all."

"Cassy, what is wrong? Where is your man tonight? Ralph tells me that you are at one table and Gordan at another." She hesitated, suddenly shaken by the unhappiness she saw in Cassy's eyes. Reaching for her hand, Renee squeezed it gently. "Forgive me, I did not mean to upset you. Ralph say I ask too many question. *Excusez-moi.*"

"No, stop apologizing. I'm fine, or at least I hope to be. Gordan and I are no longer involved. It ended a few weeks ago."

"Oh, no! Cassy, I'm so sorry. I know how much you two loved each other."

"Thank you." Cassy averted her face, then, forcing a smile, said, "It takes getting used to."

"It's not another woman, is it? That assistant? She has been after him for years. And does not try to hide it!"

Cassy shook her head no, but she could not say more, even to Renee. Not now. It hurt too much.

Squeezing her friend's hand, Renee asked, "How are you coping with this?"

Cassy shrugged. "Not as well as I would like. That was one of the reasons why I came back. I must get over my feelings for him and go on with my life."

"But, *Cheri,* how can that be? You two are both here—together?"

"Not together. He followed me," Cassy whispered, so she would not be overheard.

"What!" Before she could finish, the waiter rushed over and whispered in Renee's ear. She nodded. "Cassy, *excusez-moi.* A small problem in the kitchen. You must stop by the cottage and visit with me. Promise?"

"Yes. Are you still at the end of . . ."

"The same."

Cassy kissed her cheek. "Don't let me keep you. I know you're working."

"Come for a visit. I'm free most mornings. Off on Tuesdays. Please stop in, so we can chat."

"I will. 'Bye."

Alone again, she knew she'd had enough with pretending that everything was fine. She needed some privacy—needed to think. Her reasons for their separation might be very different than his. He had not made too much of a protest at the time. Did Jillian have something to do with why it took him weeks to contact her after their breakup? After signaling for the check, Cassy quickly signed for her meal and left.

Instead of returning to her room or going into one of the night spots available in the hotel, Cassy made her way down to the softly lit garden. The night air was a bit brisk, but refreshing. And the scents of the well-tended garden always captivated her. The sound and smell of the sea were a bonus in her estimation.

Jillian and Gordan . . . She had told herself that he was more than welcome to the woman. So why then did even the possibility bother her that he might have been involved with his lovely assistant since their breakup? She had given up all claim to the man, hadn't she?

"Excuse me," she said, suddenly, stepping back quickly after having nearly bounced off a man's chest. "I was not looking . . ."

"Cassy." Adam held her arms, steadying her. "Are you all right?"

"Yes. I was thinking and wasn't paying attention. Forgive me."

"No harm done." He chuckled before asking, "Out for a late night stroll?"

"Trying to walk off my dinner. I ate in the Martinique Room. Renee, one of my friends, is the chef there. We had a short visit."

"Another old friend. You seem to have your share," he said, pointedly.

Cassy was a little taken back, certain that he was referring to his meeting with Gordan during lunch—something he had made no mention of during their tennis match that afternoon. The very last thing she wanted to discuss was Gordan.

"It's good seeing you, Adam. If you will excuse me."

Blocking her retreat by stepping directly into her path, Adam said, "Don't you think an explanation is called for?"

"No! I don't." She was unexpectedly angry. She had enough man trouble; she did not need or want more of the same.

"No, you don't," he agreed, quietly. "You're right, you don't owe me a thing. We only met a few days ago." He sighed. "Cassy, you're such an easy person to be around. I enjoy your company." Adam's smile was engaging.

Cassy looked away then, uncomfortable with the trend of the conversation. "Have you toured the island yet?"

"Not yet. I plan to rent a car tomorrow and go into Fort de France. I hear the *z'habitants* is fabulous. I must try some."

Cassy laughed at the mention of one of her favorite local dishes.

Adam was smiling, tucking her hand into his arm and leisurely moving along the path.

Even though it was quite late, they passed couples here and there, either seated on one of the small, white, wrought-iron benches placed throughout the garden or strolling as they were on the path that eventually led down to the shore.

"I love it here. I have no idea why I haven't been back before now. Too busy I guess. The old French chef that was here then was such a great teacher. I think I finally mastered my pastry dough while I was here—something I had not quite done even while I lived in Paris."

"Tell me about Paris."

Cassy giggled. "My French was atrocious. But in spite of the language difficulty, I enjoyed my time there. Paris is so exciting. The food!" she exclaimed. "Well, it's the best in the world. The art and fashions . . ." She trailed off with a soft laugh. "You have to go, even if it's only for a short visit."

"I'm looking forward to it someday. I enjoy traveling.

Lately, I've been concentrating on the Caribbean. How long were you in France?"

"Almost a year. That's one of the perks of striving to be a world-class chef. If you wish to learn, you must travel." She giggled. "I worked my way through the country. That sounds so much better than to say I ate my way through." She sighed. "But I loved the Caribbean, especially Martinique. There is no place on earth that can compare. Perhaps it has to do with feeling an affinity for the African people who have put down their roots deep into this part of the world. I can't explain it, but I always feel so at home here."

"I understand. The islands can be addictive." He smiled down at her, saying, "Well, my friend, any time you want a volunteer to try out a new recipe on, please—call me. I bet your pastries are exceptional."

Cassy laughed. "I do try. And I'll keep that in mind. I must admit after cooking for our guests in the inn back home, it's still a challenge. But whenever I take certain things off the menu, the locals who frequent our restaurant complain, so I have to put them back. It certainly keeps me on my toes."

"I must stop by when I'm in the Bay area. I do travel that way on business from time to time."

She stopped, pulled her hand free, and laced her fingers together in front of her. Her voice was somber when she said, softly, "My life is somewhat complicated at the moment."

"I gathered that much. Kramer is very much a part of that complication," he said, dryly.

She looked away. "It's a long story and I really don't want to get into it. Let's just say it ended badly."

"I take it this was a recent ending?"

"A few weeks," she reluctantly admitted.

"When it comes to business, he's a brilliant man. When it comes down to keeping his woman, he's a fool."

"Adam, please."

"Any brother who lets a sister like you get away, has to be outta his mind. Seems to me that he finally realized it. That's why he's here, isn't it?" Adam didn't wait for a response, before he said, "Kramer's trying to get you back. Have you two been involved long?"

"Adam, I don't want to talk about Gordan. Our relationship is over. Let's talk about something else—anything."

"I've been there, Cassy. I know how it is to be in an unhappy relationship. I'm forty and I've had my share of involvements." He sighed, then started again. " What I'm trying to say, is that if you need someone to talk to, please call on me. I'd like to be your friend."

"Thank you. But, let's be honest," she said, staring up at him. "I think you want more than friendship. To be perfectly frank, I'm in no condition to even consider becoming involved with another man right now. It would not be fair to him or me."

He chuckled good naturedly, before saying. "You're right. I do want more from you than friendship. You're a lovely lady. And I would be lying if I said I'm not attracted to you. Given time, I think you'll find that I'm a patient man. I know how to wait for what I want. You're worth waiting for, Cassy."

"There are no guarantees."

"Fair enough."

Cassy frowned, biting her lip, then said, "It would not be fair to you."

What she could not very well say was that she was hopelessly in love with a man who did not understand the first thing about commitment.

"Let me be the judge of what risk I'm willing to take."

She shook her head. "I'm not into games."

"Neither am I. Aren't we already friends?"

"Yes."

Taking her hand, he linked her fingers with his. "Let's concentrate on having a good time, enjoying each other's company when we can while we're on the island."

Cassy was reluctant, wondering if she were asking for yet another complication. All she wanted was for the hurt to go away. And she wasn't willing to hurt anyone else in the process of healing.

She was so long in answering that he prompted, "Cassy?"

"Okay. I have some shopping to do tomorrow. I want to buy souvenirs for my family."

"Shall we go into Fort de France—spend the day doing a little sightseeing and shopping?"

Cassy unknowingly rewarded him with an engaging smile. "I'd like that. Around nine-thirty?"

"Great."

They were silent for a time as they slowly began to retrace their steps, rather than continue on to the path that led to the outside staircase and the beach beyond.

As wind brushed her face and ruffled her hair, Cassy said, thoughtfully, "You don't talk very much about your family, Adam. Did you come from a large family in San Diego?"

Thrilled by her interest in his personal life, he said candidly, "No. Both my parents are gone and I've never married. Too busy making money. So, it's just me and a few distant cousins scattered around California."

Adam shocked her when he said, "This would make a perfect spot for a honeymoon."

Cassy laughed. "Yes, I imagine it would. Where did that come from? Are you planning to make that move?"

"I have my eyes open, looking for that special woman. I'm at a point in my life where I realize something is missing. I've traveled, dated, and had a really good time.

My career is established. I'm a good corporation lawyer and I own my own firm." He chuckled. "Most guys would never admit that they're lonely and want more. Oh, yes, there was a time when I probably wouldn't either. As the years pass, reality has a way of smacking you in the face. The truth of the matter is that I want a wife and a family someday." His gaze rested on her when he asked, "What about you?"

"Someday," she said, around a soft sigh. "Unfortunately, life isn't always that cut-and-dried."

"Now that's where you're wrong," he teased.

"Oh?"

"Life is what you make it," he said, with a grin. "When it comes to romance there should be no games, no misunderstandings. If the ladies were as up-front as the brothers, then there wouldn't be so many problems," he finished, unable to hold back a chuckle.

"Oh, really." Cassy tried to keep a straight face and failed. She ended in a fit of giggles.

"Absolutely."

"You are sooo wrong."

"Would you care to elaborate?" He chuckled, clearly hoping she would take him up on his challenge.

"Perhaps another time. It's late and I think I'll say good night."

"I'd be happy to walk you to your door."

She smiled. "No thanks. I'm a big girl now. I won't get lost. Good night, Adam."

"Good night, Cassy. See you in the morning."

Chapter Six

Cassy enjoyed the warm breeze as they drove from the resort to the picturesque capital of Martinique, Fort de France. The Bay of Fort de France, situated at the foothills of Pitons du Carbet, was considered the commercial center of the island. They toured the city, with its narrow streets and elaborate iron work that had always reminded Cassy of New Orleans, and La Savane, the wide public square and park, with its marble statues, brilliant flowers, and open-air market. The Botanical Gallery and Geological Gallery were both high on Cassy's list of places to revisit.

Adam refused to move another step until they stopped to eat in one of the open-air cafes, sampling the spicy, Indian curry dish called *colombo*.

After that, he didn't complain when she shopped along the *rues* Antoine Siger, Victor Hugo, and Schoelcher to buy gifts for her family, including a madras-costumed doll for Mandy.

As the car picked up speed, Cassy reached for the silk scarf tied on the strap of her straw tote to cover her hair.

"Want me to close the sun roof?" Adam asked, momentarily taking his eyes from the winding coastal road. He'd chosen to take the scenic route back to the hotel.

"No, thanks. The air is refreshing. Last night's rain cooled things off nicely."

"Have fun today?"

"No doubt about it. And you?" She smiled, leaning back into the deep cushions.

"It was the bomb!" He laughed.

Cassy preferred not to recall the last time she toured Fort de France, because she had been with Gordan. Determined not to let thoughts of him spoil her day, she focused on the passing scenery.

"Cassy . . ."

"Sorry, did you say something?"

"Dinner tonight?"

Cassy hesitated. She'd genuinely enjoyed Adam's undemanding companionship. But she didn't want to rush into anything. Nor did she want to raise Adam's expectations while she was so unsure of herself.

"Not tonight. I've taken enough of your time for one day."

"I disagree."

"Another time," she said, evasively.

She looked away from his probing gaze. She'd always been one to follow her instincts. She wouldn't allow herself to be rushed or pushed into a new relationship. It was too soon for her. Plus, she did not believe in toying with anyone's feelings. Adam was a good man. He deserved more than she could comfortably give.

They were both quiet until they reached the hotel. For once, she made no protest when he walked with her to her room. At the door, he took both her hands into his.

"Thanks for sharing the day with me."

Her smile was engaging when she looked up at him and said, "I enjoyed myself. About tonight . . ."

He shook his head. "No explanation necessary. I apologize for rushing you. If you're up to tennis tomorrow, give me a call." He leaned forward to brush his mouth against her cheek. " 'Bye."

" 'Bye." Cassy watched as he walked away before inserting her key-card into the lock.

Was she making a mistake by not encouraging his pursuit? What if Adam was the man she'd been waiting for? What if she were pushing away the one man who understood the word commitment? What if . . .

She stopped on the threshold, her gaze on a beautiful crystal vase filled with a lovely arrangement of pink roses, lavender tulips, and her personal favorite, lilacs. They were simply exquisite, filling the room with their heady fragrance.

Cassy did not remember closing the door or placing her things in the empty chair near the bed or even walking to the dresser. Her fingers were shaking when she lifted the small white envelope tucked among the blooms.

She sank down onto the bed, needing the support as she stared at the sealed envelope. The name of the hotel's florist was clearly printed on the envelope.

Taking a long, fortifying breath, she slid a nail beneath the seal, then slowly eased the card out. She would have known his bold script anywhere.

"Cassy, please can we sit together and talk? Have dinner with me tonight. Seven, the penthouse . . . Gordan."

"Oooh!" Gordan knew better than anyone on earth how to get to her. He knew she loved flowers and especially adored lilacs. He also knew purple was her color in all its glorious shades, just as he had memorized the most sensitive areas of her body.

What he refused to give her was what she needed to be happy. For Cassy, there was no substitute for marriage and a family. So what was he trying to do?

She ripped the card into tiny pieces. "How dare you decide to talk now! What about all those times when I wanted to talk? What about them, Gordan Kramer? You were always too busy. Well, it's too late now."

Now that he finally recognized she meant business, he was willing to talk. Well, fine! He was welcome to talk to himself, she decided, as she wiped at angry tears.

Was she more angry at herself for still caring about him or just plain furious with him for causing her to shed even more tears? She promised herself when she boarded the plane that she was through with crying.

There was nothing left to decide. Gordan could wait until hell had frozen over before she shared so much as a crumb with him.

She had decided after weeks of torment that she had made the only decision open to her. He did not need her. Jillian was somewhere lurking in the shadows, utterly thrilled by their breakup. Now was her chance. Cassy grumbled to herself.

She jumped when the telephone suddenly rang. There was not a doubt in her mind who was on the other end. She jerked the receiver off the hook. "What?" she shouted.

"Wow! Did I call at a bad time?"

"Sis. Sorry, I'm a bit jumpy. How's everyone?"

"Couldn't be better. Mandy is standing right beside me. If I don't let her talk, neither one of us will be allowed to have a conversation without interruption. Hold on."

"Auntie?" Mandy Dean Rogers cheerfully gushed. "Are you there?"

"Hi, baby. I miss you."

"Me too. I miss you sooo much, Auntie. When are you coming home?"

"Soon. What have you been doing with yourself?"

"Riding my pony with Granddaddy whenever I can. And helping Granny with baby Kurt." She sighed. "Auntie, I'm really trying to keep out of trouble so Granny can work. And we made oatmeal pecan cookies." She said in a loud whisper, "They aren't as good as yours, Auntie."

Cassy laughed, settling back against the pillows and enjoying her great-niece's chatter. Mandy had been through so much, losing her mother at birth, yet she was part of a warm and loving family.

"Granny says I have to get off now. Love you, Auntie."

"Love you too, baby doll. Be good."

Sarah came back on the line. "Hold on, Sis. Let me get Mandy busy in another room."

Cassy frowned, knowing her sister would want details and was making sure they were not overheard.

"Is Gordan in Martinique? Is that why you sounded so angry when you answered?"

"Yes—he followed me," she admitted, then said, "Don't say it!"

"What—I told you so? No point. But, I'm not surprised and you shouldn't be either. He loves you, little sister. And what's more, you're still in love with him. Maybe, just maybe, you two can work this out."

"I don't want to talk about him. I don't want to even think about him," she whispered, fighting back tears. "He just makes me so mad!"

"What happened, honey? You sound so upset," Sarah insisted.

Cassy sighed. She could hear the worry in her sister's voice. The last thing she wanted was to upset her. "Look, don't pay me any mind. I'm okay. I spent a pleasant morning sightseeing and shopping in town with a nice man I met here, Adam Foster. He's from San Diego. And I returned to find a huge bouquet of roses and tulips and lilacs from

Gordan." She massaged her aching temples as a headache threatened. "I ran into him at lunch yesterday. A lunch, I might add, that I was sharing with Adam."

"Oh no! I bet he was surprised."

"To say the least," she said, dryly. "We went to his suite to talk—or should I say to fight it out. Guess who walked right into the middle of it—Jillian, naturally. He is so concerned about our breakup, but when he follows me he brings along his drop-dead gorgeous assistant. Give me a break! Doesn't sound to me like he's serious about anything but work."

"Jillian isn't your problem. He came after you, remember?"

"Yeah, right. And she is waiting to sink her claws into him."

"So what? I thought you decided you don't want the man anymore. Isn't that what you told me?"

Cassy frowned. "So? Why doesn't he leave me alone? I told him quite clearly how I feel and what I want. And what does he do? He leaves a note tucked into the flowers—a dinner invitation for tonight in his suite. Honestly, Sis, I'd rather starve."

"I take it the answer is no?"

"I can't. I'm not going to let him play with my emotions. I made my decision. I won't change my mind. Sarah, I need more. I deserve more." Cassy ended on a emotional sob.

"You do," Sarah agreed, then sighed, "I don't know what to say."

"There is nothing to say. It's finished between us."

"Tell me about this new guy. Are you looking for trouble or have you just plain lost your mind?"

"No! You know me better than that. I was certainly not looking for a new man—not while I am still trying to get over Gordan. Please, give me some credit for common sense. It just happened.''

"I suppose it shouldn't matter. But, I can just imagine Kurt's reactions in a similar situation. He would be livid.'' Sarah giggled.

Cassy couldn't help a giggle. "It's really not funny.''

"Are you kidding! It's hilarious. I would give anything to have seen Gordan's face.''

"I don't know who was more surprised; him at finding me with another man or me at seeing him in Martinique. What a mess.''

Sarah sobered. "It doesn't have to be. If only you and Gordan would sit down and talk this out. Perhaps, you'll both find . . .''

"No.''

"Cassandra Mosley, you have never talked to the man about your feelings. You've yelled it at him. You gave him an ultimatum and walked out on him. But have you two really talked it out?''

Cassy rolled her eyes. "Don't start with the Cassandra stuff. It's too late for talking. All the words have already been said. More words won't change his attitude. A more stubborn man has never lived.''

Sarah laughed. "No, I'm afraid my dear husband has that distinction. Cassy, just think about it. Isn't he entitled to one evening after all the two of you have shared? One evening.''

Cassy released a sigh, "I can't . . .''

"Just think about it. Now, tell me about Adam. Is he attractive?''

"Very. Six one or so. Coffee-tone skin. Forty, single, down to earth. I met him in the airport. We shared a cab to the resort. You'd like him.''

"Cassy, be careful. Don't rush into a new relationship.''

"I'm being careful. Adam is a friend. He knows that's all I'm willing to consider at this time."

"Good. I'm not surprised you were up-front with him. A Mosley trait. We both suffer from it. Must be growing up in Grandmother's house."

"How is she? Have you spoken to her?"

"She's well. I think she and Aunt Rose are planning a visit in the fall. I sure hope so. If not, when you get back we are going to have to fly down for a visit. She still has only seen pictures of the baby."

"What a wonderful idea. Unfortunately, we both can't go. One of us has to oversee the inn. Too bad we didn't think of that earlier."

Both sisters laughed.

"About dinner . . ."

Cassy sighed heavily. "I'm not making any promises. How's the little man?"

"He's such a sweet baby. He is getting so big. You won't believe how much he has grown just in the short time you've been away. Listen, I better get off of this phone."

"Thanks for calling. Give everyone a big hug and kiss for me."

"I will. You take care of yourself."

"You, too. 'Bye." Cassy slowly replaced the receiver.

Nothing had been resolved, but at least she was not still so angry that she couldn't see straight, let alone think. She decided that two aspirins and the comfort of a hot bath might not be a cure, but would go a long way toward easing her troubles.

It was not long before Cassy laid back in the tub, her head cushioned by a rolled bath towel. With her eyes closed, she let her thoughts drift—let herself daydream.

She saw herself cradling the sweetest baby. Her baby girl was dressed in pink ruffles and cooed at her. Cassy smiled, for the two of them were in a lovely garden near the beach.

She could almost smell the sea in the distance, almost feel the strength of a man's arms around them. Their baby girl had soft, amber-tone skin and thick, silky-black curls. She could almost smell the baby's fresh powder scent. Suddenly, a tear slipped beneath her lashes. Pressing a hand to trembling lips, Cassy's heart ached from sorrow and disappointment. She had been imagining the baby girl that had Gordan's square-cut chin, his velvet-brown eyes, and long, thick black lashes.

Cassy furiously wiped her eyes with wet soapy hands. "Oh, no!" she wailed. Her eyes stung from the scented soap. Sitting up quickly, she reached blindly for a towel. Her eyes were still red by the time she finished in the bathroom and wrapped herself into a robe.

She was putting drops into her eyes when the telephone rang. She picked up on the third ring. "Hello?"

"How are you?"

The smooth as silk, deep male voice nearly caused her to drop the phone, as awareness raced down her back. She said, "I'm fine, Gordan," as she struggled to slow her heart rate. She could not stop her response to the seductiveness in his tone. He wanted her. He didn't have to say it—she could feel it.

Her gaze automatically went to the flowers on the dresser. She refused to dwell on the quickening of her breathing or the way her nipples had hardened against the terry cloth covering them; even her feminine passage had tightened in anticipation—all because of the longing in his voice. Cassy was suddenly furious. It was not fair.

"I hope you enjoy the flowers."

"They're beautiful," she acknowledged, refusing to thank him for something designed to weaken her resolve.

"Can you join me tonight?"

She inhaled sharply. "That's not a good idea."

"I disagree. We must talk."

"I said all I have to say."

There was a noteworthy pause before Gordan said, "Please—this is important to me."

There was a roughness in his voice that had nothing to do with anger. But, what? Why was this so important to him? Surely, he knew she would not change her mind no matter what he had to say.

Why couldn't he just accept that they had simply grown apart, and leave it at that? There was nothing left to salvage, not even the shattered bits of her pitiful dreams. It had ended in Atlanta on her birthday.

"Baby . . ." His voice was deep with unmistakable longing.

She shut her eyes in an effort to block out the husky appeal of the endearment and the resulting memories. They had shared so much. There had been a time when she would not have believed it was possible to love a man as much as she loved Gordan.

For she had given him everything she had to offer, yet it still could not change the facts. They wanted two different things from life. Nothing could change that.

"What difference can one dinner make?"

"All the difference in the world to me. Please, give me that much."

Reluctantly, she said, "Okay. I'll see you at seven."

Gordan was nervous, more so than he had been when he had asked a girl out for the first date as an untried boy. He had cut himself grooming his beard, and it had taken nearly fifteen minutes to choose a tie, then he decided not to wear one at the last minute. He had not been this anxious when he negotiated the real estate deal for his first hotel. He would be in a position of losing a lot more than money tonight.

Money had not always come easily. He had started out

with nothing. He'd come up the hard way. No one was there to watch his back; there was no one to tell him if he was doing the wrong things while raising his little brother, Will.

He accepted the weight of responsibility as a young man and it kept him working long hours, studying whenever and wherever he could in order to finish college and keep food on the table and clothes on their backs.

Their only safety net had been that they did not have to worry about the roof above their heads. Because of their parents' hard work, their family home had been left to him. Scholarships and student loans had paid for his classes. Determined to set an example for his impressionable younger brother, plus honor his promise to his mother, along with being too stubborn to quit, Gordon had gotten through.

Once he started making money, it was as if he'd jumped on a roller coaster. It had been a rough ride straight to the top. He had grown up along the way. He had also fallen in love for the first time in his life.

He'd been drawn to Evie Sanders first by her beauty, then later by her sexy refusals. He had wanted her and he had gotten her through marriage. Unfortunately, they had married for the wrong reasons. It hadn't lasted; as a result, it had cost him his self-respect and nearly his son's love.

After years of being unable to trust, he met Cassy. She wasn't like any of the women who made a habit of chasing him down, drawn primarily because of his bank balance. From the beginning he sensed how grounded Cassy was— how real. She had no patience for pretense. The only thing she was willing to impress him with was her cooking.

At last, he had found a woman he could trust, first with his thoughts and then gradually with his heart. She was not interested in the things he could give her or what he could do for her career. She had offered friendship, and eventually, her sweet love. They cared deeply for each other. For a very long time, that had been enough.

He glanced at his watch. Six-fifty. He impatiently drummed his fingers against the iron railing encircling the balcony. He had given her two weeks—as much time as he could stand—before he came after her. He had to put an end to this nonsense—end it before he lost his blasted mind. He was not about to sit back and lose the only woman he cared about. He swore beneath his breath.

"Did you say something?" Ben Bradford asked. He was putting the finishing touches on the linen-covered dining table in one corner of the wide balcony. Thick vanilla-scented candles encased in crystal hurricane lanterns were lit on every available surface, as well as centered between an array of violets on the table.

"No," Gordan mumbled. It took all his concentration not to pace the length of the plant-rimmed enclosure. A cooling breeze brushed his throat and bearded cheeks. He took deep, calming breaths. He refused to look yet again at the thin, gold watch on his left wrist. "Everything all set?"

"Yes. Marian has everything under control in the kitchen. May I get anything for you before I uncork the wine?"

"Thank you, no."

Bradford and his wife, Marian, had worked for and traveled with him for close to fifteen years. Ben acted as chauffeur, bodyguard, manservant—whatever needed to be done, he did it.

Gordan walked inside over to the glass-top, behind-the-sofa table where a wet bar had been set up. He fingered one of the crystal decanters while eyeing the array of crystal glasses without interest. Moving restlessly to the mantel, he stared down into the candlelit grate. He was surrounded by opulence, but he was no longer sure if he had what he valued most—Cassy's love.

Was that the real problem? Had she simply stopped loving him? Acid churned in his stomach as he mulled over the distinct possibility.

How could she promise to never let anything come between them and then suddenly break her word? Was her love gone? Everything else had changed between them. Why not that? None of what was said or promised seem to matter to her. No! She had to still care for him. She had to . . .

Only Cassy could make him believe that she no longer cared. And she had failed to do so thus far. He knew her. They had shared everything. They had no secrets.

She knew his body as intimately as he knew hers. So why hadn't he seen this coming? He had no idea something was drastically wrong between them. And how did this guy Adam Foster fit into the equation?

When she confronted him in Atlanta she had certainly said nothing about another man. Cassy had won his faith in her long ago. She had never given him reason to doubt her word—that was another woman. No, he had no reason to doubt that she had met Foster here on the island. Her complaints centered around her resentment of his cramped schedule, in addition to his decision not to ever remarry.

The melodious tones of the doorbell chimed through the apartment and brought his head up sharply.

Chapter Seven

Cassy could not understand why she was so shaky as she waited outside the penthouse suite. She had asked herself the same question at least a half-dozen times. Still she had no answer. She had a single reason for coming and that was to show him once and for all that he could not change her mind. Nothing more.

Did her anxiety stem from being back in this suite—a place that held so many tender memories? She ignored the fine tremor in her hands as she waited.

"Good evening, Miss Cassy." The huge man with dark-brown skin towered over her. His eyes seemed older than time itself, as he looked at her with a mixture of compassion and understanding. Ben Bradford and his wife, Marian, had always been kind to her, seeing to her every comfort whenever she had been with Gordan.

Cassy's smile was filled with warmth as she held out her hand to him. "Good evening, Bradford. How have you been?"

Giving her hand a squeeze, he said, "We've missed you. Marian and I are both well."

Cassy nodded her thanks when she could not voice it.

"Your family—all is well?"

"Yes. My little nephew is getting so big."

He grinned. "Wonderful. Please, come in."

As Cassy moved forward, her eyes went to the tall man walking toward her. He looked exactly what he was—a self-assured, multimillionaire. He wore a custom-made dark-green suit that emphasized his long, powerfully built frame, from wide shoulders, trim midsection to seemingly endless long, hard, muscled legs. His feet were encased in custom-made butter-soft Italian leather loafers.

A fine, pale-yellow linen shirt had been left open at his throat—his only concession to the warmth of the night. It drew her attention to the beauty of his dark skin. She found herself wondering if she saw a few more strands of gray at his temples or in his well-groomed mustache and beard. If so, the gray only added to the man's dangerous allure.

Shivers of awareness raced like tiny fingers down her spine as she recalled the soft caress of his beard on her breasts, down her torso, along the tender inside of her thighs. She flushed at the unexpected rush of heat that the unwanted memory caused her. She was enormously grateful for her brown skin so that he could not detect the heat of her blushes.

She was not thrilled by the sharp images that flowed through her mind of what he looked like beneath the finely woven cloth. There could be no doubt that Gordan was a beautifully made man. He generated a heat that could be both incredibly comforting and deeply erotic. She would be lying to herself if she failed to acknowledge that she missed him. They had shared so much—made so many memories.

Forcefully pushing away intimate thoughts, Cassy tried to concentrate on only one fact. Gordan was a self-made man. He had worked tirelessly to create a highly profitable corporation, which had always come first in his life. His lady's needs would never be a priority.

"Cassy," he said, as if he were releasing a pent-up breath. His smile was charged with an elemental sexuality that was a natural part of the man. "I'm glad you came. You look lovely tonight."

"Thank you," she murmured, keenly aware of the way his dark gaze sensuously moved over her.

She had selected a lilac-colored silk sweater set and ombre crinkled skirt in shades of purple, from the palest lavender close to her waist to the deepest eggplant that bordered the midcalf-length garment. The small, self-fabric buttons that lined the front of the skirt stopped an inch above her knee. Her small feet were in open, mesh, deep-purple sandals with high chunky heels.

As he inhaled her essence, a combination of jasmine, honeysuckle, and lavender, plus her own sweet feminine scent, he realized how deeply he missed her. He felt as if a part of him had been severed. Feeling that loss, he shoved his hands into his trouser pockets so that he would not make the mistake of placing his hands on her. Gordan knew if he touched her, he could not make himself let her go. His control was just that tenuous.

"Please," he made himself say, gesturing toward the sofa. "Make yourself comfortable. May I get you a drink?"

What he did not ask was why she preferred the plain gold hoop earrings she was wearing tonight to the Brazilian amethyst earrings, which were surrounded by flawless diamonds, that he had given her for her birthday. She had thrown them at him before she walked out of his house in Atlanta.

Cassy could not fail to see the way his full lips had tightened. "Sparkling water with a twist of lime, please," she said, as she sank gracefully down onto the sofa, crossing shapely legs.

"You look beautiful tonight," he said, quietly, as he handed her a crystal tumbler. He collected a squat tumbler of cognac for himself.

"You've seen the outfit before." She shifted uncomfortably as his gaze lingered on her body. She detested each carefully placed word directed her way. He was like a little boy on his best behavior.

There was nothing childish about the way his eyes followed the swell of her full breasts or the feel of his hot gaze on their highly sensitive peaks. Her mouth tightened with annoyance, for his eyes alone had caused her nipples to tighten, ache for what he could give her.

She did not want to feel anything for this man—not ever again. Nor did she want to so much as attempt even a casual conversation with him. Gordan did not need words, for she sensed that beneath his masculine awareness there was anger. He held it just beneath the deceptively cool facade he displayed to the world; nonetheless, it was there.

Gordan made himself comfortable on the matching honey-colored silk settee, stretching his long legs out in front of him. He quietly took a sip of his drink.

"I'm glad you agreed to join me tonight. Marian has planned a special meal for us—all your favorites."

"She should not have gone to so much trouble." Cassy's gaze went to the silver tray that had been placed on the coffee table. There was a selection of salmon rosettes with mustard sauce on cut rounds of pumpernickel bread and tuna tartar on thin baked potato slices, two of her favorites.

Choked with emotions, Cassy did not think she could swallow. Instead, she focused on the soft glow from crystal-encased candles in the fireplace. The candles were in the living room, as well as out on the balcony. This was no romantic evening, she silently fumed.

As if he could read her thoughts, he said, "You're worth much more to me, Cassy, than a few flowers and candles." His voice was rough with emotion.

There was a prolonged silence. Cassy watched through the floor-to-ceiling windows as Bradford put the finishing touches on the dinner table.

"I can't understand why all of this is necessary. You know as well as I do that I won't change my mind."

"Indulge me, please." His eyes lingered on her face when he said, "Let me enjoy your company."

Cassy did not like the way her breath quickened as if he had physically caressed her skin. Before she could formulate a protest, Bradford announced dinner. Gordan rose smoothly to his feet. He held out a hand, intent on helping her rise.

Cassy knew better than to touch him. She gracefully came to her feet without his assistance. Although his mouth tightened, he said nothing. Cassy hastily looked away, leaving her purse on the coffee table, before moving ahead of him through the patio doors onto the candlelit balcony.

The fresh fragrance of orange, lemon, and lime trees, as well as the sweetness of pots of hibiscus, jasmine, and roses filled the air. The plants grew in huge copper urns, providing the perfect backdrop for the sound and smell of the sea below. There was hardly any wind, just enough to rustle the leaves in the trees.

The table was set with fine china and gleaming crystal. The centerpiece, a thick vanilla-scented candle shimmering inside crystal and encircled with tiny potted African violets, was a beautiful touch. A magnum of pink champagne was being chilled in a silver ice bucket. Everything was perfect, but there was nothing perfect about the end of a relationship.

"How charming," Cassy murmured, as Gordan held a chair for her.

As she absently caressed the velvety petals of a violet, she remembered that it was on a star-filled night such as this that she made love with him for the very first time. Alarmed, she quickly tried to push the unwelcomed thought away.

Gordan seated himself across from her. He waited until Bradford had filled their water and wine glasses and served the sweet potato and apple soup with a dollop of crème fraîche. Once they were alone, he began telling her about his son, Gordy, and how well he was doing in school. Gordan's dark face had softened with a warm smile. He also told her about the current woman his brother, Wil, was dating.

Mixed green salad with a ginger-lime dressing was followed by fettuccine with spicy lobster sauce. He kept the conversation light and easy, as if they had never disagreed.

Cassy's stomach suddenly went tight with tension when he said, "Do you remember the night we met? You were busy in the kitchen preparing a meal for me and my guests while I was entertaining. The meal had been fabulous, so much so that we just had to invite the chef to join us in a toast. You were so pretty in that lavender chef's coat and hat. Do you still remember what you prepared that night?"

Cassy carefully put down her fork. "I've had enough."

There was a heavy silence before he asked, "No dessert?"

She shook her head, not meeting his gaze.

He signaled to Bradford that they were finished.

Cassy waited until they were alone, then she said angrily, "I came tonight for one reason. Let's get it over with. Please say what you have to say, so I can go."

"What's the rush? I'm enjoying your company. But then, I have always enjoyed being with you," Gordan said, toying with her hand, which rested on the table.

Cassy pulled away, dropping her hand into her lap. "What we had is over. I don't see the point of rehashing it. We said our good-byes. Why did you invite me here tonight?"

"I didn't say good-bye, Cassy. I don't want what we have to end." His eyes held hers until she looked away.

"You can't say you've been happy with the way things have been between us?" Her disbelief was evident.

"We have problems. Just as all couples do. Why can't we at least try to work it out? We're both intelligent adults."

"For months I've been trying to explain my feelings to you. You never heard me, Gordan."

"I'm listening now. Tell me again," he invited.

"No!" she said, pushing back her chair. She went to the railing and stood staring straight ahead. The wrought-iron railing was so high it nearly reached her shoulders. In spite of the clouds in the sky, it was a clear night. The storm was inside of her.

"Why can't we talk about this?" he asked, from a few yards away. "Why are you so angry, baby? I never meant to hurt you. If I have, I'm sorry." The huskiness in his deep voice was like a caress.

Cassy took deep, fortifying breaths, hoping to soothe her frayed nerves and conceal her very feminine response to his masculine charm.

"Baby . . ."

"I don't believe you have the nerve to ask me why. We hardly ever see each other. We've grown apart, Gordan. And you ask me why?" she said, shaking from the force of her emotions. "We don't know each other anymore."

Gordan carefully placed on the table the delicate stem glass he'd been squeezing, determined to keep a tight rein on his temper. Losing control would solve nothing. He was reeling as if she had punched him in the gut. How could he honor her request? Just the thought of

letting her go hurt so much he immediately pushed it
away. He had to convince her that what they had was worth
saving. But how? She had come tonight only because of
his persistence.

There was no doubt in his mind that she had already
closed her heart to him—forgetting all that they had
shared. He had no choice to accept that he had hurt her.
Did that mean she had stopped loving him? As badly as
he wanted to know, he didn't ask—he could not.

What chance did he have of winning her back? It didn't
matter. He had to try. She was a part of him now—lodged
deep within his heart.

From the beginning, going into a relationship had not
been easy for him. He had been free of emotional entangle-
ments for quite some time. In fact, he had convinced himself that he actually preferred casual relationships. In other
words, he was careful to never let his emotions get involved,
and he was always in control. He took care of his lady
friend financially, and in return, he demanded her loyalty,
her time, and her attention when it suited him. He did
not sleep around, and he could not stand to be involved
with a woman who did—a leftover quirk from his failed
marriage.

Cassy had always been the exception. She refused to be
taken care of. She refused his gifts. The only things she
didn't refuse was his love. Despite their lengthy separations, she never gave him reason to doubt her loyalty. The
trouble was he had no idea when it had started to unravel.

"Nothing to say, Gordan?"

"We both have busy, demanding careers. It was that way
from the first. We managed before; we can manage now.
As for growing apart, that, too, can be rectified."

"Not this time."

"Yes, this time." His voice deepened when he said,
"Whenever we've been apart for a time, we make love. It

always soothed the loneliness of being separated. I need you, baby.''

Furious, she hissed, "Why do men think sex solves everything? You're wrong! It solves nothing!''

"It certainly can't make things worse.''

She swung around to face him. "I made a mistake in coming here. We've nothing to say to each other.''

"Why did you come back to Martinique? It was where we met.''

"The perfect place to correct the biggest mistake of my life.'' She averted her eyes.

"Don't you mean the perfect place to remember how wonderful it was between us? All our firsts happened here, baby. This is where we met, had our first date, and shared our first kiss. This is where we fell in love. We made love for the first time in your cottage. Remember?''

"Will you stop?''

He continued as if she had not interrupted. "I'd been celibate for so long, I'd given up on ever finding a woman who I could respect as a person. That was, until I met you.''

"You were entertaining some model the night we met. You have a short memory if you don't recall that you happened to be with your current lover.''

"She was nothing more than a friend. I was not sexually involved with her. You know that.''

"What possible difference does it make, now?''

He ignored the question. "You're very special. I knew that the first time I looked into your eyes. Four and a half years later, I still find that to be true. Why did you come back, Cassy?''

"I've told you. What I didn't expect was for you to follow me here.'' Cassy didn't think she could take much more. "There's nothing more to say. Good-bye.'' She headed for the patio doors.

"Running away again, Cassy?" He held onto her wrist before she could take more than a few steps.

"Don't touch me."

He slid his hands along her soft arms to cup her slender shoulders. "Another don't. What are you afraid of?"

"I'm not."

"Sure you are. You didn't want to have dinner with me tonight. You didn't want to talk to me. I repeat, what are you afraid of?" When she didn't respond, he whispered, "I've had my mouth and hands all over your soft sexy body, baby." His voice took on an even deeper tone and heavy lidded eyes dropped when he added, "You think I don't know you miss our lovemaking? You think I don't miss it, too? It's always there, that deep sexual awareness we share—hot, sweet . . . combustible."

His mouth was a hairbreadth away from hers and her plump breasts were pressed into his deep chest. He moved his hips against her, letting her feel the thick, unyielding strength of his sex. "Admit it."

Even though it was his arms that held her erect, she shook her head, as she ruthlessly bit her fleshy bottom lip. "There is no point to this."

Gordan groaned as he covered her lips with his. His mouth was hot, hungry, over hers, worrying the seam of her soft lips with the pointed tip of his tongue until she quivered, softly parting her lips for him. Not needing a further invitation, he dipped his tongue into the sweet cavity to caress and taste the honeyed interior.

"Oh, baby . . ." he whispered, widening his stance in order to press her body close as he cupped her bottom and squeezed. "Oh, Cassy . . ." he moaned.

Momentarily lost in the heat of his mouth, she opened her mouth even more, unwittingly rubbing the achy hard tips of her breasts against his chest. She had been empty for so long—she yearned to have him deep inside. It had been too long since their bodies had been joined intimately.

"Gordan . . ." she sighed and suckled his tongue.

He groaned, lifting her until he could move her soft mound along his throbbing penis. "Oh yes, baby. You're mine . . ."

"Stop!" she gasped, as if she were suddenly aware of what she had let happen. She pushed against his chest. "This is wrong."

Gordan's breathing was as quick and uneven as hers when he lowered her and dropped his hands to his side. He fought to bring his raging desires for her under control.

"I told you I want nothing to do with you."

He snapped, "You told me a lot of things, but your body tells me something entirely different."

"We're good in bed together. So what! It will never be enough. Never!"

He had to clench his jaw to keep the angry protest inside. He was rock hard and aching to finish what they started. "You're not making a bit of sense. Why did you just spring this on me in Atlanta? It came from out of the blue. We have not really talked about this."

"We talked the night I left. You just refuse to respect my decision."

"You issued an ultimatum. I don't call that talking." Gordan shoved his hands in his pockets. "Look, all I'm asking, Cassy, is that you give me a chance to make it right again. I had no idea you were so unhappy. Let me make it up to you. Baby, we've shared so much over the years. We love each other. Shouldn't that count for something?"

She wrapped her arms around herself as if she needed protection. "It was important once. But nothing stays the same. I need more."

She could see that she was tearing him apart; it was evident in the way he held himself. But she didn't care.

She could not afford to care, not if she wanted the home and family she'd been longing for.

He whispered, "I'll give you anything you want."

"I'm not talking about things! How many times do I have to tell you that!" She practically screamed at him, before she gained a small measure of control. "It's my understanding your name is unavailable." Her bitterness was evident in her tone. "I can't help wanting a husband and family."

He restlessly paced the perimeter of the balcony. His features looked as if they were permanently fixed in a scowl.

"Why didn't you tell me in the beginning? Why weren't you up-front about this?"

"People change, Gordan. Evidently, I'm not the same woman I was four and a half years ago. I don't know why!"

"You were fine until you turned thirty-nine!"

"Well, sue me!"

He did not dignify the outburst with an answer. "I realize that I've been selfish, always depending on you to fly to me. I can change that, baby. It's just that I've started a new project in . . ."

"There is always a new project with you. Finally, it doesn't matter to me anymore. I no longer care."

"Don't say that." He paused long enough to run an unsteady hand over his beard. "What did you expect— that I'd neglect my business?"

"Never that." Her voice was tinged with sarcasm. "Good night." This time she made it through the patio doors and into the living room.

He was right behind her. "You know why I can't marry again. I've told you what Evie put me through. You have my heart; why isn't that enough? Why can't we find a compromise on this?"

Cassy paused, not wanting to talk about his beautiful,

vindictive ex-wife. Evie had done everything within her power to keep him, and when that failed, she settled for trying to destroy his relationship with their son.

"There isn't one."

"What about what we've meant to each other over the years—what we've shared? I need you. What is so wrong with living together? Lots of people do it."

"Gordan, you have what you want—a wonderful son who adores you, a close relationship with your brother, and a loyal staff, including an eager assistant. With a little effort on your part, I'm sure Jillian would be willing to fill my shoes. Since she doesn't appear to be the maternal type, I don't think you have to worry about marriage." Cassy glared up at him. "It's my turn to go after what I want."

Gordan said nothing, not trusting himself to hold on to his temper.

Cassy continued. "I don't understand why you're fighting me on this. We both know I'm nothing more than an inconvenience to you. Why can't you admit that what we have hasn't been working?"

"Is it Adam Foster? Is he why you've stopped loving me?" A muscle jumped in his bearded jaw. "Tell me," he snarled, "what does he give you that I can't?"

Cassy gasped, her eyes wide with hurt and disbelief. "I told you that I've known the man less than a week."

"Sorry." He quickly apologized. "I should not have said that. But, Cassy, his sudden appearance is awfully convenient. The man is from California." His laughter held no humor as he interpreted her incredulous expression. "What? Didn't you think that I would have him checked out?"

"What Adam hasn't done is hurt me!" She flung the words at him. "He keeps his promises. At least he can marry me and give me the family I want," she flung angrily from over her shoulder, as she grabbed her purse and headed for the door.

All she wanted was to get as far away from him as she could. And she told herself that she was thrilled that he made no move to stop her. Cassy had reached the foyer when she hesitated. But she knew she could not leave this way. The implications she had tossed around weighed heavy on her heart. She had tried to hurt him, and she had seen the pain of betrayal. He was not an easy man to read, but his emotions were reflected in the depths of his eyes.

Slowly, she turned to face him. His large frame still shadowed the patio doors as he stared at her.

"I'm sorry. I should not have thrown Adam in your face like that. This has nothing to do with him."

Although deep inside he knew the truth, he nevertheless needed the words. "Why the apology?"

Chapter Eight

"My life has never been about lies or half-truths. I refuse to start now, even when you make me so angry I can't think straight." She flung her arms wide in an empty gesture of frustration. She was close to tears when she whispered, "Don't you think we've hurt each other enough? Gordan, please—let it end now . . . tonight."

It took every ounce of his self-control not to go to her and jerk her back into his arms, where she belonged. She was asking for too much and leaving him with nothing.

"No. But I realize I've made mistakes. All I ask is for some of your time."

"What?"

"What better place to find each other again than in Martinique? Isn't that why you came back to the island— back to Kramer House?"

Closing her eyes for a moment, she tried to collect herself. She had asked herself that same question since the day she had arrived. Unfortunately, she still didn't know the answer. Her voice was as steady as she could make it. "I'm not one of your projects—I don't need fixing."

"If you wanted nothing to do with me you certainly would not be here, in my hotel. Now would you, baby?"

"I can leave in the morning."

"And prove nothing."

"My family made the arrangements for this vacation, not me. The airline ticket was nonrefundable. Unlike you, I can't just throw money around. Besides, I needed time alone. It started here. It has to . . ." Cassy stopped abruptly and looked away. "I certainly did not expect you to follow me."

"You should have." He wanted her back in his life, in his bed. They belonged together. "Consider my request, Cassy. You owe me that much."

"This is not just another wildly romantic vacation we're discussing, only to have nothing change when it's over. This is my life."

"After what we've meant to each other, all I'm asking is for some of your time, baby."

"I've given you years out of my life—years that I can't get back."

"I'm talking about time together here on the island. Please—just think about it."

She nodded before she slipped out the door.

Gordan had no idea how long he stood unmoving, his body stiff with tension. He was barely aware of the servants clearing the outside table. Or the candles being extinguished. He stared for the longest time at the door Cassy had disappeared through. He could not believe how badly his attempt at reconciliation had gone.

"May I get you anything before I say good night?" Bradford asked.

Gordan shrugged out of his jacket and dropped it on the back of the couch. He began to unbutton his shirt then released the diamond cuff links, dropped them into his pocket, and rolled his sleeves above his elbows.

"Gordan?"

"Sorry. What did you say?"

"May I get you something before I say good night?"

"I could use a brandy. On second thought, bring the bottle and a second glass." Gordan settled in one of the leather wingback armchairs, propping his feet on the wide ottoman.

He was tired—dog tired, to be exact. It could have been that the constant traveling had finally caught up with him. More likely, it was his breakup with Cassy. At the moment, he couldn't muster up enough energy to care about anything, including the demands of the very profitable corporation he headed.

Had he ever felt more alone—even after the divorce? He had met his ex-wife during his college years. He was on a scholarship at Morehouse and Evie attended Spelman. Even with the responsibility of a much younger brother, he'd managed to keep his grades up and work a full-time job at one of the local hotels. Marriage should have been the last thing on his mind.

Like a love-sick fool, he married, straight out of college, a stunningly beautiful spoiled young woman, used to having everything she wanted. She had little patience with the motherless twelve-year-old, Wil. It was a mistake from start to finish. Nine years of his life had been wasted. The only good thing that had come out of it was his son, Gordy.

After an extremely nasty and bitter divorce, Gordan spent years trying to forget he'd ever been that stupid in the first place. He was too blasted angry with himself to let any woman get close to him. The first couple of years after the divorce, he had a series of relationships with some of the most glamorous women in the world, although he'd always practiced safe sex. He was not about to play fast and loose with his health.

But his lack of trust had gotten so bad that for several years before he met Cassy he had opted for celibacy. It was less risky, emotionally. The women he'd been seen with were nothing more than friends, including the woman he had been with the night he had met Cassy.

Cassy . . . With her, he'd finally understood what love really meant. For the first time in a very long time, he had allowed himself to be vulnerable to a woman. But then, Cassy was special. He was able to share his thoughts and his feelings with her. She didn't judge him; she accepted him. And they had been so happy together. That was, until recently.

How could he had been so blind to her unhappiness that he let her slip away from him? What had he been thinking? Did he think that he could neglect her for months at a time and she would always be there for him, like a custom-made suit? Perhaps that was the problem. He hadn't been thinking.

"Here we are," Bradford said, handing him the snifter of brandy, before he placed the bottle on the table between the two armchairs and made himself comfortable in the other chair.

"I blew it, Bradford."

"Maybe if you gave Miss Cassy some time to reconsider?" he offered, lifting his own glass to his lips. He had worked for Gordan since his salad days when he was just opening his first hotel. He and Marian had looked after Wil when Gordan had to be away on business. The two men respected each other, and Gordan had come to depend on Bradford's level head and keen judgment. It had been his ex-wife who had hired the couple, but at the time of the divorce, they had chosen to work for Gordan.

"She was not exactly in a receptive mood," he said, dryly, staring at the liquor in his glass rather than drinking it.

The two settled into a comfortable silence, Bradford thoughtful while Gordan brooded.

"She can't turn off her feelings that quickly."

Gordan's laughter was filled with bitterness. "Believe it. I have no one to blame but myself. I missed all the signals. I didn't even see it coming. I didn't know she was unhappy until it was too late."

Their silence stretched on until Bradford said, "My Marian almost put me down a few years back."

Gordan looked at him. Marian Bradford had worked alongside her husband for many years. They both seemed to enjoy the travel and each other. Gordan had often marveled at their devotion to each other. Marian was an excellent cook and was very good with Gordy when he visited.

"What happened?"

"I didn't let her leave me, that's for sure."

Gordan grinned. "How'd you stop her?"

"Found out what was wrong and fixed it. In other words, I made her fall in love with me all over again."

"Yeah?"

"Yeah." Rising to his feet, Bradford said, "I suggest you figure out what you did right the first time and get busy." He picked up the discarded suit coat before he said, formally, "Good night."

" 'Night, Bradford. And thanks."

Gordan slowly drained his glass. Reaching for the cordless telephone, he dialed, without bothering to check the time. "Hey," he said, when the sleepy, deep male voice came on the line.

"What's wrong?" Wilham Kramer asked.

"Why do you ask?"

Wil grumbled, "You don't usually call me this late unless there's a problem. What's wrong?"

"You alone?"

"Does it matter?"

"Just curious."

"Yeah. Is it Gordy?" Concern was evident in his voice.

"No. Sorry, I should have paid more attention to the time."

"It's all right, bro. Something is bothering you. Start talking."

"It's Cassy. She was not pleased to see me."

His brother knew about their separation. "I hope you haven't made it worse by losing your temper."

"Probably. I couldn't find the right words to make it better. She's fighting me every step of the way. She wants out and she's not willing to reconsider."

"Can you blame her? She loves you, man. Why can't you get it through your head once and for all that Cassy isn't Evie and that you should marry the lady?"

"You know why," he grated, harshly. "You know how the marriage ended. And what it did to me." Gordan didn't add that it nearly destroyed him. He didn't have to; his brother had been an eyewitness. It took years to pull himself together emotionally.

"So you goin' to sit back like a chump and let your woman walk?"

"Hell, no!"

"Well? How are you goin' to get her back?"

"I don't know. I just know I have to. I can't lose her, Wil."

"Do you want me to try talking to her? She still likes me."

Gordan surprised himself when he chuckled. "If only it were that simple. This is something I have to do myself.

Only, how? Bradford had some interesting advice. He suggested I repeat whatever it was that worked the first time."

Wil laughed. "Can't hurt. Try it."

"Yeah," he said, thoughtfully, then asked, "Everything okay with you?"

"Absolutely. I've got sense enough not to fall in love."

"I can just imagine what Dad would say to that. Our folks were in love, or did you forget that?"

Wil chuckled, "Point taken. But how many women are there like Mama and Cassy? Very few. A man can get a little tired of the 'I'm gorgeous and what can you do for me' crap the sisters are dishing up." He let out a loud yawn. "If you need me, I'm here."

"Yeah, I know. 'Night." Gordan replaced the receiver before refilling his glass. Wil had grown into a man of whom their parents would have been proud.

"Cassy . . ." he said, softly, thinking of the sparkling brown depths of her beautiful eyes the night they met.

He'd been fully engrossed in obtaining the property of one of his dinner guests, Howard Parham—business, pure and simple. It was a choice strip of land in Bali, which included a pristine white beach. As he recalled, his guest was interested in developing condominium complexes on that property.

Bradford had overseen the meal, as was his custom, including the hiring of the hotel's French pastry chef to concoct a mouth-watering dessert for a guest known for his sweet tooth.

At the time, Gordan had been seeing a lithe, African beauty, well known for her glorious cheekbones. Sonja had no objection to his lifestyle or his very expensive presents. She made herself available to him whenever he needed a hostess. She had a very successful runway career, working almost exclusively in Paris, London, and Milan, and she enjoyed aligning herself with wealthy men.

The classic French cuisine had been exceptional. Gordan, as well as his guests, had fallen in love with the exquisitely creamy and rich tropical pie brimming with freshly grated coconut and sweet and tangy pineapple in a buttery, rich, flaky crust. Gordan smiled at the memory; everyone had raved about the perfect ending to a delicious meal— everyone, that was, but the constantly dieting Sonja. Howard had insisted on meeting the chef. Gordan always believed the man had been trying to steal the chef from under his nose.

He had been the one shocked when the chef who joined them on the balcony turned out to be an exceptionally lovely woman. Cassy was simply beautiful. The remainder of the evening, he had made polite conversation, but his mind, for once, had not been on business.

He was thinking of a woman of average height with a genuine warmth that was reflected in her dark eyes and in her captivating smile. Her eyes twinkled with humor. She was a confident woman, comfortable with herself and proud of her culinary achievements. He had been both immediately fascinated by and attracted to her.

Gordan smiled, thoughtfully. He had been livid when he got around to remembering that she was one of his employees. He did not date members of his staff. It had been a rule he had not even considered breaking until he met Cassy.

Over the years he had grown tired of women who were interested in what he could give them rather than a genuine interest in him. Celibacy had not been a hardship. Empty, emotionless sex had no appeal.

He had known from the beginning that Cassandra Mosley was different. He had no idea what it was about her that caught and held his attention. Perhaps it was her open, friendly attitude toward life; it certainly was not her delectable, curvy figure, simply because it had been concealed beneath her starched cotton chef garb. Even her hair had been hidden. Whatever it was, he knew that he wanted to know everything there was to know about her. His sexual appetite for her was unrelenting.

For the first time in memory his business took a back seat to his personal life. He devoted himself to spending as much time as he could with Cassy. He devoted himself to winning her over.

Gordan chuckled, closing his eyes as if to savor the sweetness of those weeks of discovery. They had spent hours exploring the island, getting to know each other, while slowly but steadfastly falling in love. For the most part, he worked around her hours in the restaurant. She had flatly refused when he suggested that she take a paid leave from her duties.

She had been adamant, refusing to allow him to manipulate her schedule to suit himself. She let him know that she had a temper and was not afraid to stand up for herself or what she believed in.

It got so bad that when they were not together, he had a difficult time keeping his mind off of her. Cassy was never far from his thoughts. Many things had changed over the years, but even after all this time, that was the one thing that remained the same.

Also, his desire for her had not altered. If he lived to be a hundred he would never forget that first time she took him inside her body. Gordan whispered her name aloud as he leaned back in his chair with his eyes closed. He could almost see her as she stood in front of him on that long-ago night when she had finally said yes.

She'd been so beautiful. His breath quickened and his nostrils flared, as if he could not only see her but also smell her woman's scent. They had spent the evening together, and ended it with a walk on the beach, or so he thought at the time. After the drive to the colorful cottage situated a few miles from the hotel, she'd invited him inside. Neither of them wanted the night to end as the others before it, with both of them alone. When she invited him in, he was not about to refuse.

Her cottage was small, consisting of a sitting area, a combined kitchen and dining room, and a single bedroom with connecting bath. Once he was seated on the settee, she asked if he cared for something to drink.

Gordan had had enough of waiting. He wanted her—wanted her so intensely that he could not get past that need. He had held a hand out to her, and she had come to him without hesitation. She stood between his spread thighs, her small, delicate fingers intertwined with his. Although she smiled, she was trembling when she leaned forward and pressed her mouth to his.

"Please—I want to be with you." Then she told him, "You see, Gordan Kramer—I'm in love with you."

There had been no holding back—they wanted each other too much. Gordan had pulled her onto his lap and deep inside his heart. He had never experienced anything more wonderful or fulfilling than making her his that first time. Knowing he had her trust and her love had been worth the weeks it had taken him to convince her to become his lady. She suited him perfectly both inside and outside of the bedroom.

For a time, his life had been full, balanced between his son, his work, and his lady. He had been happy—happier than he ever thought possible. When they were not together, he looked forward to their next time together.

As time passed, he had managed to even convince himself that the distance didn't matter. As far as he was concerned, she was more than worth the wait involved until they could see each other again.

He had not been prepared for things to change between them. Perhaps he had even taken what they had for granted. Yet, the demands of a successful business had eventually taken a toll on his free time. He needed to be in South Africa or St. Thomas or Jamaica or Atlanta. He could not get to Martinique, or later, the San Francisco Bay area, where she had relocated when she left the island.

He sighed wearily. How had he gone from thinking nothing could come between them to watching it crumble without being able to put a stop to it?

Even after their confrontation in Atlanta, he had not taken her as seriously as he should have. It had been easier to console himself with the thought that once she had time to cool off, reconsider, she would remember how much they meant to each other.

For the first time, he had no choice but to face the fact that what was wrong between them he might not be able to fix. If nothing else, he knew Cassy had a mind of her own.

He had failed to recognize that they had been in transition for some time. Was it any wonder that they had gradually moved away from their emotional connection? Could they find it again?

Gordan took a deep swallow from his glass, letting the liquor burn its way down his throat; hopefully it would dull the ache in his heart. He needed her. She was a part of him. When had he stopped mattering to her? He certainly had not seen it coming. He had missed all the clues along the way. If he ran his business the way he did his personal life, he would have been bankrupt long ago.

She had been cool and lovely tonight, never letting her eyes meet his for more than an instant. Her voice remained soft and unemotional with only occasional flashes of temper. Her soft body had stiffened when he got too close. Cassy had become a master at keeping him at a distance.

She had gone positively rigid when he cupped her shoulders. It was almost as if she could no longer tolerate his touch. He swore bitterly. He hated the changes in her. The further she pushed him away, the closer he wanted to be.

Gordan growled with frustration deep in his throat, like a wounded animal, as he wondered how he could possibly do what she wanted. How could he let her go? How?

Gordan felt as if he were losing the fight against his own deepening despair. Was it true? Had she stopped loving him? Why else would she decide she no longer wanted him in her life? Surging to his feet, he went out onto the balcony. As he stood at the rail, staring out into the night, waves of mounting fear and despair rushed over him. What if it were already too late? What if he'd lost her? What kind of life would he have without her? No!

"I can't let her go," he mumbled, aloud. Not yet, not until she convinced him that she had stopped loving him. Not until then.

If he could gain her trust once, he could do so again. He would woo her back into his arms and into his life, just as he had done four years ago. Only this time, he intended to keep her there.

Cassy could not stop shaking, even after she let herself into her room and locked the door firmly behind her. She was overreacting and she knew it. She had practically run from the penthouse as if Gordan was in hot pursuit. She had gone into the classic fright-and-flight pattern after the shock she had received.

How could he have implied that she had been seeing Adam behind his back? And how could she have deliberately let him think she was after Adam? There had been no reason to bring the other man into the conversation.

Her decision to end the relationship had nothing to do with anyone other than the two of them.

Cassy was furious with herself for even mentioning the other man's name, throwing him up to Gordan just because she was hurt and angry. She was a better woman than that.

Her decision to move on had been coming for some time. There was always something keeping them apart— problems with his ex-wife trying to turn his son against him, his career, or her career. Always something.

Gordan's anger tonight had nothing to do with caring. He was not about to stand quietly by and let any woman walk all over him. And that, in a sense, was what he thought she had done. In his estimation, she had stepped all over his ego and onto his pride. Adding that to her claim to be interested in another man so soon after their breakup was just too much. She might as well have thrown salt onto an open wound, considering the way his marriage had ended. She had not meant to hurt him.

Couldn't he see that walking away was the hardest thing she had ever done? She had loved that man too hard and too long. Letting go had been sheer torment. Yet, there were no alternatives for them. And the sooner he accepted it, the easier it would be for both of them.

As she sank into a nearby armchair, Cassy knew she needed more—deserved better. She had to remain strong. And she would.

After all, she had survived worse. The loss of her mother at a young age had been heartbreaking. As a young girl, Cassy missed her father, who had been so crushed by his wife's death that he sent his girls to be cared for by his mother in California, a long way from DC, where they had been born.

It had been harder on Cassy than Sarah because she was younger and did not understand. Thank goodness, they had their grandmother's love to help pull them both through the loss of their mother.

Sarah had gone back to live with their father and stepmother and twin brothers when she was eighteen, while Cassy had stayed on with their grandmother. Cassy's first time away had been after high school graduation when she had gone to culinary art college in upstate New York.

She had dated during her vagabond years while she'd been learning her craft. She had met cosmopolitan, sophisticated black men from all over the world. Yet, none of them could touch Gordan's seductive, masculine charm. He was suave, extremely male, confident in himself and his appeal to the opposite sex.

She had been in love only once before she met Gordan. It had been while she was living and working at a world-famous hotel in Paris. Van was also a chef and from New Orleans. He was a very handsome black man, who owned a restaurant in the heart of the city of lights. It was a fabulous place. Cassy went there for the first time with friends and loved it because of the reminders of home. Van specialized in down-home Louisiana, fire-in-the-belly kind of Creole cuisine.

Van was so handsome and had no shortage of female friends. But he had taken a particular liking to Cassy. He had shown her the wildly romantic city. He had also taken her virginity and given nothing of his own heart in return. She had come to Paris, young, filled with dreams, and naive; she'd left vowing to never let another man get that close again.

For the next ten years, although she dated, she concentrated on making a name for herself as a chef, pushing away all those girlhood thoughts of a home and family of her own.

She had been working in Toronto when she had been approached by Kenneth Kittman, manager of Kramer

House—Martinique. While in the city on business, he had
sampled several of her desserts. He offered her a job on
the spot. She had been thrilled that her reputation as a
pastry chef was growing and she was on her way. And she
was not about to turn down this opportunity.

Naturally, she had heard of the black multimillionaire
who headed Kramer Corporation; who hadn't? The man
had been written up in *Ebony, Black Enterprise,* and *The Wall
Street Journal.*

When she received the request to prepare a special meal
in the owner's penthouse kitchen, it was an honor.
Together, Cassy and the Bradfords had planned a menu
for that special night. And she had been determined to
do her very best. What she had not planned on was meeting
Gordan Kramer.

He had taken things further by dining often in the
French restaurant, inviting her to join him for coffee and
dessert. Cassy was just beginning to realize that the boss
man was interested in more than her cooking.

She not been prepared for his undivided attention.
Although flattered by his interest, she was quickly overwhelmed by his blatant male charm; yet, she was determined to use her head and not let his wealth or good looks
influence her. The last thing she needed was some rich
playboy, playing with her emotions.

Gordan slowly but steadfastly eliminated her doubts until
she could see not what he owned nor his social status, but
the man behind it all. It was only then that she fell for
him. And she fell hard. There were no half measures on
her part.

Wiping away tears, she accepted that she had come a
long way from Oakland and her roots if she had to resort
to half-truths to get her way. It had been a lousy thing to
do and she had not been able to carry it off. Who either

of them became involved with should not matter. Neither
Jillian's nor Adam's name should have been spoken.

It was not that she was being stupid. A man in Gordan's
position would have absolutely no problem replacing her.
There was no doubt about it. Gordan was a very attractive
man.

Jillian was waiting for him to get Cassy out of his system.
Any fool could see how much his lovely assistant cared for
him. And Cassy was nobody's fool.

What was surprising was that Jillian had not already made
a move on him. Cassy was certainly no longer a deterrent.
The Jillians and the Sonjas of the world were welcome to
the man.

Cassy's mistake was that she had stayed so long. She
should have left him over a year ago when she recognized
that she was not a priority. She was not even on his list. It
was only after she could no longer travel to him that she
had to face the truth.

Cassy shuddered. She had wasted years wishing and hoping that Gordan would change. No more! She was moving
on, going after what she needed in life. All she had to
figure out was how to stop loving him.

When Gordan had touched her on the patio, her heart
had virtually stopped beating. It had taken all her resolve
not to let him see just how responsive she was to him—
and she'd failed. She had started trembling in awareness
before he had taken her into his arms. But then, it had
always been that way between them. Tonight had been no
different. He had caressed her and she had melted deep
inside.

Cassy closed her eyes as provocative memories of their
loving flashed through her mind. Gordan knew exactly
where and how to touch her—how to pleasure her in and
out of bed. For a time during the evening, she had wanted

nothing more than to let him do what he did so well—
make love with her.

He had always been with a sensuous and considerate
lover. Physically, he could take care of all her sexual needs;
unfortunately, she would end up an emotional wreck—
worse off than she was now.

What did he mean when he said she owed him that
much? It was true she had sprung her decision on him.
And it was true it had taken her a while to build up the
nerve to tell him what she wanted, while knowing he
wanted just the opposite. And it was true she had been
very hurt and angry when she had issued that ultimatum.

Perhaps she had not been particularly fair to him. But
did that mean she owed him the time he was asking for?
Was she strong enough to do that much and no more?
Hadn't the kisses on the balcony shown her, as nothing
else could, how vulnerable she was to the man?

The intrusion of the bedside telephone startled her.
"Hello?"

"Hi. I hope I didn't wake you. It's Adam."

"No, you didn't. Did you have an enjoyable evening?"

"Impossible not to. It was ladies' night in the hotel's
jazz club. I'd hoped I'd run into you."

"It's late, Adam."

"Can I interest you in a little club-hopping tomorrow
night?"

Cassy stopped, swallowing an automatic refusal. She felt
as if she was cheating on Gordan, which was ridiculous.
She had no reason to feel guilty.

"Cassy?"

Why not? What better way to get over one man than
with another? It was clear that what she had been doing
was not working to any measurable degree.

"Thank you, Adam. I'd love to go out with you tomorrow
evening."

"Wonderful. Nine?"

"Fine. I'm looking forward to it."

"So am I. Sorry I called so late."

"Not a problem. 'Bye."

Chapter Nine

It was nearly a week after she had seen Renee in the Martinique Room that Cassy set out for the Halleys' cottage. She considered taking a taxi or one of the hotel shuttles, but she decided the walk would do her good. The sun was just breaking through the clouds when she reached the cottage, which was less than a half mile down from where she had lived while she worked on the island.

Using the brass knocker mounted on the door, she decided that she had been lucky it hadn't rained, after all.

"Cassy! *Bonjour!* It's about time you showed yourself," Renee scolded her, with a welcoming smile and kiss on both cheeks. She stepped back so that Cassy could enter the roomy three-bedroom cottage she shared with her husband and son, now that their older daughter no longer lived on the island. "Come inside, *Cheri*. Did you walk?"

"Yes. I decided to walk off some of the extra calories I have been indulging in lately." Cassy giggled, "Lounging on the beach and shopping doesn't exactly work up a sweat, if you know what I mean."

Renee laughed. "Island men like a woman with a few curves on her."

The cottage was as colorful and comfortable as Cassy remembered. On the bright pink, blue, and green braided area-rug was a large rattan sofa and matching love seat, cushioned in heavy dusty-rose cotton. Positioned in front of the bay windows were two deep, cushioned, floral-patterned armchairs. Large tropical plants were everywhere.

"Oh, Renee, I see you haven't lost your talent with plants." As always, Cassy was charmed by Renee's lovely accent and natural beauty. Her speech, as well as her taste, was a delightful mixture of both her African and French roots. "Your ferns and the ficus trees are huge. I bet your garden is still as fabulous as ever."

Renee laughed. She'd been busy arranging wild flowers in the vase on the side table near the windows when Cassy knocked. "It is so good to have you here. But, as you know, it takes no great talent. Of course, everything grows beautifully in Martinique, *oui?*" Ceiling fans hummed quietly overhead and the blinds were partly closed to keep the room cool and comfortable.

Cassy was not surprised by the Halleys' prosperity. Gordan was more than a fair employer. He believed in only the best, which meant hiring talented people and paying accordingly. Kramer Corporation provided cottages for its staff. The Kramer hotels and resort complexes were almost cities within themselves.

"Please, sit down."

"May I see your garden?"

"Oui! Come."

The two were dressed much the same in cool gauze sleeveless dresses—Cassy's was white piped in plum while

Renee's was orange. They hooked arms as Renee led the way through the cool dining room, past the large kitchen and out the screened backdoor. Birds fluttered high in the tree-lined border of the property and bougainvillea, hibiscus, and wild orchids were in abundance.

"Renee, it's as beautiful as I remembered. And what was that delectable smell in the kitchen?"

"I was doing some baking earlier. Sit." Renee indicated the lawn furniture positioned beneath a majestic palm tree, semi-enclosed by the flowering shrubs. Once they sat side by side on the slider, she said eagerly, "We have so much to catch up on. Tell me all about that wonderful inn of yours, that you wrote me about. Did you bring pictures?"

Cassy grinned. "As a matter of fact, I did. It's called Parkside Garden Inn. You and Ralph must come to visit."

She searched through her tote bag, before she pulled out a small photo album to give to her friend. As the two settled back, Cassy told Renee about the inn and showed her pictures of the rooms, the gardens, and her family including her little nephew.

"What a charming family. Everything is *magnifique!* And the roses. They are huge. Is this where you have your herb garden?" Renee asked, pointing to a photo.

"Yes. Just a few steps away from the kitchen door. I love it. My sister, Sarah, and I both enjoy gardening. But there is so much to do these days, we hardly have any free time anymore. This is our dining room. As you can see, we chose the shades of pink that are in the rose garden since the room opens right into that section of the garden."

"What a charming place—more like home than a hotel. Congratulations. You and Sarah have done well for yourselves."

Cassy was practically beaming. "Thank you. It's a tremendous amount of work, but we're pleased."

"Ralph and I will come for a visit the next time we're in the States, I promise."

"I would love that. I'd like you to meet my family."

"It's so good to be able to sit down together and talk. Tell me, do you only serve breakfast?"

"No, we have a fully staffed restaurant. We often have local clientele, especially during dinner on the weekends." She laughed. "It keeps us busy." Cassy smiled. "That little one is my great-niece, Mandy. That is my sister with her husband, Kurt. This was taken on their wedding day."

"What a happy family. So much love."

"Speaking of families, it seems as if yours is doing very well. Ralph told me about Ria and André. You must be thrilled."

"Oui! Thanks to Gordan, both are thrilled with their jobs. *Excusez-moi* for a moment while I get the iced mint tea."

After placing the photo album on a side table, Cassy chided herself because of the way her heart had raced at the mention of Gordan's name. He was known for looking after his own. It was one of the reasons she believed he was so successful. He had always . . .

She made herself stop right there. *You need to get over it, girl.* She had gone out with Adam the past couple evenings and even managed to enjoy herself. Adam was good company and had made no demands on her. For that, she was grateful. She would be the first to admit that she was not ready for an emotional involvement with a new man. If only she had met him at another time when she . . .

"Here we are, *Cheri.*" Renee placed a tray on the table and poured the iced beverage.

"Thanks." Cassy took a long drink. Eyeing the frosted lemon bars, she teased, "I thought this was your day off?"

Renee giggled. *"Oui,* but there is always enough time to

make treats for those we love," she said, as she poured the iced drink, then offered the pastry.

"Mmm," Cassy said, tasting the bar. "Is Ralph working today?"

Renee shook her head. "No, he is out with ..." She hesitated, then quickly added, "fishing with a friend."

Taking a deep breath, Cassy sighed, "I've missed the island."

"What made you come back?"

"The trip was a birthday gift from my family." Cassy went on to explain about her sister's difficult pregnancy and recovery.

"How are Sarah and the baby?"

"Wonderful."

"The four of us used to have so much fun. Do you remember the times when Gordan took us out deep sea fishing on his boat?" She giggled. "You had that huge snapper on the line and had no idea what to do with it."

Cassy looked away. "I'd rather not ... remember."

Renee took her hand. "What happened? You and Gordan were so happy for so long. Now suddenly you are both here on the island but you're not together."

Cassy jumped to her feet and walked over to one of the rose bushes. Caressing a single bloom, she bent to inhale the fragrant scent, then she said, "It doesn't matter anymore. It's over."

"Non, I don't think either one of you is happy. Look at you. The instant I mention the man's name you start trembling. This is not idle curiosity. Please, perhaps I can be of help. Ralph and I have had our share of disagreements."

She tried to smile at her friend, but failed. Perhaps, Renee was right. "This is more than a disagreement."

"Is that why I've seen you with another man? Is he the reason you've broken it off with Gordan?"

"No! Our breakup has nothing to do with Adam. I met

him here, my first day back in Martinique. We're friends—
nothing more." Cassy shivered, rubbing goose pimples on
her arms despite the sun overhead.

Renee came up to her and gave her a hug. *"Pardon.* I
didn't mean to upset you."

Cassy returned the hug, needing the comfort. "I'm sorry,
also. But I had no other choice. I could not go on with
things being the way they were between us. Gordan has
become so successful—so busy. He didn't have time for a
relationship. His work, his son, and Jillian, his assistant—
whom he spends ten to twelve hours a day with—have
taken up all his time." She shrugged. "It had come to the
point I started to wonder what he needed me for." She
admitted, "I had been working long hours also. And I
could no longer get away easily, especially when my sister
was ill." Cassy bit her lip before admitting, "It didn't seem
to matter to him if we don't see each other for months
and months. Besides, we want two different things from
life. He doesn't want a wife or more children. I started
asking myself, what was the point of it all. I want those
things."

"Family is very much a part of your life. It's only natural
that you would want a husband and children, eventually."

"We were happy, the first couple of years. Then everything changed. It wasn't all his fault. I don't mean to say
that. For too long we didn't have time to even see each
other, and we settled for telephone calls. That was not
enough."

"Come, let's sit down." Renee ushered her back to the
glider. "Relax. We'll speak of other things. Pleasant things.
What is your menu like at your inn?"

They talked about cooking and family, for a time.

"How have you and Ralph remained close for so many
years? The two of you are still so much in love."

Renee giggled like a young girl. "We work at it. We

always take time away from work, just to be together and think only about each other. We always vacation alone, no kids. Something we both look forward to."

"That's wonderful. My sister has been lucky, also. She fell in love all over again with her high school sweetheart. And now they're married and very happy. So I know it can happen."

"Perhaps it has happened for you?"

Cassy didn't even consider exploring that avenue of thought. It was simpler, less painful, not to believe.

"It is not easy to stop loving someone, my friend, even when our minds tell us it is for the best."

Cassy managed to force a smile, deciding to change their focus. "I take it Ralph will bring dinner tonight. What if the fish are not biting?"

"I have confidence in him." Then she shrugged. "But just in case they all get away from him, I have a pork roast in the freezer." They both laughed. "Won't you stay and share our evening meal? It will give us a chance to cook together again."

"I'd love to. It seems like ages since we've played around in the kitchen. I never would have gotten the hang of local cuisine without your help. I've even made several of your favorites at the inn, with wonderful results."

"*Marveilleax!* How often do you change your menu? I imagine that you have some returning guests who expect certain dishes to be on . . ."

They heard Ralph calling Renee from inside the house. "Where are you, *Cheri?*"

"In the garden," she called. She whispered, "Want to make a wager—fish or pork?"

Cassy giggled, "I'd probably lose."

Ralph's large frame filled the back doorway when he saw Cassy. With a huge smile on his dark face, he said, "Cassy! It's about time you came to visit."

Before she could formulate an answer, she caught sight
of the taller man behind him. Cassy's entire body stiffened
as her eyes locked with Gordan's an instant before Ralph
swept her off her feet.

"Ralph, put me down!" Cassy laughed.

She could not believe her bad luck. Why today of all
days? She hadn't heard from or seen him in days. Even
though Gordan had been friends with the Halleys for years,
she was shocked that he had taken valuable time away from
his precious business to go fishing with Ralph.

Ralph chuckled, kissing both her cheeks. "It is good to
have you here in our home. It has been too long!"

Renee greeted Gordan with a kiss on both cheeks.
"Where is our dinner? What! You two been out all day
and no fish? Do I have to get the roast out of the freezer?"
With her hands on her hips, she looked from one man to
the other. "Well?"

Gordan laughed, but his gaze was on Cassy. He said,
"Hello, Cassy. Renee, you'll find four large snappers waiting in the kitchen for your special touch."

"Splendid. We'll have a special dinner. Cassy and I were
just talking about cooking together again." She asked
Cassy, "Ready to get started?" From over her shoulder, as
she urged Cassy along with her toward the house, she said,
"Gordan, you're staying to eat with us, aren't you?"

"I'm looking forward to it."

"Wonderful. *Cheri*, get Gordan a cold beer, *s'il vous
plait.*"

Cassy was struggling with her feelings. What could she
do? She couldn't back out now after she'd promised to
stay. Why did he have to spoil it for her? She had been
looking forward to a relaxing meal with old friends.

Once they were in the kitchen out of hearing range,
Renee said, "I'm sorry. I had no idea Ralph would bring

Gordan home with him. And I couldn't very well not invite him to stay."

Cassy patted her friend's arm. "Don't worry about it. After all, we're only talking about a meal. Now, let me wash my hands and we can get started."

In no time, Cassy, covered by an apron, began mixing and kneading dough for an exquisitely flaky pie crust, while Renee washed and seasoned the fish and prepared an array of vegetables. They chatted while they worked, careful not to mention the man that Cassy could see through the picture window relaxing in the garden with his host.

"Hmm, something smells good," André Halley said, as he came into the kitchen. He kissed his mother's cheek and grinned at Cassy.

"One of your favorites. But I thought you had a date tonight," Renee replied.

"I do. I stopped to change. What's that?" he asked, eyeing the fluffy, meringue-topped pie Cassy was putting into the oven.

"Banana creme."

"Too bad you're not staying for dinner," Renee teased.

"Mama! You've got to save me some."

Renee shrugged. "You know your father."

"You're a hard woman. Talk to her, Cassy." With that, he was gone.

"I think it's only a matter of time until I'll be a mother-in-law."

"Really? Who?"

"Gretchen Divan. She works in the hotel's business office. She transferred in from the Jamaica hotel."

"An island girl?"

"She's from New York."

Cassy helped her friend carry in the china and cutlery

and table linen into the dining room. "Sounds interesting." Together, they set the table.

"Will you call the men?" Renee asked, when they were ready to serve.

Cassy nodded, taking off her apron. She took a deep breath, wishing she were anywhere but near Gordan. Her stomach was already in knots, and they hadn't even sat down to eat.

A meal shared with old and dear friends should have been enjoyable. Unfortunately, she could not get past her awareness of the man seated directly across the table. She did no more than pick at her food. She told herself that she was glad that everyone else seemed to be having a great time.

She couldn't imagine being more uncomfortable. Every single time she looked up, her eyes collided with Gordan's. She was the one that looked away. Why didn't he just leave?

The ladies went into the sitting room while the men cleared the table. Cassy busied herself by studying Renee's collection of cookbooks on the bookshelf. It was an effort to keep a smile on her face. The task was becoming more difficult with each minute that passed.

Cassy asked, restlessly wandering from one plant to the next, "Are you sure you wouldn't like me to help with the dishes?"

"That's Ralph's job—loading the dishwasher. Besides, you're our guest. I want you to sit beside me and try to relax."

Although Cassy sat, she was far from tranquil. "I really should be getting back to the hotel. It's getting late."

"Oh, here is Ralph with the coffee and your delicious dessert. I can hardly wait. Your technique with pastries is flawless. I have to have another lesson before you leave the island."

Cassy smiled her thanks. "That's easily arranged."

"This is a real treat. Wouldn't you agree, Gordan?" Ralph asked, placing the tray on the low table in front of his wife.

"There is no better way to end an exquisite meal," Gordan said, smoothly.

Cassy clasped her hands in her lap but made no comment.

After the praise had died down, and they had indulged their senses in the creamy dessert, they chatted about the changes to the island, as Ralph refilled their cups with more fragrant, strong, hot coffee.

Cassy had had enough. Rising, she said, "I really must get back." She kissed both of her hosts. "Thank you, both, for a lovely evening. You two always make me feel so welcome."

"What's the hurry? Another engagement later?" Gordan asked, pointedly. They were all on their feet now.

"No, but it's late." Furious with herself for answering, she said, "Besides, it's a long walk back to the hotel."

Gordan said, "I'd be happy to drive you."

"Un moment, I'll get your purse from the garden," Ralph offered.

When she spoke to Gordan, she chose not to meet his piercing gaze, but focused instead on his bearded chin. "It's a beautiful night. I prefer walking. Besides, you haven't finished your coffee."

"I'm truly sorry," Renee said, close to Cassy's ear. "Must you leave so soon?"

She whispered back, "It's not your fault. I have to go."

In a normal voice, Renee said, "I enjoyed our visit, Cassy. I hope we can get together again before you go back home."

Accepting her tote bag, she squeezed both of their hands in turn, before she said, "Good night." Then she hurried out.

Cassy tried as hard as she could to concentrate on nothing more important than the gravel road winding its way toward the hotel. The road was almost deserted at this time of day. The sound of the sea was close at hand.

She had forgotten her sun hat, but she was not about to go back for it. She would rather toss herself into the sea than face another evening like this one. It had been so difficult that she would not have been surprised if she had battle scars. Since he would not leave, she should have. But she could not have hurt the Halleys that way. They were good people.

She tried telling herself that seeing Gordan again had absolutely no effect on her; unfortunately, she knew better. Her knees were still shaking, and she did not want to recall the way her heart had pounded when his eyes lingered on her throughout the meal.

She didn't have to remember exactly how his pale-blue knit shirt had hugged his wide chest and muscular arms, or the way soft, well-washed jeans had hugged his muscular thighs and long legs. There was not a thing wrong with her eyesight.

Furious, she quickened her steps. She reminded herself that she did not make her decisions based on her estrogen levels. She had left Gordan Kramer for a reason that didn't have a thing to do with the way a pair of jeans cupped his prominent sex. He might look like a man, but he was nothing more than a well-oiled machine that thrived on it's work. Why did he have to force his company on . . .

"Cassy . . ."

She jumped at the sound of the male voice coming from the open car window. Refusing to glance his way or so much as acknowledge she had heard him, she kept right on walking.

"Cassy . . ."

When he didn't take the hint and drive away, she flung from over her shoulder, "I don't want a ride."

Gordan didn't say another word. Pressing on the accelerator, he sent the sleek, convertible black sports car moving ahead of her.

"Hallelujah!"

He'd finally gotten the point. After a look at the thickening clouds and the ominous rumble of thunder overhead, she hurried her pace even more. When she rounded the blind curve in the road that was blocked by towering flowering shrubs, she saw Gordan. He was leaning against the car, his arms casually crossed over his chest.

Enraged by what she considered sheer male arrogance, she hissed, "What part of 'no' don't you understand?" Ignoring the deepening shadows, she persisted, "I told you ..." She'd broken off so abruptly that her teeth clinked together. Gordan held her photo album in one hand and her straw hat in the other.

"It looks like we're in for rain. I thought you might need these. Renee found them after you left," he said, calmly.

"Thanks," she said, begrudgingly. Determined to put distance between them, she paused only long enough to collect her belongings.

"I'm not letting you walk back to the hotel alone. We either walk together or ride. The choice is yours."

That got her attention. She hesitated, then said, "I don't believe I need your permission."

"We're not in New York or DC, but you're still a beautiful woman and you're alone at night."

"It's not even fully dark yet."

"I'm not leaving you, baby."

Cassy raised her chin, preparing for a confrontation, then looked away. In fact, she was silent so long that he said her name.

"Does everything have to always go your way, Gordan?"

She had barely taken a half dozen steps when he pocketed his keys and fell into step behind her. "Why are you doing this?"

"You know why."

Cassy pressed her lips together.

"I really enjoyed being with Ralph and Renee. It's been a long time since the four of us spent time together. We used to have a ball together. I've been doing a lot of thinking these past few days. You're right, Cassy. I've been taking too many things for granted—you especially. I'm sorry."

She didn't make a comment, but merely kept her eyes straight ahead while trying not to internalize what he'd said.

"I said . . ."

"I heard you. But it's too late. I don't care anymore."

Gordan went on to say, "I've done a lot of remembering. There was a time when we both were so hopeful, so pleased we had finally found each other. We were a lot alike. We'd both had bad experiences with someone else. We were determined to get it right this time."

"So?"

"I wanted you from the first moment I saw you, baby. You were beautiful, but it was much more than the physical. You were warm and rich in spirit, generous with your smiles and laughter." He chuckled, "Do you remember how surprised you were the first time I asked you out? You asked me if I were serious."

"I was thrown off balance. I thought you were captivated by my cooking. Wanted me to become your personal chef."

"I was captivated by you. You were different from the other women I had dated."

"Well, you got one thing right. I was very different from the pencil-thin high-maintenance model you were seeing at the time. Her shoes cost more than everything I wore on our first date. I couldn't compete."

"You didn't have to try. It was you, Cassy. I wanted to be with you—only you. That hasn't changed. You've never given me reason to doubt that it was me you wanted. Not my income or level of success. It has always meant a lot to me. I just haven't taken the time to tell you how much it has meant recently. You're right. I've been neglectful."

Cassy closed her eyes briefly as if she could escape the sincerity she heard in his voice. She forced herself to say, "It no longer matters." She felt badly that she could not be completely open with him. But how could she when she could not let him weaken her resolve. She sought protection in anger. "I've had about as much as one woman can take."

Quirking a brow, he asked, "Why? Because I won't let you walk all over me? Or because I won't take no for an answer?"

Cassy's mouth dropped open. Then she jerked her chin up in a show of defiance. "Because you refuse to take me seriously."

"That is not true."

"It is true! You haven't heard what I've been telling you for months!"

"I heard you, baby. I just didn't know it was so important to you." He turned her so he could look at her in the meager light. "Cassy . . ."

She tried to push him away.

"Stop it!" he exclaimed.

"We don't have to touch in order to talk!" she replied.

His jaw was tight. "You've done everything you can think of to push me away from you. But some things you can't hide. I felt the way you responded to me the other night on the balcony. Everything may not have gone your way in our relationship, but that doesn't change how we feel about each other." He whispered close to her ear. "I missed you, baby. It's been so long since we've held each other, loved each other. When are you going to stop punishing us both? We can work this out, if we try."

Here they were in the middle of a desert road, halfway between the hotel and the Halleys' cottage, and she was shaking like a leaf in a gale. None of it was making very much sense.

Cassy tried to ignore the longing in his dark eyes. She said, "I don't want to try. All I want is to forget we ever met."

"You can't meant that, Cassy."

"It doesn't matter anymore, Gordan. None of it matters. You can't have everything you want. I'm not part of the million-dollar corporation you are used to controlling. You can't have me."

Gordan's muscles went taut as he fought the urge to prove his point by pulling her against him and grinding his mouth against hers. Instead, he lowered his head until he was nearly eye-level with her. "I know how to go after what I want. Make no mistake, lady. I want you back."

"I'm not one of your business projects. I'm a flesh and blood woman. I want to be first in my man's life. I won't ever again make do with less."

They glared at each other as the sky cracked with lightning.

"This is crazy! You're leaving an expensive car with the top down on the side of a road to prove a point. One of us needs to use a little common sense." Cassy whirled and started back.

Gordan followed, deep in thought. The car or the threat of rain was not the problem. His inability to fill her needs were. Again and again, she had flung the accusation at him that he didn't consider her a priority in his life. The lady was right.

He had made her a priority—that was, until he felt she was firmly fixed into his life. Once he knew he had her, he had gradually let business demands and his son come before her.

How many times had he assured himself that she would understand why he had to fly here or there and not meet her as they had planned? But she had not understood. And he was now facing a future without her.

Gordan reached the car ahead of her, opening the passenger door for her. He waited until she was inside before closing the door and going around to the driver's side.

Gordan had barely managed to get the car-top up before the rain started. He made no effort to start the car, but sat as if he were deep in thought.

"Is there a problem? Shouldn't we get moving before it gets any worse?"

"Can it get any worse? Nothing has been right for me since you walked out on me in Atlanta."

"Don't. We've both said enough."

"It hasn't all been said." He traced a lean finger along her jaw line. "Baby, I had no idea that you weren't happy."

"But I tried to tell you."

He shook his head. "Evidently, I was not paying attention. I assumed that you had been busy, absorbed in all that you had to do while your sister was unable to work. Later, I thought you were just caught up in the new baby. I didn't realize you were unhappy with me and our relationship." He whispered, "I assumed once things settled down around you, then things would go back to the way they had always been—with you flying to see me on the weekends. I was wrong."

In the deepening shadows, she could just barely make out the despair etched on his strong African features.

"Baby, I'm truly sorry." He caressed her cheek and was

grateful that she did not pull away. "At least, let me make it up to you—please."

She watched sheets of rain pelt the windshield. Eventually, she said, "Your way of making up means giving me something expensive. That's not what I want. Expensive gifts won't change anything between us. What really matters to me can't be bought."

"Yeah, I finally figured that out about you," he said, dryly. "Sorry, I've been so dense. When I said let me make it up to you, I meant let me try and change our situation. I want us to start getting to know each other all over again. That involves spending time together."

Cassy blinked back tears. There was a time when that was all she wanted—it would have been enough. Unfortunately, there was no longer a simple solution to the problem.

Gordan's stomach felt as if it were in knots as he waited for her response. He consoled himself with the assurance that she was here in the car with him, listening to his request.

"We'll only end up hurting each other more. Frankly, I don't know about you, but I don't think I can handle any more heartache."

Gordan's heart ached, all right. He struggled with a combination of impatience and frustration. He ached to have her back where she belonged—in his arms.

Suddenly they were more like sparring partners than lovers. He had advanced; she retaliated. He had insisted; she had refused out right. The argument left him cold and unapproachable while she had been burning hot with temper and outrage. And they both were alone and hurting.

He kept his hands braced on the steering wheel when he said, "We've both made mistakes. But the feelings have not changed. At least, they haven't for me. Cassy, I still love you. Let me prove to you that I can change. Will you give me that chance?"

Cassy whispered, "I don't know. I just don't know right now. Please, just take me back to the hotel."

Gordan held the wheel so tight, his hands hurt from the pressure. A sob rose in his throat, but he managed to suppress the raw sound. He forced himself to start the engine and put the car into gear.

How could he let her go? He had no idea how many times he asked himself that question before he brought the car to a stop in the wide, well-lit drive. Without a word, he handed the keys to the uniformed attendant. He waited silently while Cassy swung her gorgeous legs out of the car.

Side by side, they entered the luxurious lobby that was busy with activity, even at this hour of the evening. As they crossed the lobby, Gordan said nothing. He escorted her to the bank of public elevators.

"Good night." He would have walked away if Cassy had not touched his arm. He stopped, his eyes immediately locked with hers. "Yes?"

Cassy winced from the pain mirrored there. She had to clear her throat before she could say, "Tell me why . . . ," she was careful to whisper so she would not be overheard, ". . . you think spending time together will make a difference."

Gordan didn't speak. He couldn't just then. He did not trust his voice. He was in too much pain.

"Gordan . . ." she persisted.

Absently, he stroked his bearded jaw. He finally said, so quietly that she had to lean forward in order to hear him, "We deserve to at least try it. We owe each other that much after so many years together."

"Okay," she reluctantly agreed. "Would you care to take a drive with me tomorrow—perhaps have lunch out?

Doesn't matter where. Perhaps, Club Nautique-Les Pieds
Dans I'Eau? Or Le Robert?''

Gordan's dark eyes caressed her face, then he grinned.
"Yes. What time?"

"Is ten too early?"

Gordan heard the challenge in her voice and knew she
expected him to back down. The next day was Monday—
a working day. Well, she was wrong. No matter what was
on his schedule, it was not as important as she was to him.
He had a point to make.

"I'll pick you up at ten."

Cassy nodded, before she walked away.

Gordan made no effort to follow her, but he followed
the sexy sway of her soft, round bottom until she disappeared from view.

He went over to the courtesy telephones and lifted a
receiver. The telephone rang several times without answer.
He had just put it down when he felt a tug on his arm.
He turned with a smile, hoping to see Cassy.

"Hello," Jillian said. "Have a nice day on the boat?"

"Hi. I just called your room."

"Oh, really?" she beamed, liking the sound of that.
"Would you like to join me for a nightcap? I was on my
way to the Sunset Lounge."

"Fine." Gordan fell into step with her.

Jillian casually looped her arm through his. "Did you
enjoy your day off?"

Gordan shrugged. What he wanted was to be with Cassy.
He had spent most of his day wondering if she was spending
her day with Adam Foster. He had not been able to relax
and enjoy being on the water. He'd been thrilled that he
allowed Ralph to talk him into staying for dinner.

Finally, he could breathe a little easier. Cassy was willing
to give him a chance. He was determined to make the
most of it.

When they entered the low-lit seclusion of the lounge, they found empty seats at one of the small tables against the wall. Soft music was playing in the background.

Once they had ordered their drinks, Jillian leaned forward, aware of the way her tank-styled black, knit dress dipped low in front. "Why did you call? Or should I ask, what did you have in mind?" Her dark lashes flickered seductively down over lovely dark eyes.

Gordan looked surprised when she repeated his name. "Did you say something?"

"You called my room?"

"Yeah. Did anything important come up today?"

"Nothing unusual. Trudy called. She will be back at her desk in the morning, and the latest figures on the South African project were faxed in. The sea island construction ran into a problem with the contractors, but Wil has flown down to take care of it. Lingston called. He didn't say it, but I suspect he's after the management spot in Jamaica. My bet is that he's heard that Paul Smith is next in line. You know how the gossip mill works at corporate. There was a call from your broker. A call from your son. I left a written report of what happened today and the latest reports with Bradford."

"Thanks." He pulled out a small leather notepad and pen from his pocket and began outlining instructions for the rest of the week. He ended with, "Cancel all my appointments and conference calls for the week."

Jillian's eyes had gone wide but she quickly took notes on what needed to be done. Then she almost asked, "But what are you . . . ," then, at the last moment, thought better of questioning him.

Gordan leaned back in his chair, then said, "As of now, I'm on vacation."

"For how long?"

Gordan lifted a brow. "Until I tell you differently. You're

in charge of day to day operations. Management will report
to Wil. You'll leave a written report with Bradford at the
end of the day. I will contact you when necessary—not the
other way around. I expect you to work with Trudy without
problems.''

"But . . .''

Gordan held up his hand. The cocktail waitress put down
their drinks and left. "What's the matter, Jillian? Don't
you think you can handle the office on your own?" There
was no doubt that he had issued a challenge.

Jillian straightened her spine, dropping her lashes—
thus hiding her fury. He'd been grooming her for a vice
presidency. This was her opportunity to prove herself. This
would be her chance to go it alone.

"I know I can handle it," she said, with confidence.

"Good, then we don't have a problem." Gordan ignored
his drink as he stood, reached into his pocket, and dropped
a bill on the table. " 'Night.''

Jillian watched as Gordan disappeared through the
entrance-way. She was furious. This vacation had everything to do with that empty-headed little witch. Did he
think she didn't know? He was going after Cassy.

How could he be so blind? Why couldn't he see that
that cook was not woman enough for him? She lacked the
sophistication, the elegance, of a true lady. She was not
the kind of woman meant to be on the arm of a man like
Gordan Kramer.

There was not a doubt in her mind that this sudden
need for time off had everything to do with Cassandra
Mosley. The woman had managed to tie him up in knots,
yet again. Jillian was so angry she wanted to throw something. She settled for draining the fancy fruit juice and
rum concoction in front of her. She had made her play

and failed. But she had not given up—not yet. There had to be a way.

Here she was on one of the most romantic islands in the world. There was more moonlight, dark-blue star-filled sky, and ocean breeze than any one woman could stand without a man. Correction. She took note of a funny-looking little man, who was seated beside a dumpy woman, staring at her. Jillian suppressed a shiver of revulsion.

Taking her drink, she weaved her way between the tables, her destination the highly polished glass and chrome bar. Settling herself on one of the velvet covered bar chairs, she motioned to the bartender. "Another one, please." The seats on either side of her were both empty. She told herself she needed the privacy to think—to plan. She would figure out a way to stop the hussy in her tracks. They had already broken up. But that was only half the battle. They were not sleeping together—or, at least, she hoped not.

What to do? She was fast running out of options, if she wanted the man and her job. Jillian had worked hard to position herself near the power, in this case, Gordan Kramer. She had succeeded far beyond her wildest dreams. She was not only his personal assistant, but was close to becoming one of the company's corporate vice presidents. What an accomplishment that would be if she made it at thirty-three. That had not been her original goal.

After coming to work for Gordan, her goals had changed—or, rather, she had changed. She'd always been on the lookout for a powerful man—someone who could afford to keep her in jewels and the luxury she was entitled to. Gordan had been perfect. But she soon discovered her beauty alone was not enough of an attraction. He surrounded himself with competent people.

When it came to women he was attracted to intelligence.

He admired a woman who knew how to handle herself—
a woman who didn't need a man but merely wanted one.

Determined to prove herself, she moved up in the company by using her brain power and was proud of her accom-
plishments. In all honesty, her only frustration had been
that Gordan had not made a single move toward her. There
was always a professional distance—a distance that she
hated, but grudgingly respected him for it.

The man was a machine. He not only thrived on business,
but excelled at it. Gordan Kramer *was* Kramer Corporation, that's why his sudden need to take an unplanned
vacation was disturbing.

This little holiday of his would give her the opportunity
to show her stuff. What an opportunity. But she wanted
more. She wanted the man himself. They would make such
an unstoppable team. Why couldn't he see that?

Jillian knew she was every bit as beautiful as Cassandra
Mosley. And she was also smarter. She knew the hotel
business. She would be an asset to him. If only she hadn't
left so many hints; she had told her father to expect that
the company and the man would be hers someday. But
she had been so hopeful after Gordan's breakup with
Cassy. She knew it was merely a matter of time until he
looked her way.

Well, she just had to work harder, like her father had
taught her how to get what she wanted. She could earn
her father's approval. And she would have it all—the love,
the approval, and the acceptance she craved.

If only Cassy would give up and go back to California.
It was all her fault, anyway. Why did she have to vacation
in Martinique, right under Gordan's nose? What Jillian
could not understand was that the girl had had him, yet
she was not smart enough to keep him. What more did
Cassy want? All she had to do was smile at the man and

he would buy her anything she wanted—cars, houses, expensive jewels—anything.

As she nursed her drink, she wondered what it would be like to have that kind of love and devotion directed her way.

She had considered his younger brother, Wilham, but quickly dismissed it. Although he was more approachable than his older brother, he was also rough around the edges. He liked to get his hands dirty—he liked the construction end of the business. He did not have the smooth sophistication of the older man. It was a shame.

She let out a soft sigh, lifting her drink and sipping. The man a few seats down caught her interest. He looked familiar, but she could not quite place him. Where had she seen him before? He didn't work for the resort, so where?

Jillian smiled. He was the man who had been lunching with Cassy. He was the new man in Cassy's life. Yet, tonight he looked as alone and melancholy as she felt.

Just how serious was he about Cassy? How often did they see each other? Were they lovers? And how much did Gordan know?

Jillian eased from her chair and moved down the bar. "Is this seat taken?" She had to ask twice before she gained his attention.

Adam lifted his head from the draft beer he'd been brooding into and met the eyes of a beautiful woman. "No, not at all."

Jillian smiled as she sat beside him and crossed her shapely legs. "Vacation or business?"

"Vacation," he supplied, returning his attention to his beer.

"I'm Jillian Harris," she said, offering him a slim-fingered, manicured hand.

"Adam—Adam Foster," he smiled, taking her hand. "Would you care for another drink?"

Jillian shook her head. "I'm fine." The conversational ball dropped then. Since he made no effort to revive it, she said, "Are you enjoying the hotel and resort? We at Kramer House do try to please."

Adam's brow lifted. "No problems. So, you work for the hotel?"

Jillian smiled. "I work for Gordan Kramer. I'm his personal assistant."

"I see," Adam said, dryly.

"Did I say something wrong?" she asked, all wide-eyed and innocent.

"Kramer," was all he said.

"Now I know where I saw you before. You were lunching with Cassandra Mosley. Are you close friends?"

"Friends, yes."

"A friend can make a vacation very romantic, if it's the right friend."

Adam shrugged. "Are you sure you wouldn't care for another drink?"

"No, but thank you. How long have you known Cassy? Or are you from Oakland?"

"We met here at Le Lamentin airport. We shared a cab to the hotel. You're full of questions, Jillian. May I ask why?"

She smiled, while quietly assessing him. She stared into his deep-set, intelligent, dark-brown eyes before moving on to his firm, strong chin. Her gaze lingered on his thick, well-shaped mouth. This was no fool to be easily led. She dropped her long, silky dark-brown lashes as she decided just how much she needed to tell him. If she clammed up, would he do the same?

"What do you do, Adam?"

"I'm a corporate lawyer." He named a well-known and

profitable computer company as one of his clients. "Another question, not an answer."

She smiled, seductively. "I've worked for Gordan for nearly six years now—and cared for him almost as long. I suppose curiosity got the better of me. When I saw you with his ex-lady, well . . ." She let her voice slip away.

Adam studied her at length, from her pretty eyes and her high-sculpted cheekbones, to her small nose and pouty, full lips. Her long, dark-auburn hair had been swept up into an elegant chignon. He said somewhat dryly, "Kramer is a very lucky man. He has two gorgeous women in his corner. Is the brother aware of your interest?"

"Somewhat. It was my understanding that Cassy's involvement with him was over and that she has moved on," she said, expectantly.

"The possibilities are endless."

"Excuse me?"

"I don't betray a confidence."

"Even when it might prove beneficial?"

"Even then."

"Perhaps if we put our heads together, we might be able to swing the odds in our direction."

"Sorry. I'm not in the game-playing business. Good night, Ms. Harris."

Chapter Ten

"You're early," Cassy said, as she opened the door. She struggled not to notice the way Gordan's pale-green tee shirt hugged his wide shoulders and broad chest or the snug fit of his black jeans following the lines of his thighs. She quickly looked away from his prominent sex. He wore heavy leather sandals on bare feet. The man worked out and swam daily, and it showed. He believed in keeping his body as well-toned as his mind.

Stepping back, she said, "Come in."

"I'm fine. No hurry," he said softly, leaning a shoulder against the open doorjamb. His dark eyes followed the way she filled out a pair of yellow walking shorts, before lifting to the neat, white, blouse, embroidered with yellow butterflies and daisies.

Gordan decided the sun streaking in through the patio doors could not compete with her radiance and dark beauty. His breath had quickened when he inhaled her scent. She smelled like flowers mingled with her own clean womanly scent, which never failed to gain his attention.

As he watched her move around the room collecting her things, he did not need to study the shape of her breasts or the sway of her hips. He knew all her sweet secrets.

He had awakened alone, after spending half the night painfully aroused, throbbing for what had been his for so long. He came into contact with beautiful women every day of the week, but there was only one Cassy. He knew what he wanted—he wanted her back. He needed her back.

Yet, as badly as he wanted her beneath him, he had no option but to curb his impatience. He assured himself that this time, when they were together again, it would be different. It would be better. No more long separations. No more weeks without her sweet smiles. Together they would find a way. He planned to give her as much of his time and attention as possible.

Gordan's square-cut jaw lifted with ruthless intent. His African forefathers had fought to their deaths for the freedom that they believed was their God-given right. He pushed aside his doubts and fears that he might not succeed. That Cassy might not give him a second chance.

He grinned suddenly as he watched her tuck a short nighty away. They used to laugh over the tiny lace panties she liked to wear beneath them because, more often than not, he would hide them from her, claiming she didn't need the panties—or the nighty, for that matter.

"You have to be kidding." he teased, as she tried and failed to get all her things into a tiny, white, long-strapped purse.

"What?" She knew what he was going to say, and her eyes challenged him.

"Baby, I didn't bring a jacket. How much do you think I can get into these pockets?" He patted his lean hips.

It was a familiar conversation that they had had many times. She adored pretty little purses that held almost nothing, and she liked to use his pockets to take care of the overflow.

Cassy couldn't help smiling as she draped her bag across her body. "I don't need your help," she tossed back, before she placed an oblong silk scarf, patterned with butterflies, over her throat, then smoothed her wavy, chin-length curls. "Ready?"

"Yes, I am. What?" she asked, noting the way he was eyeing her feet.

Gordan lifted a heavy brow, chuckling deep in his throat. "Sandals? You know you hate to get those pretty feet dirty."

Changing the subject, she said, "I'm ready. Sorry, if I kept you waiting. I'm not usually late."

He chuckled; he couldn't stop himself. "Really? It's hardly the first time."

Cassandra Mosley had kept him waiting for weeks before they made love that first time.

"I have no idea who you are confusing me with!" she protested, before moving past him into the hallway.

He laughed throatily. "I couldn't confuse you with anyone. You're one special lady."

She ignored him, waiting.

"Got your keycard?"

"Right here." She frowned at the way he just smiled and had not explained, but merely closed the door behind them before starting down the corridor. "Well?" she prompted. "When did I keep you waiting?"

"More times than I care to remember."

"That's not an answer. I'm very prompt. I'm always on time for work. My meals are quick and skillfully prepared. I've never missed a plane while we were together. You, Mr.

Kramer, are dead wrong." Cassy crossed her arms beneath her breasts.

He roared with laughter, throwing his head back, his chest rumbling, before he recovered himself to say, "Here's the elevator. How's that for service?"

As they began their descent, Cassy couldn't stop herself from smiling. "Will you stop laughing at me and tell me just one time I was late?"

"You don't want to know."

The doors slid open on a lower floor and an older couple joined them.

"Yes, I do," Cassy said softly, leaning closer so her voice would not carry.

Gordan smiled, enjoying the sparkle in her lovely eyes. Cassy clearly was miffed at him. She opened her mouth to speak when several more people joined them on the elevator before it continued its descent. They were the last to enter the busy lobby.

"Sometimes, Gordan, you . . ."

"Excuse me, Mr. Kramer, but we have a problem," Kenneth Kittman interrupted them.

Cassy's playful mood evaporated as quickly as someone could pop a soap bubble. She was not surprised. She expected as much. She did not even have to strain to remember how often Gordan had taken time away from the business to be with her. It happened so seldom that it was practically nonexistent. With Gordan, business always came first.

She could see that he was not pleased. A scowl dominated his dark, lean, good looks. He apparently did not welcome the intrusion.

Before Gordan could speak, the hotel manager said, "It will only take a moment of your time."

"No."

"But, sir . . ."

Gordan held up his hand, and he said quietly but distinctly, "I said no. If you can't handle this hotel then I expect your resignation in the morning. Good day."

Kenneth Kittman was not the only one in shock. Cassy considered checking Gordan's forehead to see if he might be ill. Gordan cupped her elbow, steered her through the lobby, and out into the sunshine.

Cassy could only blink in disbelief.

"Close your pretty mouth before I kiss you right here. I promised you a day away from the resort and that's exactly what you're going to have."

Cassy could not believe it. He had threatened to fire his hotel manager if he could not do his job, and he had meant it. There had been steel in his voice.

Gordan thanked the attendant who had brought his car around. He paused long enough to hold the door for Cassy, before he walked to the driver's side of the car and slid behind the steering column.

It took Cassy a moment to collect herself. Gordan was evidently determined to prove something to her. They were buckled in and on the road with the convertible top down when Cassy recalled their discussion in the elevator.

"You're full of surprises today. First, you make unfounded remarks about how often I've kept you waiting, then you walk out on a business problem without a backward glance. What's next?" she asked, as she covered her hair with a scarf.

Gordan flicked his turn signal before he slowed the car and eased to a stop on the shoulder of the road.

"Gordan?"

He shifted, as much as the seatbelt would allow, until he was facing her, his long arm rested behind her shoulders. "No big secret. Baby, we both know you have kept

An important message from the ARABESQUE Editor

Dear Arabesque Reader,

Because you've chosen to read one of our Arabesque romance novels, we'd like to say "thank you"! And, as a special way to thank you, we've selected four more of the books you love so well to send you for FREE!

Please enjoy them with our compliments, and thank you for continuing to enjoy Arabesque...the soul of romance.

Karen Thomas
Senior Editor,
Arabesque Romance Novels

Check out our website at
www.arabesquebooks.com

ARABESQUE
®
A PRODUCT OF
BET
BOOKS

SPECIAL OFFER!
4 FREE BOOKS

3 QUICK STEPS
TO RECEIVE YOUR "THANK YOU" GIFT
FROM THE EDITOR

Send this card back and you'll receive 4 FREE Arabesque
novels! The introductory shipment of 4 Arabesque novels – a
$23.96 value – is yours absolutely FREE!

There's no catch. You're under no obligation to buy anything.
You'll receive your introductory shipment of 4 Arabesque
novels absolutely FREE (plus $1.99 to offset the costs of
shipping & handling). And you don't have to make any
minimum number of purchases—not even one!

We hope that after receiving your books you'll want to
remain an Arabesque subscriber. But the choice is yours to
continue or cancel, anytime at all! So why not take us up on
our invitation to receive 4 Arabesque Romance Novels, with
no risk of any kind. You'll be glad you did!

Call us
TOLL-FREE
at 1-800-770-1963

THE EDITOR'S "THANK YOU" GIFT INCLUDES:

- 4 books absolutely FREE (plus $1.99 for shipping and handling)
- A FREE newsletter, *Arabesque Romance News*, filled with author interviews, book previews, special offers, and more!
- No risks or obligations. You're free to cancel whenever you wish... with no questions asked.

BOOK CERTIFICATE

Yes! Please send me 4 FREE Arabesque novels (plus $1.99 for shipping & handling). I understand I am under no obligation to purchase any books, as explained on the back of this card.

Name _____

Address _____ Apt. _____

City _____ State _____ Zip _____

Telephone ( ) _____

Signature _____

Offer limited to one per household and not valid to current subscribers. All orders subject to approval. Terms, offer, & price subject to change. Offer valid only in the U.S.

Thank you!

AN063A

Accepting the four introductory books for FREE (plus $1.99 to offset the cost of shipping & handling) places you under no obligation to buy anything. You may keep the books and return the shipping statement marked "cancelled". If you do not cancel, about a month later we will send 4 additional Arabesque novels, and you will be billed the preferred subscriber's price of just $4.00 per title. That's $16.00 for all 4 books for a savings of 33% off the cover price (Plus $1.99 for shipping and handling). You may cancel at any time, but if you choose to continue, every month we'll send you 4 more books, which you may either purchase at the preferred discount price. . . or return to us and cancel your subscription.

THE ARABESQUE ROMANCE CLUB: HERE'S HOW IT WORKS

ARABESQUE ROMANCE BOOK CLUB
P.O. Box 5214
Clifton NJ 07015-5214

PLACE
STAMP
HERE

me cooling my heels many times in the past." He laughed, caressing her nape. "Admit it. You, my sweet, became good at keeping me hard and hungry while you spent hours in the tub, then perfumed your skin with lotions, and did whatever it is women do to drive men out of their minds with need."

She jerked her gaze away from him, concentrating on the passing cars—anything but him. "You were right. I would have rather not known."

He pressed a kiss against the side of her neck, close to her ear, saying huskily, "Aw, don't be that way. You've never heard me complain, have you? Because you, my love, have always been worth the wait." He chuckled throatily, "Except for the first time we made love. You kept me on edge for weeks before you were willing to admit that you needed me as badly as I needed you."

Cassy offered thanks for her dark skin, which could conceal the flush that heated her face and throat. Much to her relief, he put the car back in gear and eased out into the flow of traffic. Cassy did not have a clue as to what she was feeling. She was a bundle of raw nerves as she tried to regain control of her emotions.

His deep voice, his recollections of a sweeter time, combined with the feel of his mouth on her skin were more than she could cope with right now. She was much too vulnerable to him. Her breathing had actually accelerated, and her breasts felt swollen; the nipples had tightened and tingled with awareness. Goose bumps had raced down her spine at the feel of his open mouth against her flesh, while her woman's center had pulsed with sweet expectation.

Cassy did not want to remember the many layers of intimacies they had once shared. Those deep, erotic thoughts would only remind her of what she could no longer have. It was very simple. They did not belong to each other anymore. They would never be lovers again.

162

Bette Ford

There was no purpose to indulging in memories of what they had once shared.

Despite her best efforts, her thoughts slid back to the night they became lovers. Her sexual experience with men had been embarrassingly limited for a thirty-four-year-old woman. Until then, she had been consumed with building her culinary career.

She had thought she knew what it was to be in love. But she'd been wrong. Falling in love with Gordan had been completely different. While in Paris, she had been drawn to Van Campbell because he was another African American and he reminded her of home. Their interlude had had more to do with the romantic elements of Paris than real love. And she ended up hurt and feeling like a fool. It also hadn't taken her long to learn that sex was a major disappointment.

Cassy had not been in a hurry to repeat the experience. She had dated other men since her time in Paris and before she met Gordan. She just hadn't bothered to sleep with any of them.

When Gordan had come into her life, all that had changed. To her amazement, she found herself wanting Gordan's lovemaking long before it happened. Gordan had made her sizzle with needs she could not begin to understand. He was the only man she could not walk away from. She loved him.

And then it happened. They had not caught so much as a glimpse of each other that day. He worked in his suite while she prepared an elaborate luncheon and dinner buffet for a group of businessmen staying at the hotel.

It had been quite late when they finally had gotten together. They had gone out for a meal and then walked hand in hand on the beach. She should have been exhausted, but she wasn't. When Gordan brought her back to her cottage, she invited him inside. She prepared their drinks—cognac for him and wine for her—not wanting the night to end. When she returned, he slipped his arms around her waist and pulled her down onto his lap.

"What are you doing?" she had asked.

"Making you mine. Any objections?"

Cassy could have told him there was no need because she was already his, but the words had not come. Cassy suddenly shivered in the warmth of the hot sun as she recalled how he had attacked her senses with one hot, sweet kiss after another. To this day, she had no idea what happened to those drinks. All she remembered was how good his mouth felt on hers as he lifted her and carried her into her bedroom.

Gordan glanced longingly at Cassy before returning his gaze to the road. He could not help wondering what she was thinking and if she were remembering their first time, as he had been. Could she have forgotten?

He had been wild for her. Week after week of unrelenting need had eventually taken its toil on him, twisting him into such a state that his hunger for her was endlessly painful.

He had no idea how he had maintained self-control, but it had been critical that he prove himself to her. Her trust was important to him. For the first time in his adult life, he wanted a woman's love more than he wanted her body. Cassy had been more than worth the wait.

Gordan discovered that he had never needed a woman more. He let out a slow breath as he recalled that night. The instant he had tasted Cassy's sweet mouth, his control shattered. He had taken kiss after kiss, his tongue stroking hers again and again, until he began to suckle. He shifted uncomfortably in his seat as he remembered the way he had slowly penetrated her unbelievably tight sheath.

Gordan had no idea who had undressed whom. All he clearly recalled was that they were finally bare skin to bare skin. Her wonderful breasts were crushed against his chest. He could not stop himself from moving against her softness. Her sweet moans had nearly destroyed what was left of his control. He groaned from the memory.

"Did you say something?"

He was so long in responding that Cassy looked at him and repeated his name.

"No, I was just remembering our first night as lovers."

Startled, Cassy made no response. If his thoughts were anywhere near as intimate as hers had been, she did not want to know about them. Their lovemaking was the very last thing she was prepared to discuss with him—ever. Why had he bothered to bring up the subject? What did he think she was made of—granite? She had been in love with him at the time . . .

Cassy had wanted Gordan that night—more than she believed it was possible for a woman to desire a man. The instant he had touched her, she had understood what it meant to be in love.

Resistance? She had forgotten the meaning of the word. The feel of him against her had been consuming. His skin was supple, smooth as silk, and incredibly hot against hers. Cassy had never known how highly sensitive her breasts could feel until Gordan had caressed them, cradled them, and then worried the aching nipples with the hot wash of his tongue, before he took each peak deep into the heat of his mouth to apply the most exquisite suction.

She shivered from the memory, for she had nearly gone out of her mind from the intensity of the pleasure. It had been sharp and potent and she had not wanted

him to stop. How was it possible for a woman to gain so
much pleasure from a man's mouth? And it was only the
beginning.

Gordan had taken such care with her. He had caressed
the entire length of her body repeatedly before he lingered
in that damp place between her thighs. She had been more
than ready for him—yet, he continuously caressed her
before he parted the fleshy folds of her sex. The second
he touched her there, whatever reluctance she had been
harboring dissolved. She remembered calling out his
name—then he was slowly filling her body with his steel
hard sex.

"Nothing to say, Cassy?"

She blinked in surprise before she could say, "Absolutely
not."

Closing her eyes, she tried to stop the vivid memories,
tried not to recall the feel of him deep inside her body.
It was hopeless. Her thoughts were as vibrant as the sensa-
tions she had experienced that night. He had pleasured
her.

Gordan was not her first lover, but he was the one to
bring her to completion and show her what it really meant
to be a woman. She had experienced pleasures she had
only read about, fantasized about—as he took her from
one shattering climax to the next. She had not known her
body was capable of such incredible pleasure.

She had thought she was prepared, but how could a
woman ready herself for the lovemaking of the one man
she would love with all her heart? Cassy had no choice but
to accept the truth. Without question, she had fallen utterly
under Gordan Kramer's spell.

Even now, she had to press a hand to her lips to hold
in a sob of anguish at the loss. In spite of the heartache
and disappointment he had caused her, she still wanted
the man.

I have to calm down, she told herself over and over, as
her heart raced. She had to be able to think rationally.
The potency of their desire for each other had always been
there, from the instant they had looked into each other's
eyes. It was not an issue. Life was more than what took
place in the bedroom.

What she needed was a man she could count on to be
there day in and day out—a man able to share all the ups
and downs that life offered. She needed someone who was
not afraid to give his woman not just his body and his love
but to honor her with his name and child. Gordan was
not that man.

"I've never thought of you as a coward." His voice was
huskier than he would have liked, but he was also aroused
and uncomfortable.

"What?"

"You remember that night just as I do. It was the night
we acknowledged that we were in love. Why not be honest
about it?"

Fed up with this entire conversation, she asked a question of her own. "Why take time off today? I can't imagine
you taking an entire day away from your work. I'm sure
there are any number of things waiting for your attention,
such as Kenneth's little problem at the hotel."

"Changing the subject won't change what we've meant
to each other."

"Why today?" she repeated, as if he had not spoken.

"The sky is blue, the sun is out. Why not?"

"Kenneth had every reason to expect you to stop and
take care of the problem. It's something you have always
done. Nothing else has ever been as important to you as
Kramer Corporation. What did you do with Jillian while
you're spending a work day playin' hooky?"

"Why are you deliberately trying to antagonize me?"

"I'm trying to understand what's going on."

"There is nothing complicated about it. I made my choice. I want to be with you, baby. I want you back."

"So you're willing to do whatever it takes to win me back? Even willing to go so far as to take time away from your precious business?"

"Whatever it takes." His eyes momentarily locked with hers before he returned his gaze to the roadway.

"Why waste the time? I'm only a temporary challenge. It's evident that once you win me over, so to speak, it's back to doing exactly what you have always done before our breakup."

A muscle jumped in his cheek. "That's not what I intend."

"It's what will happen."

Gordan did not voice the quick retort rising in his throat. He was not going to let her make him angry—nor was he going to forget the reason why he had wanted to spend this day with her.

He reached out and squeezed the hand resting in her lap. Quietly, he said, "You're wrong. But can't we forget our problems for a few hours? Let's just concentrate on enjoying the day—each other. Is one carefree day too much to ask for?"

"Gordan . . ."

"Please . . ."

Finally, she said, "Okay."

After acknowledging to herself that a few hours could not change how she felt or what she wanted, she settled back to enjoy the view. Even though they were no longer close, she was willing to go through the motions if that's

what it would take to convince him that she would not—
could not—compromise on this.

A day off for fun! Who was he trying to fool—her or
himself? Gordan was not about to change his life for anyone. She was the woman he claimed to love, but as far as
she was concerned, he could not love her the way she
longed to be loved.

When a man was in love with a woman, he naturally
wanted her to be a part of his life and he wanted to be
part of hers. In her mind, that meant marriage. What
he had mistaken for love was nothing more than sexual
compatibility.

Cassy clung to the belief that a single day or even a
month away from his business would not convince her that
he was willing to make a change. After years of observing
him, how could she possibly think he even wanted to
change? He was perfectly happy with his life.

She was the one who had changed. She was no longer
willing to believe in fairy tales. As long as she remembered
that, they both might get through this fun-filled day still
speaking to each other.

"I've been coming to this island for years, yet I never
tire of it. There is always something new to see and enjoy."
He smiled. "The days are sweet and the nights are sweeter.
I never fail to miss this place when I go back to Atlanta."
He paused before admitting, "I've been considering build-
ing a house here. I've surprised you, haven't I?"

"A bit." She longed to say it didn't matter what she
thought, for she knew they would never share a home.
That particular fantasy had been crushed when he refused
to even consider a life-long commitment.

"You don't think it's a good idea?"

"I don't know. I honestly thought you preferred the
traveling. I can't imagine you settling in one place for long.
It doesn't fit with your corporate image."

Gordan's mouth tightened, but he did not comment.

Uncomfortable with the prolonged silence, Cassy said, "I expected you to tell me to bring my hiking boots today. Your idea of a day off, as I recall, is more like an invigorating climb up Monte Pelee." Looking away from the rolling hills, she laughed, "I have not forgiven you for the five-hour hike to the summit you took me on when I was living on the island."

Gordan chuckled. "Nothing so strenuous today. I thought you might enjoy the southern view of the island. Leave the mountains in the northern region for another day. Have you gone hiking on this trip?"

"No. I have been into Fort de France, shopping, sightseeing, and lots of eating. I may have to go on a diet when I get back home."

"Never that. Consider it as developing even more dangerous curves." He took his gaze off the road to eye her figure.

"I'd much rather you keep your eyes on the road—it's safer." She smiled, "I couldn't resist visiting the Botanical Gallery and the Geological Gallery again, while I was here."

They were passing yet another fishing village, then rows of cane fields dotted the landscape. Everything was so wonderfully green and lush.

"Where are we going? This is not the way to Le Robert or Club Nautique-Les Pieds Dans l'Eau."

"It's a surprise."

"I hate surprises. Tell me. We are going south, aren't we, to Maison de La Canne—or La Pagerie?"

"Nope."

"Is that the Caribbean or the Atlantic?" she asked, pointing to the water along the coastal road.

"Caribbean," he conceded.

"We are going south. Pointe du Bout is so pretty."

"Nope."

"Where?"

"Les Trois-Ilets." he grinned. "Does that meet with Mademoiselle's approval?"

"Oui," she said, settling back in her seat.

Cassy gradually relaxed and started enjoying the beauty of her surroundings. The village was in full bloom— enchanting, Cassy decided. They toured one of the refineries used by the area's sugar plantations and had a late lunch at a tiny restaurant well known for buttery, hot croissants along with freshly caught, steamed crayfish and rock lobster, eased down with icy-cold sips of the local beer.

When they left the restaurant, she hit him playfully on the arm. "Will you stop teasing me about my French? I'm out of practice."

Gordan grinned. "Yeah, sure. Do you remember the last time we were here?"

Cassy nodded, sobering instantly. She did not want to recall how happy they once were together or how very much in love. It hurt too much.

She said, "Let's not take another walk down memory lane. It's getting late, Gordan. We have to drive back."

They were enjoying each other's company a bit too much for her peace of mind. There was no way she was going to forget why they were spending the day together. It didn't have a thing to do with how they had once felt about each other. She was merely keeping a promise. Nothing more.

"What's the rush? I thought you might like to visit Empress Josephine's birthplace in La Pagerie and her home, since we're so close."

Reluctantly, she admitted, "I have plans for the evening."

Chapter Eleven

Unable to look past the disappointment she glimpsed in his eyes, Cassy found herself agreeing to a brief tour before returning to the hotel. It wasn't until they were back in the car and Cassy was buckled into her seat that Gordan surprised her by leaning forward to brush his mouth over hers.

At the sound of her soft gasp, he could not stop himself. He had to taste her sweetness. Even though he was greedy for all of her, he forced himself to be content with stroking his tongue over hers. Without conscious thought, he released her seatbelt and gathered her close until her soft breasts were pressed into his chest. He ignored the pulsating heat in his groin and the hard beat of his heart. He told himself he could wait—he had to. Gordan eased away while he still could and started the car.

Cassy had no idea how she got through the brief tour of La Pagerie without revealing her inner turmoil. Cassy

tried not to think about his reaction to her plans for the
evening and failed.

Even the lovely view could not distract her as they drove
back. She did not want to consider that she had hurt him.
She did not want to care about him at all. If she let herself
care again, she could not survive the emotional devastation.
She would not throw away her plans for the future. She
could not.

"I'm glad we did this today. You made me realize how
long it has been since I've taken time away from the job.
My last vacation was when we went to New Orleans. We
haven't taken a real vacation together in two years, since
you and your sister started the inn."

"Are you blaming me?" Cassy knew she sounded as if
she were spoiling for a fight, but she didn't care.

"I'm not blaming either one of us. We've barely had an
occasional weekend in ages. That kind of distance takes a
toll on a relationship." He sighed, before he said quietly,
"Baby, this isn't about blame. We've both been too caught
up in our work." Then he said dryly, "Not that I've been
productive since our split—just the opposite."

"So that's why you're here, isn't it? Finally, you admit
that this whole day has been designed so that you can get
your life back on track." Her voice practically vibrated
from the intensity of her emotions. She could not contain
the hurt and anger that churned inside of her.

Gordan swore beneath his breath. He kept both hands
on the wheel, but after a glance in the rearview mirror,
he slowed the car enough to turn onto a deserted road
that was no bigger than a farm track. Eventually, he stopped
the car beside a cane field.

His eyes were focused straight ahead when he said, "I've
told you why I wanted to see you today. It has nothing to
do with getting my life back on track, although I will be

the first to admit that I want you back in my life. I've made no secret about it.''

"Oh, please. Why pretend? We both know that as soon as you get what you want, things will go back to the way they have always been between us—me in Oakland and you flying all over the place like some Sahara nomad.'' Cassy was trembling with rage when she yanked on her seatbelt, trying to free herself, but her hands were shaking too badly. She hissed at him, ''Well, Kramer, I'm not one of your business deals gone bad! I'm not some project! I also have wants and needs—needs you can't begin to satisfy. I'm not dropping back in your lap like a ripe coconut. Now, will you please start this blasted car and take me back to the hotel. I want this day over sooner, not later.''

"Since you seem to be an authority on why I'm here, why don't you tell me why you're with me today? You hate me so much, why in the hell did you bother to spend the day with me? Huh?''

"You asked me.''

A muscle jumped in his beard-covered cheek. Judging by the outrage stamped on her small features he knew he was wasting his breath, nevertheless he asked, ''Why?''

"I'm sorry I came. I would like to go back to the hotel.''

"Not until you're honest with me. You're here for a reason, Cassy. What is it?''

"It was my stupid attempt at trying to be fair.''

Gordan did not like her response. It wasn't what he wanted to hear. She evidently had made a decision. When was he going to get around to believing her?

"Am I supposed to thank you for your thoughtfulness? Is that the idea?''

"Gordan, this entire conversation is a complete waste of time. Take me back!''

He did not move a muscle. He maintained his grip on the steering wheel as he battled mounting frustration. She had done her level best to cut him off at the knees. It was as if she was determined to keep him from developing any kind of momentum toward a reconciliation.

When Gordan shifted in his seat, releasing his seat belt, he reached over and released hers. Before she could even offer a protest, she was across his lap, her back against his door, her breasts pressed into his chest.

Gordan was finished debating the issue. He took her mouth in a series of slow, drugging kisses. He kept right on kissing her, and when she moaned, he deepened the kiss, stroking her tongue with his, savoring her sweetness. Her slender arms found their way up to encircle the strong column of his neck. He moved his chest against her tight, pointy nipples as he sucked her tongue.

"Don't . . ." She managed to break free and turned her head away.

"Don't what—take off every stitch of clothing you are wearing so that I can take you here? Or is it, don't make you feel? What you don't want, Cassy, are reminders of how much you want my mouth on your breasts or lower." He pressed her hips against his throbbing shaft. "Does that tell you how much I've missed you, baby?"

His mouth was heavy, relentless, as he licked her lips before suckling the lower one. He tasted her as he had been wanting to do the entire day, feasting on her sweetness. All he knew was that he had to have her. He was empty without her.

"Cassy . . ." He groaned, finally allowing them both the liberty to breathe. He placed warm kisses down the length of her throat, sponging the mole he found at the tender base, before he traveled back up to kiss, then tongue, the sensitive place behind her ear.

"You want me, baby," he said, huskily, as he opened button after button on her blouse and unhooked the front closure of her bra. "Your nipples are hard, tight with hunger, for what I can give you."

He explored the incredibly soft, full globes, first with his eyes then his mouth. He placed hot, wet kisses all over them, in turn, before he tenderly squeezed each dark-brown peak between his fingertips, applying just enough pressure to cause her to gasp and whimper for more. He laved each nipple with the velvety roughness of his tongue until it was glistening, and she was quivering in his arms. Only then did he take the hard, sweet tip into the warmth of his mouth, providing an intense suction.

"Gordan . . . ," she sobbed, cradling his head in her hand. There was no hesitation on his part as he turned his attention to her other nipple. He didn't lift his head even when he sensed that she was close to climaxing. He slid a hand beneath the hem of her shorts, up her thigh, to cup her soft mound. He could feel the damp heat of her through the silk of her panties, as he rhythmically squeezed her softness.

Cassy whimpered, eyes tightly closed. "Please, baby. Please. I need you—now."

"I can't take you here," he said against her mouth, his breathing as uneven as hers. "We're going back to the hotel. And I promise you, I won't stop until you are a part of me. I want you to climax with me deep inside of you. I want to feel your sweetness."

Cassy's eyes flew open, and she stared into the burning heat of his dark gaze. She had almost let him . . . It couldn't be happening all over again.

"No!"

Using both hands, she pushed her way out of his arms and scrambled off his lap, across the seat and out of the car, nearly falling in the process. She fumbled, trying to straighten out her clothes. Her hands were shaking so badly, she could hardly stand up, let alone close her buttons. She took off down the farm track.

Gordan got out of the car as quickly as he could, considering his erection. He called her name, but when she didn't even slow down, his long legs soon caught up with her.

Swinging her around to face him, he held on. "What are you doing—running away, yet again? What is it with you? Just when are you going to accept that there is a reason why we can't keep our hands off each other? It's more than just sex. That's why it hurts so much."

"I won't do this anymore. It doesn't solve anything," she snarled at him. "It's not what I want anymore." Her small hands were balled at her sides.

"Really? You sure felt like a willing participant." When she lifted her chin, stubbornly refusing to make a comment, he said impatiently, "Admit it. You want me as badly as I want you. I know you, baby. I know the sounds you make deep in your throat when you're close to finishing. There is no question about the fact that I'm hard and aching and you're damp and ready. We both know I could have made you climax back there in that car with my mouth alone. Stop playing this game with me. Stop punishing me, because I won't make the same mistake again!"

His mouth was hard and insistent on hers. He stopped when he tasted her tears. "Baby, please don't."

"I can't . . ." She was trembling all over.

He released a rush of air from his lungs while he held on to her. "What you mean is, you won't."

Cassy was crying so hard that he bent to pick her up and carry her back to the car. He settled her in the passenger seat before he took his place in the driver's seat.

Cassy barely remembered accepting his pristine, white handkerchief. She was so miserable, but at the same time relieved that they were finally underway. What was she

going to do? How was he ever going to take her seriously,
after she let him touch her?

Although she blamed him, she could not excuse herself.
She could have stopped him, but she had not. She did
more than allow his caresses and kisses. She savored each
one—had been as eager as he was to once again be a part
of each other. She had wanted him.

How could she have forgotten even for an instant how
potent and dangerous their attraction was to her peace of
mind? What was it about the man that pulled her deep
into those self-destructive flames?

There was no getting around the fact that they'd given
in to an intense hunger and indescribable yearning for
completion. They had nearly made love in his car. He had
been the one to set limits—to stop it. Cassy hung her head,
her face and neck hot with mortification.

It had been a mistake for her to go out with him today.
She should have known better. Her body had wanted what
her mind had told her was wrong. She was still too vulnerable to the man; she cared too much for him.

Why Gordan? She had no trouble telling any other man
no and meaning it. Yet, her sensuous response to him was
indisputable, she decided, miserably, as she blinked away
scalding, hot tears.

Taking deep breaths, she tried to calm herself and figure
out what she needed to do next. The most obvious thing
was not to let it happen again. That meant not to let him
near her again.

"My guess is that you've decided not to see me again
once we reach the hotel complex. Am I right?"

"It sounds like a winner to me," she answered, flip-
pantly, in a weak attempt to conceal hurt feelings.

He was silent for so long that she peeked at him through
her lashes. His jaw was tight and his knuckles were pale
against his dark skin. There was no need to speculate on

his mood. He was furious with her. Or had she managed
to hurt him, yet again?

She had never meant to hurt him. Gordan was a fine
man. He had so many good qualities that she admired.
But his desires were not her own. How could she make
him see that what she was doing was not designed to hurt
him but to protect herself?

Although feeling the need to defend herself, she swallowed the apology rising in her throat. She had made the
only decision she could, under the circumstances. Her
entire future depended on her not backing down, even
though it was hurting them both. There could be no turning back for her, not if she wanted a husband and family
of her own someday.

She strongly believed that for any marriage to work in
this day and age, the couple had to put their love for each
other first. With that unshakable core of love, together
they could survive anything that life had to offer. She had
seen the proof of it in her parents' marriage and suspected
it had been there in her grandparents' marriage. In her
sister's case, even though she and her husband put their
love for each other first, there was still plenty of love available for Mandy and baby Kurt. And that's what Cassy
wanted for herself.

Today had been an exception to Gordan's normal
operating procedure. It was only a minor diversion, meant
only to sway her to his way of thinking. It was not as if she
doubted his sincerity. Gordan truly wanted her back, but
on his terms. He wanted her to fit into his lifestyle.

And Cassy couldn't even blame him for it, for she had
been his lady for years. He knew what to expect from her.
And, even more important to him, he knew he could trust
her. He saw no reason for that to change.

Their arrangement met his needs, for the most part. He
was willing to make one small concession—that they live

together. Cassy sighed wearily. She knew, as well as she knew her name, that if she agreed to come back to making herself available to him as she had done early in their relationship, Gordan would probably back down on the living-together issue. He just wanted to see more of her. But his agenda was his alone—never hers.

Much of the past four and a half years, she had felt as if she had been caught in a whirlwind of private planes, limousines, luxurious hotels, and romantic Caribbean nights. He had taken her on lavish vacations all over the world. And she had gone eagerly because of the way she felt about him. For her it had always been about feelings—their unshakable love.

But life was also about change. Being with him was no longer enough. It was time Cassy took care of her own future. Time she found the emotional strength needed to deal with Gordan's seductive method of persuasion.

Perhaps it was time to go home. Although she was just beginning to recognize her mistake in coming back to Martinique, she would not let it get the best of her. She could not let him win.

And it really should not matter how many times she saw Gordan while she was here. He could not offer her what she wanted. Her future did not include him or what he wanted her to do with her life. He could not have power over her because she would not give it to him.

"We're back," he said, quietly. He was holding on to his temper—just barely.

Cassy maintained her silence the entire way to her hotel room. Although she would have preferred he did not see her to her door, she was not about to start screaming in the lobby or venting her outrage in the crowded elevator. No. Her grandmother had taught her to carry herself as a lady at all times. Besides, she was not one to make a scene and embarrass them both.

The instant the door closed behind them, she turned, ready to face him down. She found herself pulled against his chest.

"I've had about enough of you manhandling me."

"And I've had enough of your pretense."

"Why are you tossing that accusation at me? I told you in Atlanta how I felt—what I wanted. There was never any pretense."

"Only that you have no feeling for me anymore. Is that what this Foster thing is about, Cassy? Is it designed to make me jealous and force me to do what you want?"

"No! How can you say that? I'm not trying to manipulate you. Why can't you get it through your thick head that this is not about you at all? It's about me. It's about what I want."

"We wanted the same thing on that deserted road. We wanted each other."

"Why are you acting this way? I've moved on, Gordan. I've moved on without you."

"So Foster is my replacement—is that it?"

"I never said that."

"You didn't have to," he snarled. His hands on her shoulders were not hurtful but were unyielding. He lowered his head and hissed, "You have a date with Foster, tonight. Fine. But, lady, you will go to him with the taste of my kisses and my touch."

Chapter Twelve

Cassy's mouth dropped open, but before she could collect her defenses, Gordan's full lips settled over hers.

There was no reluctance on his part. Gordan's mouth moved insistently over hers, demanding her surrender.

Cassy's soft whimpers of protest caused him to be gentle, and soothe her with tenderness. He groaned heavily, his tongue forging a place in the deep recesses of her mouth. He stroked her tongue with his over and over again.

He didn't stop until he could feel the resistance leave her smaller frame. Only then did he cup her round hips, squeezing her and pressing her against him. He moved the hard pads of his chest against her softness, but it was not enough—not nearly enough.

"Cassy . . ." he whispered, lifting her until he could press her soft mound along his pulsating sex. Her arms had automatically gone to his broad shoulders to help support her.

"Baby . . ." He groaned as his large frame trembled from the intimate contact. "Do you want me?" he whispered, his face buried in her neck, as he angled her until he could moved her down the length of his penis, causing both of them to shiver from the erotic contact. "Can he make you feel the way I do?"

Cassy stiffened, then recovered enough to say, "Put me down."

"What?"

"This is not some macho game. And I won't let you use me to prove a point." Pushing against him until he let her slide slowly down the length of his body, she was so shaky she would have fallen if he had not been holding her.

Gordan's burning hot gaze challenged hers. He studied the flashes of temper and sparks of desire reflected in her dark-brown eyes. With his gaze on her mouth, he said, "I'll make it easy for you. Tell me you don't want me as much as I want you and I'll walk out of the door right now."

Cassy eased as far away as he permitted. "This doesn't have anything to do with desire."

Rubbing the back of his hands over the hard, pointy tips of her breasts, he said, "It has everything to do with the way we feel about each other. You're just too stubborn to admit it."

Cassy shook her head in denial.

"Baby, you need me just as much as I need you," he whispered huskily. He had worried her nipples until they stood out, even through layers of clothing.

Cassy had no idea how she managed it, for she was not only fighting him but herself as well, but she said, "If I were stupid enough to go to bed with you right this instant, it wouldn't make a difference. Unless, you've changed your mind?" Judging by his look of surprise, that certainly was not the case. She forced herself to say "I didn't think so. Please—just go."

Gordan's eyes shot furious sparks at her, but his arms dropped to his side, then he turned and walked out of the door, slamming it behind him.

"Great crowd," Adam said, close to Cassy's ear. Taking her hand, he threaded their way through the mesh of people to a corner table in the jazz club. The rhythmic vibrations from the Zouk jazz beat, with its Creole lyrics and powerful beat of steel drums, came from a local band. The dance floor was as crowded as the rest of the club. It was only one of several available to hotel guests.

Cassy's smile was a bit strained when she slid into the empty chair he held for her.

"Something to drink?"

"Yes. White wine, please."

She should have followed her instincts and canceled. She was not exactly in a festive mood. The loud music was beginning to wear on her ragged nerves. But she had given her word, and it would have been wrong to back out at the last minute, just because she was emotionally drained from her encounter with Gordan.

Determined to make the best of things, she dressed with care, choosing a white silk sheath and short gold jacket. Both the knee-length hem and bodice of the dress were embroidered in a gold, Greek key pattern. She wore a citrine tennis bracelet set in fourteen-karat gold and citrine-and-gold stud earrings.

She had studied herself in the mirror to make sure that there were no lingering signs of her earlier crying jags. She had soothed her swollen lids with a cool cloth soaked in lemon juice and ice water. There was nothing she could do about her swollen bottom lip, where Gordan had suckled her mouth. She trembled from the memory.

"Are you all right?"

Cassy blinked in surprise, asking a bit defensively, "Why do you ask?"

"You've been kinda quiet all evening. And you barely touched your dinner."

What could she say? Certainly not the truth, that she'd enjoyed a late leisurely lunch with Gordan. She shrugged, "No appetite."

"Tell me about your day." When her smooth forehead creased into a frown, and she reached for her wineglass, Adam smiled, "That bad, hmmm? Let's talk about something else. The weather was in the low eighties and sunny. Not a cloud in sight," he teased.

"I'm sorry, Adam. I don't mean to be difficult. It might be best if I called it a night." She realized how tired she was.

When she reached for her tiny, white, beaded evening bag, he said, "Don't go. Come on, let's get out on the dance floor. Forget our troubles. We're here to have fun, remember?"

Cassy nodded. There was nothing she would like more than to forget the day she had spent with Gordan—forget all that had been said, the feel of him, how close she had come to letting him make love with her. Too close.

She really tried to relax, and she moved with ease to the sultry beat of the island music. She was unaware of the man leaning against the wall in the back of the room, watching her. As one song moved into the next, Cassy tried to focus on nothing more than enjoying herself and losing herself in the music.

Adam was a good dancer, and the night was warm and fragrant. The patio doors were open and a cooling breeze filtered through. In spite of the press of bodies on the dance floor, Cassy was enjoying herself. She was relieved when the music slowed so she could catch her breath. She closed her eyes and swayed to the beat.

"May I?" Gordan's deep voice caused her heart to slam in her chest.

She was thrown off balance, so much so that she nearly tripped over Adam's feet. He steadied her as his gaze shifted from Cassy to Gordan, before he nodded and stepped away.

Cassy was upset, and it showed when Gordan took her into his arms, his hands settled on her waist. She braced her hands on his shoulders, taking care not to rest her cheek against his chest.

Neither of them spoke as he skillfully guided her to the slow, seductive allure of the music. Cassy would not let herself relax in his arms. They had danced many times before, and there was a natural alignment as they moved easily across the floor—but not this time.

She was weary from their conflict and longed to rest her head on his chest, with her face against the sensitive hollow at the base of his throat, thus giving herself permission to enjoy the music, the magic of the night, and this man. She did none of these things.

She could lie to herself—deny that she missed being in his arms and that his long, hard body did not feel right against her own. But she did not. Unwelcomed thoughts of the very last time the two of them had made love intruded. She was forced to admit how close she had been earlier that day to doing what came naturally. The last thing she needed right now was to feel the prominent ridge of his sex pressed against her as he moved with her on the dance floor.

Her voice shook when she said, "I need some air."

Gordan led her through the crowd to the open French doors that opened onto a veranda.

"Cassy?"

"I'm fine on my own." She went to stand on the shallow stairs that led down to one of the garden paths. She could feel him behind her. She turned to ask, "Did you follow me here tonight?"

"Yeah."

He wore white linen slacks and a dark gold, collarless, silk shirt left open down to the middle of his chest. She was still trying to forget the pine fragrance of his soap, combined with his own clean male scent that she could not get away from on the dance floor. She watched as he absently stroked his bearded cheek. She closed her eyes for an instant, not wanting to remember how soft his beard felt against her bare skin.

"But, why? You knew I would be with Adam."

"I thought if I saw for myself . . ." his voice trailed away as if he could not finish.

"Gordan, why can't you accept that things will never be the same for us?" Frustrated by his silence, she persisted, "I've chosen to be with Adam tonight. You're not being fair to him."

His eyes flared with temper. "How could you be with him when you know what she put me through?"

Cassy had no problem knowing the "she" he meant was none other than his ex-wife. Her temper was every bit as fiery as his. "How dare you stand there and accuse me of being like her? I don't look like her, talk like her, or feel like her. And I sure would never cheat on my husband with our child and his young brother right down the hall!" Cassy was livid. She pressed a finger into his chest. "I didn't go out with another man until after we broke up and you know it! My name is Cassy—not Evie."

His voice was cool, to the point of almost being brittle, when he said, "Good night, Cassy. I'll see you at the pier at nine."

"Wait!" She ran after him before he disappeared into the garden. "I didn't agree to spend any more time with you. Besides, it's not a good idea for us to continue seeing each other."

"You agreed to give me a chance. What's the problem? Are you afraid to spend time with me?"

"I just don't think it's wise."

"You gave me your word. Are you backing out?"

Cassy hesitated, knowing that was exactly what she would like to do. "It's not a good idea."

He repeated, "Are you backing out?"

She lifted her chin. "No."

"Then I'll see you on the boat. Bring your swimsuit," he said, as he walked away.

Cassy resisted the urge to follow him. He was right. She had agreed to give him a chance. But it was too soon, especially after spending the day with him and almost letting him . . . No! She was not going there. It was best forgotten.

What was she going to do? she puzzled, as she made her way back up the stairs to the veranda. Leaning against the low railing, she felt trapped. Gordan's determination was rock hard and her feelings for him were way too volital for her.

Cassy jumped when she felt hands on her shoulders. Turning, she gasped. "Adam! You scared me."

"Sorry. You okay?"

"Yes. I needed some fresh air. The dance floor was crammed with people."

"Where's Kramer?"

"Gone."

She was not up to talking about Gordan, especially not with Adam. She did not want to even think about Gordan. She glanced at a laughing couple, arms around each other, hurrying down the stairs before disappearing into the dimly lit garden. It made her heart ache for what was lost to her. Maybe it wouldn't hurt so much if she had not known what it was to be so deeply in love and to have that precious gift returned.

"Cassy?"

She looked at Adam as if she had forgotten he was there. "Please don't let me stop you, if you prefer to go back inside and dance."

"You're hardly keeping me from anything." He frowned, then said, "Care to walk down to the shore with me?"

She nodded absently. "I left my purse inside."

"I have it." He removed it from his pocket.

"Thanks."

She was lost in thought as she walked with him. When they reached the beach, she kicked off her shoes and let her stocking feet sink into the cushiony warmth of the sand. They walked for a time, enjoying the cooling rise of the wind and the sounds of the birds overhead.

She glanced at Adam. "Do you think you'll ever come back to Martinique?"

"It's a possibility. When I get home, I'll probably get so caught up in my work that it will be another year before I decide to travel for pleasure."

"Why do men do that?"

"What?"

"Become so engrossed in their work that they forget their families and friends—everything but the work."

"You're kidding, aren't you?"

She shook her head, pushing a wavy curl out of her eyes. "No. I'm serious. I really would like to know. The only man I know who puts his wife first, followed by family, then his work, is my brother-in-law. Even my father works too hard, and sometimes forgets my stepmother's needs. Maybe I'm wrong, but I think so many marriages fail because both partners don't put their spouse first, especially in cases of a second marriage when children are involved. Men are notorious for forgetting they have wives and kids. Their careers are what matters. Isn't that what you would do?"

"No!" Adam insisted, then stopped. "Hey, this isn't about me, or even men in general. It's about Kramer. You're still in love with the man, aren't you?"

"Yes . . . ," Cassy reluctantly admitted. "I don't want to be. And I certainly don't intend to stay that way. It's just going to take a little more time than I first believed."

"I'm probably going to hate myself for pointing this out, but have you ever considered that the brother might be willing to change?"

"Absolutely not. I know better."

"Kramer isn't walking away. He's tougher than that. What if he loves you?"

"Why are you saying these things to me? Whose side are you on, anyway?"

Adam chuckled, shaking his head. "It's not a fondness for Kramer, that's for sure. Cassy, you're a very special lady. As much as I want you in my life, I also want you to be happy. You deserve that."

Cassy reached out to squeeze his hand. "You're a wonderful man. I wish I had met you first."

"That makes two of us." He took her hand and lifted it to his mouth. He kissed the center of her palm. Then he said, somewhat wistfully, "San Diego is not that far from Oakland. If you need me, all you have to do is call, Cassy."

She smiled up at him, wishing she could give him the love he deserved. "Thanks. I appreciate your friendship. I didn't mean to be unfair to you. I like you, Adam."

"I've had women in my life, but none like you. What I'm trying to say is, I can wait. I'm willing to give you the time you need. You see, Cassy, I believe you're more than worth the wait."

Cassy blinked away unexpected tears. Her emotions were so close to the surface. "Adam, don't." She took a deep breath, before she said, "I have tried to be honest with you from the beginning. But I'm not handling anything very well at the moment."

How could she when she was constantly fighting her feelings for Gordan? She was beginning to wonder if she would ever be emotionally free of the man. Comparatively speaking, it seemed so much easier the night she decided to walk away in Atlanta.

This torment seemed to have no end in sight, especially since Gordan had arrived in Martinique. She wanted the pain to end. She wanted her life back. She was tired of hurting every waking hour of the day. Gordan was not the only one hurt by this. She was sporting her own emotional scars.

"I understand. But I must warn you, I'm not giving up."

Cassy would have thrown her hands up in the air if they were free or she had the energy. Right now, she was carrying her shoes in one hand with her purse tucked under her arm, while Adam had held on to the other one. What she was burdened with was a heavy heart. If only she could curl up and sleep—make the whole world go away for awhile. Or, at least until she felt stronger and more able to cope with it. She couldn't even remember the last time she had had a full night's sleep.

"Please, God," she prayed aloud. "Save me from mule-headed men."

Adam chuckled. "Your trouble is that you're attracted to the strong, opinionated types."

She laughed. "Maybe. But I think it's time I said good night."

"May I walk you to your door?"

"Yes."

Once they were outside her door, Adam surprised her when he pressed his mouth against hers. Cassy was too stunned to move. But she recovered quickly when his tongue brushed her lips, and she stepped back. Her eyes were filled with accusation.

"I thought you understood."

"I do understand. But I would not be a man if I didn't try to change your mind."

"Only time can do that," she said sadly, angrier with herself than with him. "Good night, Adam."

Chapter Thirteen

"You're late," Gordan said, as he offered a hand to help her to board the cabin cruiser.

He could not hide the anger and resentment that had been his companions during the night. He hated the fact that she had spent the evening with another man, and he detested himself for wondering if she might have done more than danced.

Cassy did not need the reminder. She had been awake most of the night, unable to shut down her brain. It was near dawn before she had finally dropped off. She would probably still be in bed if it had not been for the wake-up call she had received from the front desk.

"Well?"

"Leave me alone," she snapped, then wished she could bite her tongue. "I'm sorry. I had a late night."

She wanted to scream that it was all his fault. He had ruined the evening for her when he had cut in on her and Adam on the dance floor. It had gone downhill from there.

It took all his strength to hold onto his temper and not demand to know precisely what she meant by a late night. Only his respect for her as a woman, and his awareness that once the words were spoken he could not take them back, kept him silent.

He took a deep breath, concentrating on nothing but breathing. He knew once he calmed down and started using his head instead of his emotions he would have his answer. Cassy had not shared a bed with Foster. He knew what kind of woman she was. She could never sleep with one man while caring about another. That was simply not her way. Despite their estrangement, he knew she still had feelings for him. She would not be here if she did not. What he did not know was if she was still in love with him.

Last night, Cassy had accused him of confusing her with his ex-wife. Was she right? Was that what he'd been doing?

"Come on. You can stow your things below while I cast off."

Cassy felt his dark, penetrating eyes move over her. She wore white cargo shorts and a lavender tee shirt. On her feet were purple, floral sneakers, and her hair had been tucked under a lavender baseball cap. Her swimsuit, towel, personal items, and cosmetics were in a bright, floral, canvas tote bag. She hadn't bothered with makeup, other than a touch of mascara and a plum lipstick.

"Will I do?" she challenged, meeting his heated gaze.

He grinned, his first smile of the day. "No doubt about it."

She scolded herself for noticing that he looked long and muscular in snug-fitting, cut-off jeans and a white tee shirt. She sternly reminded herself as she raced down the stairs to the lower level that his long, dark legs and powerful biceps were of no interest to her.

Below deck was as spacious as she remembered, housing the salon area furnished in navy leather armchairs and a sofa, and a galley complete with compact sink, refrigerator, and stove. His cabin held a built-in king-sized bed and chest of drawers. There was also a head with all the amenities, including a large shower stall.

When she heard the sound of the engine and felt the movement of the boat, she dropped her bag beside a pale-blue armchair in the bedroom then headed for the stairs.

She found Gordan seated at the helm. He glanced at her before returning his attention to the wheel.

"Where are we headed?"

He smiled. "Thought you would enjoy a trip to Cap Enrage' near Case Pointe. It's a perfect day to get in some snorkeling, fishing, or just plain swimming."

"Sounds wonderful. What was in the huge picnic basket I saw on the table in the galley?" she asked, grateful for the shield of her sunglasses.

She had been staring at the wide expanse of Gordan's chest. His shirt was draped over the back of his chair. She forced herself to concentrate on only the beauty of the island's irregular coastline and the richness of the blue-green sea.

"Bradford packed our lunch. How did your evening end?"

"Are you asking if I slept with Adam?"

"I don't need to ask. You're a bit testy, aren't you, baby?"

"Don't push."

Gordan was focusing on steering them around the reefs and out into the open sea.

"What do you mean, you don't have to ask? Do you have someone checking under my bed at night?"

"Hardly. You don't sleep around any more than I do. If we didn't have anything else in this relationship, we have trust. We couldn't have made it as long as we have without it."

"News flash! We're not in a relationship, Gordan Kramer." There was more than a hint of sarcasm in her tone.

He shrugged. "Certain things have changed and others have not. I don't have to tell you that you're not the type of woman to jump from one man's bed into another. And then there's the fact that we still care for one another."

Cassy didn't respond. There was no need for a verbal confirmation. They both recognized the truth.

Cassy tried to relax and do nothing more strenuous than enjoy the breeze and the beauty of the sky and sea around her. She failed. She was out of sorts and just plain tired— downright evil would be what her grandmother would have said, without bothering to mince her words.

Cassy was quickly getting to the point where she could not stand herself. More than once she had gone so far as to toy with the idea of taking the next plane back to California and safety.

What she was tired of was fighting her feelings for Gordan. She wanted her life back. She would much rather be worrying about next week's menu than wondering if this was the day he crushed her carefully built defenses. She was no closer to getting over the man than she had been the day she arrived on the island. Nothing was working as she planned.

"How interested are you in Foster?"

"What is your problem?"

"You're my problem, damn it! How do you think I felt when I found you on the dance floor with that guy's hands all over you?"

"Not all over me! I've told you on more than one occasion that Adam and I are friends. Please drop it."

"And I've told you that the man wants you in his bed."

Cassy stared straight ahead, refusing to get into yet another argument. She preferred to listen to the hum of the motor, the water lapping against the side of the boat, and the sea gulls overhead.

"What's the matter? Is the truth too difficult to take?"

"I haven't thrown Jillian in your face. Leave Adam out of this. It has been obvious to everyone but you that your assistant wants to offer her assistance in your bedroom!" Instantly, she was furious with herself for her own lack of control.

"There hasn't been and never will be anything remotely personal about my relationship with Jillian. She isn't the woman I stay awake night after night wanting in bed with me."

Folding her arms over her chest defensively, she did not want to care who he slept with. It was no longer her concern. But she could not hide the truth from herself. She cared—too much.

"Can we please talk about something else?"

Gordan's eyes locked with hers when he said, "I hate every moment you spend with him and not with me." He sighed, before changing the topic, "There's an ice chest of cool drinks on deck. Help yourself."

Relieved, she jumped at the diversion. "What would you like?"

"Beer."

Cassy did not like what their separation had done to them. She hated the fighting and missed the closeness they had once shared. It could not be helped, she decided, as she selected a soft drink for herself and a local beer for him.

"Thanks," he mumbled, when she passed him the opened bottle.

"What kind of fish are you after?"

He lifted a brow. "Anything that jumps on my hook. Are you going to join me? I'll bait that nasty old hook for you," he teased.

"You know perfectly well, I'm not squeamish about food. I just don't like getting that friendly with my food source."

Gordan chuckled. "Ralph and I have gone out a few times since I've been back. It's a welcome break for both of us. Maybe, I can get Wil to come with me next time. He needs a break."

"I can't believe my ears. Both Kramer men taking time away from the corporation. Are you sure you feel all right?"

He grinned. "I can't say that I'm shocked at your attitude. I wasn't born the president and CEO of Kramer Corporation, baby."

"You've come a long way."

"I sure hope not. I don't plan on ever forgetting that my parents couldn't afford to send me to college and that both of them died before I finished high school. I always want to remember that I not only worked my way through, but I had Wil to take care of as well." He said thoughtfully, "I hate that neither of our parents lived to share our success. I, especially, wanted my mother to know that Wil and I both made something of our lives. And that we appreciated the sacrifices she and Dad made for us."

Cassy blinked away unexpected tears. "They know. Even though they are gone, they'll always be a part of both you and Wil. They would have been proud of the men you've become."

Their eyes locked for a moment, hers with tenderness, his with yearning. Cassy was the first to look away.

"Want a turn at the wheel?"

"It's been a while."

"Come here. I'll show you." He eased back until she was cradled between his thighs. Once she was settled, he showed her how to maneuver the boat.

She laughed, "It's coming back."

His hands rested on either side of her. He could not

resist dropping his head, in order to place a tender kiss where her neck and shoulder met.

"Sorry," he said, softly. "I didn't mean to lose my cool last night. I was jealous."

Cassy had to work to keep her breath even, while trying to overlook the butterflies in her stomach and the so-familiar ache in her womanly center. As she struggled against the magnetic pull of his masculinity, she was cognizant of every single place where their bodies touched. Her breasts felt heavy and her nipples ached for the feel of his large hands on them. It had been too long since she was able to relish in and savor all that made him so gloriously male.

"Cassy?"

Suddenly angry, she asked, "Why did you say that?"

"Hold her steady. That's right." Gordan's voice was rough with desire when he lifted her and slid out from beneath her.

"Gordan?"

"There is no mystery, baby. I don't want our time together to be spent fighting."

"That's easily solved. You can take me back."

He surprised her when he pressed his mouth against the side of her throat, then said close to her ear, "Come on, baby. Let's enjoy each other. You're right—we haven't done nearly enough of that. And it's my fault. When you couldn't travel to me, I should have come to you. We needed to see each other."

She studied him. She didn't know how she felt about the sincere regret she heard in his voice. It was so unexpected. At one time, she would have danced with joy to hear those words.

Placing his hands over hers on the wheel, he teased, "Hey, baby. You do have to look were you're going now and then."

"Sorry."

"How's that beautiful niece of yours? You haven't shown me any recent pictures."

"Mandy is wonderful," she grinned, every bit the proud aunt. "She's growing so fast. And smart. Her teacher said . . . ," she hesitated. "You know I tend to get carried away. Both Mandy and baby Kurt are doing well."

"Your sister looked well when I saw her."

"She has fully recovered. And Gordy—how is he?"

"Great. Still on the honor roll in high school. In a few more years he will be part of the Kramer Corporation."

"What if he does not want to be part of the company? What if he wants to study law or medicine?"

"I don't have a problem with that. It took too long for me to gain his trust for me to want to force him into anything. His career choices are his own."

"I'm glad."

"Cassy, I have regrets. If I had not married the first woman who caught my eye at college, I wouldn't have my son. Yet, that marriage was a mistake. Baby, you know that. You also know what Evie did to make me distrust marriage and women. If it were not for you, I don't think even to this day, I would ever be able to believe in a woman. You were the one who changed that."

"Gordan, you did marry Evie and, as a result, you have a wonderful son. Besides, even if you hadn't married, you would have found some other reason for not wanting to make that particular commitment."

"How can you say that? I had an excellent example in my parents. My father died when I was young, but he was one of the hardest working men I've ever known. He taught me what it was to be a man. Taught me how to take care of myself and my family. Family meant everything to him." Looking at her, he persisted, "Cassy, I grew up seeing how

it's possible for a man and woman to believe in each other
and love one another. It isn't love I've lost faith in.''

She hated herself for saying it, but she could not seem
to stop the words from coming from that raw, tender place
in her heart that would not heal, "We're not all like Evie."

"I know that, even if you don't think so. But, believe
me when I say you have no idea what that kind of betrayal
can do to a man." The hand he brushed over his hair
shook from the intensity of his emotions. "I knew early
on that Evie and I didn't share the same values. But, I
thought what we felt for each other would help us work
out the differences. I couldn't have been more wrong."

When Cassy looked as if she would have interrupted, he
said, "Please, let me say this. I don't know if I ever told
you this before, but I suspected that she was unfaithful long
before I walked in on her. Things weren't good between us
for a long time. I was away a lot of the time, trying to build
the business. It took years to establish myself. Those years
took a heavy toll on my marriage. Evie was not the patient
type. I suppose she became so frustrated with me not being
there that she sought out the attention I couldn't give her
on a regular basis."

"Surely, you don't still blame yourself?"

"No. But once I suspected that she was cheating on me,
it ended for me emotionally and physically. I never once
felt anything for her after that. Cassy, that was six months
before I caught her." He sighed heavily. "For half a year,
I couldn't make myself sleep in the same room with her.
I stayed in the marriage because I thought I was doing
what was right for my son and my brother. But I was wrong.
Staying made things worse. Wil knew what was going on,
only he was afraid to tell me, afraid of hurting me. And my
staying caused him unnecessary grief because he blamed
himself for not telling me."

"Oh, no. He was still in his teens then?"

"That's right. But old enough to know right from wrong. Hell, I will never forget the night, I came home early from a business trip. Gordy was still in diapers and asleep. Wil was in another part of the house. Evie was in bed with some guy she picked up in a bar. It wasn't about feelings. I might have accepted that. But not this—never this. All she cared about was keeping my name and my money. What she didn't want were the responsibilities of marriage."

His face was stark with emotion when he said, "Afterward, she had the nerve to insist she still loved me. She couldn't understand why I didn't want her in my life. When it ends, it usually ends badly. At least, it did in my case. Divorce changes people—and not for the better."

Cassy longed to scream, "I'm nothing like her!" but it was a waste of energy. She could not make him see what he did not want to see. Instead, she said, "You're absolutely correct. No one should ever consider going into marriage if they believe it can't work. Will you take over, please? I need to freshen up."

Gordan watched in mute frustration as she disappeared below.

As Cassy sank into the leather armchair, she dropped her head into her hands. She was a wreck. She had nearly burst into tears in front of him. Her throat and eyes burned from holding back.

Why was she putting herself through this? Her being here with him today was reckless. She should have known better than to let him talk her into spending any more time with him. Being near him left her hurting and yearning for what could never be.

How could any woman want a man so desperately that she would consider marrying him after he'd admitted he did not want to be married? With that kind of marriage, the couple would be lucky if it lasted through the honeymoon.

What had she been thinking? There was absolutely no chance of marriage with Gordan. He was not about to propose to her—not even to stop her from walking out of his life for good. No way! The corporate genius had opted to take the persuasive high road—love and commitment without the benefit of marriage.

But then, he had never tried to conceal his feelings about marriage. She had known and dealt with it for nearly five years. She was the one who had changed—not him. Had she been trying to change him when she issued that ultimatum? If that was the case, it certainly hadn't worked. It was past time to accept the bitter truth. Gordan would never change. Hadn't she already learned that lesson? Now she had to figure out how to move on emotionally.

By the time Cassy had herself under control, Gordan had dropped anchor and provided two fishing rods and reels. A bucket of bait was close at hand.

"You game?"

"No, thank you. But please don't let me stop you."

Taking the deck chair beside her, he said, "I've never consciously compared you to Evie. My not wanting to remarry is not about you, it's about me. I don't take failure lightly."

"Doesn't matter anymore. I stopped letting it matter in Atlanta." She deliberately changed the subject. "How's the South African deal?"

"Slower than slow. Baby, the last thing I want to talk about is business."

She laughed, but there was no humor in her eyes. "So, how long is this vacation supposed to last before you have to get back to the real world of high powered business deals and circling the globe in that private jet of yours? A week? Two? Three?"

"As long as it takes," he said, somewhat huskily eyeing the fullness of her soft lips. "Come on, play with me." He chuckled throatily at her expression, pointing to the fishing gear. "What did you think I meant?"

She shrugged, determined to ignore the chills that had raced along her spine. "I told you . . ."

"I know you don't like to get too friendly with your food. Would it help if I promised to throw them all back? Don't worry, we won't starve."

"Then, why bother?"

"The sheer fun of it. Don't tell me you've forgotten how to have fun?"

"My idea of fun does not include a fishing rod."

Cassy eventually gave in, and they spent an enjoyable couple of hours doing what he called, playing at fishing.

"This is the way men have been taking care of their women for generations, going back to nature. Hunting, fishing, providing," he boasted, with more than his fair share of arrogance.

Cassy fluttered her lashes at him. "Man stuff, huh?"

"Exactly. That's the trouble with the world—women don't want men to be men."

"What's so wrong with a woman wanting to take care of herself?"

"Confuses the natural order of things," he said, thinking about how much he hoped she would give up her job in order to travel with him and let him provide for her.

"Tell me, do you just make up this junk or is this just a man thing?"

"Makes perfect sense," he said, with a grin.

She giggled, "None whatsoever. Ready for lunch?"

"Trying to change the subject?"

"Absolutely. I'm hungry. So, what did the Bradfords select for our dining enjoyment?"

"You don't think I had anything to do with it?" he teased, as he went below.

She followed, finding herself saying playfully, "The only time I've ever known you to cook was when we worked in the kitchen together."

Flushed by the heated way he looked at her, she moved ahead of him into the galley. She went to the sink to wash her hands.

"Here or on deck?" he asked, taking the bar of soap she handed him before she began drying her hands on a paper towel.

"Picnics are always more fun." She looked around. "What should I bring?"

"Grab the wine from the refrigerator. I'll bring the basket. It's heavy."

Within no time, they were relaxing in the sun, sharing a bottle of Chardonnay. Inside the basket was a selection of fresh fruit, along with cold roasted chicken and a crisp green salad.

"Mmm, this is so good. You'd better hang on to the Bradfords. They are irreplaceable."

"Who I'm tryin' to hang on to is my lady. How am I doin'?"

"Why did you have to spoil it? You think I like arguing with you?" She began repacking the basket.

"Then, why fight me on this?"

"You know why. Are you finished?"

He felt as if he had hardly gotten started. He had waited too many years to find the woman that was right for him. He was not about to give up. He was not made that way.

"Yeah. Did anyone ever tell you that you're one stubborn female?"

Cassy suddenly laughed. "Yes, you. But I took it as a compliment."

He threw his head back and laughed until his side hurt.

"Grandma would say something about the pot and the kettle being the same color. Or do you like the 'takes one to know one' theory better?"

"Okay . . . okay," he said, throwing his hands up. "Be right back." He took the remains of their lunch below.

She stood staring out into the endless blue, where the sky seemed to meet the water, letting her thoughts drift.

When he came to stand behind her, he said, "I never get tired of being on the water. There is nothing more soothing. Maybe one day I will take that long voyage that I keep promising myself."

"Do you have regrets, Gordan?" The question was spoken so softly that it was a wonder he even heard it.

"My share," he said, with a release of pent-up air. "Cassy—I don't want either one of us . . ."

Before he could finish, she pressed her hand against his lips, shaking her head, then said, "Please, forget I asked. I'm hot. I'm going below to change into my suit. Can I interest you in a little snorkeling?"

"And give up all this fun?" He indicated the fishing gear.

She wrinkled her nose. "To each his own. Excuse me." She disappeared below.

As Gordan put away the fishing gear, he found he could not ignore the thought of her changing in the cabin below. He wanted her. Nothing could alter that, not the fact that she spent last evening with another man nor that she was not eager to spend time with him.

There was a time when he didn't think he could love a woman more than he had once loved Evie. The dissolution of his marriage did not hurt as much as the pain he felt when he learned that Cassy was going out with another man. He would rather have taken a knife in the gut.

But he had admitted only to himself, not long after he and Cassy became intimate, that she meant more to him than Evie ever had. He could trust Cassy. He trusted her in a way he had stopped believing was possible. The strange part of it was, the trust had happened early on in their relationship. As soon as he fully accepted that Cassy was a woman of her word, the barriers around his heart had crumbled.

Cassy had done that. In the blink of an eye, she had been anchored deep inside his heart. That had not changed. He had had many opportunities over the years to be with other women. He had never been tempted. His feelings for Cassy went too deep. If he couldn't have her, then he could wait until they could be together again.

If Cassy had done what Evie had done to him, there was no way he could have looked away for six months. He would have been in her face and had his fist down the other guy's throat in a heartbeat.

Just the thought of another man one day claiming her for his wife and having the right to make love with her night after night ate at him. It didn't bear thinking about.

Gordan had spent the night brooding, furious that she was with Foster and not with him. What he had done was nearly drive himself out of his mind from a mixture of equal parts frustration, jealousy, and feelings of pure help-lessness. Was it any wonder he had awakened that morning with a hangover and a heavy heart? Yet, it had not stopped the wanting.

He had walked away from other women for less. He had vowed long ago to never share a woman again. She either wanted him or she didn't. In his estimation, it had always been that simple. Yet, there was nothing simplistic about what he felt for Cassy. It was a shock to him to acknowledge that he could not walk away from her.

For weeks, he'd clung to the hope that if he could get her to appreciate what they had—that it would be enough to hang on to. But his back was against the wall, leaving him no choice but to accept that he was running out of options. As difficult as it was, he forced himself to consider there may not be a choice. He might have to let her go. Gordan let out an involuntary moan, as he struggled to hold in the scalding tears filling his throat and burning his tightly closed eyelids. How?

Cassy laughed, startling him, as she eyed the snorkeling equipment he had set out. "I see you changed your mind." Her dark eyes flashed playful sparkles at him. "You are coming, aren't you?"

She had changed into a purple one-piece swimsuit, piped in white, that dipped into a low vee in the front and was cut high at the hip, drawing his eyes to the length of her shapely legs and gently rounded hips. Gordan's reaction was immediately and utterly male.

Gordan forced himself to relax, slowly flexing his fingers, which had been balled at his side. He grinned. "I like that suit. Is it new?"

"Uh-huh. Coming?"

He studied the movement of her shapely bottom as she crossed to the back of the boat, then he whistled. The back consisted of crisscross straps down the smooth expanse of her creamy-brown back. The trouble was, he knew what was concealed beneath. His teeth clenched in mute frustration as he thought about how long it had been since he had been deep inside of her. He needed her.

Balancing on the swim platform, she pulled on fins and grabbed one of the snorkeling masks. He watched her pretty dark eyes move down his chest to linger on his hips, as he unsnapped his shorts and let them drop to the deck.

She briefly explored the snug swim brief that hugged the lines of his manhood, before she quickly lowered her gaze.

Gordan closed his own eyes as he fought for control. He felt as if she had actually stroked the length of his pulsating penis before she had quickly diverted her eyes. He held in an agonizing groan. He wanted so much more than her eyes on him. His body had prepared itself to take her, right here and right now. He was rock hard with hunger for her feminine heat. There was no way she could have failed to notice what she alone could do to him with no more than a glance.

"Hurry," she called, tossing him a set of fins before she jumped over the side.

Gordan had recovered somewhat by the time he dived in after Cassy. He surfaced a few yards away from where she floated on her back.

"Feels good." His strokes were long and even.

"Fabulous." She treaded water as she put on her snorkeling mask.

"Ready?" he asked, before adjusting his own mask.

She nodded.

They moved comfortably together through the water. Gordan shortened his strokes in order to stay at her side. Cassy particularly enjoyed viewing the tropical fish, while Gordan enjoyed watching her. The sun was lower in the sky when they returned to the boat. He was right behind her as they climbed the outside ladder onto the platform.

"You okay?"

"Couldn't be better," she nodded, breathlessly. "Just haven't done any underwater swimming in a while. I'm out of practice."

"Just another ordinary day in paradise," he drawled. Removing thick beach towels from beneath one of the built-in storage benches, he wrapped one around her, dropping a tender kiss on her nape before collecting his own towel.

She shivered, then said, "I'm going to shower and change."

His voice was gruff, heavy with desire when he said, "Make yourself at home. You'll find everything you need in the cabin."

"Thanks ..." Her heart raced when she caught his heated dark eyes on her.

Her breath quickened in delightful anticipation while her breasts suddenly felt heavy with need, as memories of his unique loving filled her head.

Pushing those dangerous thoughts away, she hurried below deck while she could still go. She was tired, so weary of pretending she did not know his hard, muscled body as well as she knew her own. She had to forget that his desire for her had not been just in his hungry gaze but in the prominent, hard ridge of his manhood outlined in his damp trunks.

What she needed was to be as far away from this boat—away from him—as quickly as possible. She was not strong enough to fight his needs and her own as well. It was just too difficult.

Trying not to think or feel, she walked through the spacious cabin into the bath. Nevertheless, as she took off her suit and hung it on a towel bar to dry, her thoughts were of a man who managed to both fill her heart and ruin her dreams.

She had given her word and tried to be fair enough to keep it. But spending time with him felt as if it were little by little ripping her heart out. How was she going to recover? How was she to forget? She had too many memories as it was; she did not need to add more.

Stepping into the surprisingly roomy, dual-head shower stall, she closed her eyes, doing nothing more than letting the soothing rush of warm water flow over her body.

While she had been trying to be fair to him, what had

she done to herself? She needed no reminders of what
she would leave behind when she left this island and him.

She was so lost in thought, she failed to hear the sound
of the bathroom door opening then closing.

Chapter Fourteen

As Gordan's hungry gaze caressed Cassy through the frosted glass, he did not consider the right or wrong of what he was about to do. After easing damp, snug-fitting, navy briefs down his hips and his legs, he opened one of the built-in vanity drawers to remove a foil packet. He took a deep breath before he opened the stall door and stepped inside.

Standing with her back to the door and her head down, Cassy jumped when she felt his mouth at her nape and his hands on either side of her waist. She did not need to turn around to identify Gordan, for she knew his touch, yet she turned to face him nonetheless.

"You shouldn't be here."

Her heart pounded wildly in her chest. For a brief moment, she thought she'd conjured him up. She'd been wanting him so badly. But Gordan was no figment of her imagination. His chest was firm and hot against her palms.

And she could feel his hands on her spine, holding her close.

As if he had every right to be there, he picked up a honey-and-pine-scented bar of soap and began soaping her throat, down her back, over the ripe curves of her hips.

"Gordan!" she gasped, as he caressed and squeezed her before he moved lower.

His mouth was so hot—hotter than the temperature of the water cascading over them. He took kiss after kiss, each deeper than the last. When he broke the seal of their lips, he scorched a path with his tongue down the length of her neck to the scented base of her throat.

She tried and failed to formulate a protest. She could barely stand, let alone manage more than a small gasp, which was swallowed beneath the onslaught of yet another tongue-stroking kiss. The kiss went on and on as her tongue slipped into his mouth, and she stroked his.

"Cassy . . . ," he groaned, dropping his head to lave the ultrasensitive place behind her ear. His soapy hands slid up and down her back as he whispered, "I need you. I've missed you."

He spread her thighs with one of his until her mound, covered by thick, ebony curls, brushed the heat of his own body, his shaft against her stomach.

Trembling, Cassy told herself she needed to regain her equilibrium, ignore his drugging kisses and the sizzling-hot pleasure of his muscular frame pressed against her from chest to hips. She even managed to wedge some space between the wide expanse of his brown chest and her hard nipples.

"We can't."

"No?" he questioned, as he kissed her again and again. "You're not enjoying this? What about this?" With soapy hands, he cupped and squeezed her breasts, then gently tugged her aching nipples between his thumbs and forefingers. Then he dropped down to lick each full globe, lingering on the underside of each breast.

"This . . . isn't . . . a . . . solution," she barely managed to get out.

"It is our only answer," he rasped huskily, before he laved one plump, dark-chocolate-brown nipple repeatedly, then took it deep into the heat of his mouth to suck. Cassy cried out. The suction was strong and unrelenting, just the way he knew she liked it. If he had not been holding her she would have fallen.

"Ooohhhh . . ." she cried, cradling his head in her hands. But he did not stop until she was a mass of nerves, whimpering from the pleasure. Only then did he turn his attention to the other taut nipple. He seduced her with the hot magic of his mouth.

Her caressing fingertips moved from his shoulders to the hardness of his flat, dark nipples. When he looked into her eyes, she kissed him then gave him the same kind of enjoyment that he had given her. She tugged one small nipple while she licked the other one. She enjoyed his responsive groans. Pausing to soap her hands, she moved down his back, reacquainting herself with his lean waist and firm buttocks.

Relishing in his deep, throaty moans, she closed her eyes and indulged her sense of feel. Her small hands soaped his hard concave stomach before moving through the thicket of hair surrounding his sex.

He shuddered with pleasure as she caressed lower and lower while inhaling his wonderfully male scent.

"Cassy." He caught her hands, placing them on either side of the throbbing length of his penis. "Stroke me, baby."

Cassy could feel the tremors in his large frame and feel the pounding of his heart close to her ear, where her cheek rested on his chest. She needed no instructions—she knew how he liked to be touched, the exact pressure he enjoyed. No, there was no mystery, but many erotic memories of shared pleasure.

Small, soapy hands trembled as she cupped and gently squeezed the heaviness below his shaft before moving to encircle him. She stroked her hands from the broad, sensitive tip of his sex to the thick base.

"Cassy!" he called out in pleasure, then he was forced to still her slippery, sweet caresses. "It feels so good—too good."

Gordan held her against his chest with his eyes closed while he waited for his breathing to even out and his heart rate to slow. Close to her ear, he whispered throatily, "Do you want me, baby—want me inside of you?"

She trembled in his arms, her mouth against his throat. He played in the curls covering her plump mound. She moaned his name as he caressed then parted the fleshy folds, before he slid a soapy finger deep inside, stroking her. When she was slick, burning for him and whimpering his name, only then did he use a fingertip to rub the tiny pearl at the top of her mound.

Cassy quivered in his arms as she approached climax. He didn't stop until she fully embraced that release and shuddered in his arms as she called his name. Before she could compose herself, his lips were on hers and he kissed her again and again.

Only then did he tongue her earlobe and tell her how she pleased him, and how desperately he wanted her sweetness. Cassy was barely able to breathe, let alone think, when he returned his attention to the aching tips of her breasts worried them with his fingertips, then sucked.

"Please . . . ," she whispered, as she stroked his jutting shaft. "Please . . . please."

He placed her hands on his shoulders, then lifted her

leg and bent his knees in order to position himself between her silky smooth thighs.

"Look at me," he insisted.

When her sultry, dark eyes met his, Gordan pushed the crown of his sex between her wet folds and into the opening of her incredible tight heat. He growled from deep in his throat, gritting his teeth against the sheer pleasure. He was almost where he needed to be—nearly a part of her. Ignoring the thundering beat of his own heart and the demands of his body to take what was his alone, Gordan waited.

Panting, he said, "Is this what you want?"

Cassy was beyond speech, breathless and eager for him to give her the one thing she had denied herself for so long—the full hard length of his manhood. She wanted it. She wanted all of him.

"Is it?" he groaned.

"Yes . . . oh, yes," she sobbed.

She locked her arms around his neck and her legs around his waist. His mouth covered hers to seal in her scream as he filled the emptiness deep inside of her. Cradling her hips with eyes tightly closed, he concentrated on nothing more than giving them the utmost pleasure. He needed this—he needed her. His thrusts were deep and continuous while Cassy's face was against his throat. She tongued the strong brown column of his neck as she clung to his powerful shoulders. He threw back his head, relishing the feel of her as she gave him the most erotic of caresses.

When she tightened around him, he said through clenched teeth, "You feel so good—so good."

He covered her mouth with his, stroking her tongue as deeply and as expertly as he stroked her deep inside. Only the need for air caused him to raise his head. He looked at her as he loved her. She had never looked more beautiful to him. There was nothing to compare with what she gave him.

"You filled my heart," he said, around a shudder. As he quickened his thrusts, he whispered close to her ear, "Feel . . . feel how much I need you."

All Cassy could focus on was the all-encompassing pleasure mounting inside of her, as he gave with every powerful thrust of his body. Her head was filled with his scent and her mouth relished his taste. She was surrounded by him, both inside and out. Her chest was pressed so close to his that even the flow of water could not come between them. They were one.

When he rolled his hips and surged even deeper, Cassy contracted around him, convulsing as she reached one shattering climax after another. Gordan shouted hoarsely as her final release triggered his, and he drove himself as deep as he could inside of her. Numbing pleasure overwhelmed. By slow degrees, their awareness of each other and their surroundings returned.

The water was cooling as Cassy lowered her legs to the tile flooring. She inhaled deeply, turning her back to him and her face into the spray. Hoping to collect herself and her mixture of feelings, she retrieved the soap and began cleaning her skin.

Gordan's large hands took over the task, and he massaged her neck and shoulders, down her spine, her buttocks, her thighs and calves, even her feet. She was so weak that she leaned her head against the tile, her eyes tightly closed. She gasped when she felt his soapy fingers enter her tender sheath from behind. She considered protesting but couldn't muster the strength. Her legs felt rubbery, barely able to support her.

Gordan soaped her front, caressing her throat, her breasts, down her ribcage to her stomach, and on to her mound, before moving down her smooth thighs. When he began cleansing his own body, she could do no more than rest against the shower wall. She also could not look away from him, as if she were memorizing him—categorizing him in her mind. Nor could she fail to notice that his manhood was once again thick, heavy with desire.

After switching off the water, Gordan stepped out of the stall and collected bath sheets from a heated towel bar. He quickly wrapped Cassy inside the thick folds. As he dried himself, he watched as she sank onto the closed lid of the tank.

"Ready?"

Cassy could barely manage a nod, feeling both physically and emotionally drained. One part of her told her to run— to get as far away from him as she could—yet, another part of her insisted that she stay at his side, where she had been longing to be, for as long as he would have her.

He swept her up into his arms and carried her into the cabin. And she let him, not offering even a whimper of protest. He had flung a towel around his neck and, after he put her down beside the king-size bed, he used it to dry her hair.

"Baby?" He handed her a wide-tooth comb.

"It was wrong," she said, looking away from him. But she could not say, "I should not want you or this," as she worked the comb through her thick, wavy curls.

"It was what we needed," he insisted quietly, pulling back the spread and top sheet.

Cassy kept her back to him as she worked the comb through her hair, hoping to find some answers—some understanding as to why she still wanted him so badly.

He pulled her up and into his arms. He waited until her beautiful, sad eyes met his, before he said, "I love you," an instant before he took one slow, deep kiss after another. "And you love me."

"I can't . . ." She could not finish. Whispering out of a

sense of sheer desperation, she said, "There are other considerations."

"None more important than what we feel for each other."

He pressed a series of sizzling-hot kisses along her shoulders, lingering at her collarbone, his open mouth at her throat. "I can't express to you how much I've missed you."

Pushing away the towel that had been tucked between her breasts, he replaced it with his mouth, tonguing that scented hollow. Then he lifted her and placed her in the center of the bed.

"I don't want this," she said, with lips wet and swollen from his kisses. "It solves nothing."

"Then prove it to me," he said, following her down onto the bed. He licked the sensitive place behind her ear before he took the lobe inside his mouth to suckle.

Cassy was a trembling mass of nerves. "Once was . . ."

"Not nearly enough," he finished for her, then moved down to lick one of her pointy, hard nipples. He took his time and laved the aching tip again and again, before he drew it into his mouth to suck as if the peak was as sweet as a drop of chocolate. Gordan was not content until he performed the same hot magic on the other nipple.

He lingered in the hollow between the swells of her breasts to bathe her skin with the heat of his tongue. Cassy was gasping for breath by the time he moved down to lick her navel. He placed wet kiss after kiss there before he moved down past the thick curls covering her femininity.

"Is it enough?" he crooned, as he paused to look at her.

With eyes tightly closed, Cassy didn't respond because she could not find the words. When he caressed her thighs, she parted them for him. He pressed his lips along the length of her leg, tantalizing her first with the warm sweep of his lips and beard and then with his tongue. He licked the tender inside of her thigh, close enough but not touching her woman's center.

He hesitated. "If you want me to stop, tell me," he said, his voice heavy with desire.

When his hot, dark gaze locked with hers, there was no doubt in her mind that he wanted to taste her as desperately as she wanted him to. She could not control her tremors, nor could she deny him any more than she could deny herself.

"Let me . . ."

"Yes," she whispered, dropping her thick lashes and biting her bottom lip in anticipation.

There was no reluctance as he cupped her mound, then worried the soft petals of her sex with the blunt tips of his fingers. She moaned when he opened her and dropped his head to sample her sweet essence with first his lips then the hot caress of his tongue.

Cassy gasped his name, unable to contain the pulsating pleasure that spiralled out of control. Then he drew the sensitive pearl at the top of her mound into the heat of his mouth to suckle. Pleasure went on and on until she couldn't seem to get enough air in her lungs, yet she screamed as she climaxed, feeling as if she were shattering into a million tiny pieces. She cradled his dark head in her hands, stroking his hair. Gordan did not move until she was calm, comforting her with tenderness.

When he rose to position himself over her, she could not stop touching his large, dark frame. There was no way she could even pretend that she had not wanted him—missed him in this way.

He dropped his head and licked the place where her shoulder and neck joined. He rasped in her ear, "I can't get enough of you."

She could feel the pressure of his manhood against her

side. She pressed her mouth against his bearded cheek, sliding her tongue inside his mouth. "Love me . . ."

Gordan paused long enough to sheath himself in a condom before he surged into her damp heat and filled the emptiness. His unrelenting steel hardness overwhelmed her.

"Take me . . . all of me," he demanded, balancing his weight on his forearms.

"Oh . . . yes," she whimpered, lifting her thighs to his waist, opening herself completely to him. There was no part of herself that she could hold back. She needed him. "Hurry . . ."

He groaned with deep appreciation, for she had taken his entire pulsating length. But that appreciation was short-lived as she tightened around him, demanding he complete what had only just begun. He slowly withdrew, only to return, again and again. His hard thrusts caused her to quiver in his arms as she moved with him stroke for stroke. Her hands smoothed over his deep chest and wide shoulders as she responded, without question, to him.

"Gordan . . . ," she begged, tightening even more around him as she felt her climax building.

He shuddered as he rotated powerfully against her. "Now . . . ," he insisted. "Come with me now." His movements insisted as his body quivered. "Cassy . . . now!"

Cassy gasped his name, convulsing with him as dazzling white-hot shards of pleasure engulfed them. They held on to each other, breathing heavily.

As her body gradually cooled, only then did she realize that his body was still very much a part of hers. Her eyes were tightly closed as she finally accepted what she had let happen. She released a breath when he disengaged their bodies and eased down beside her on the bed.

She turned on her side, needing to understand. Physically, she was satiated, but her thoughts were in turmoil.

Sex was obviously not the answer, for if it was, she would have never left him in the first place.

Gordan pressed a tender kiss against her nape, his legs tangled with hers and one arm around her waist. He said, "What do you think about spending a few weeks in Bali? Just the two of us—no business, no family, no interruptions. Huh?"

Suddenly, Cassy was moving. She was off the bed before Gordan had a chance to blink. He watched as she collected her bag from the armchair and disappeared inside the bathroom.

"Baby?" When he turned the knob, he discovered it was locked.

Cassy did not emerge until she was completely dressed. Gordan had also dressed in a pair of jeans and short-sleeve shirt. He paced while he waited.

"What's up with the door?" he said.

"Gordan, I clearly wasn't doing much thinking when I went to bed with you. Maybe I hoped that you would change your mind. That you actually understood me and what I wanted and needed." She laughed, but at her own stupidity. How could she be so gullible where he was concerned? He kissed the right place and her brain stopped. She had no self-control with him.

Scowling, he snarled, "What the hell happened here? I thought that we just reconciled."

She snapped, "We did what we always do after being apart for a time."

"I don't get it! Weren't we close to reaching a compromise?" He did not like having his best efforts thrown back in his face.

"Your idea of a compromise is a few weeks in Bali, followed by back to more of the same. No way!"

"We love and need each other!" he yelled at her.

"There's nothing wrong with my hearing." She glared back at him.

Smoothing a hand over his hair, he let out a rush of air. "Okay, okay. If we can just . . ."

"I should not have let you anywhere near me, feeling as I do. I apologize for that." Cassy was dangerously close to breaking down. She could barely look at him. "I'd like to go back to the hotel. Now."

"Is that your answer for everything? Walk away and pretend it didn't happen?" he asked, furiously.

"What I'm doing is finally facing some facts. I refuse to keep banging my head against this same brick wall. I want marriage and babies of my own. I want to come first with my husband. What I don't want is to be romanced in some exotic place, unless it's on a honeymoon." She lifted her chin. "I will matter in a man's life—just not yours, Gordan Kramer."

His fists were balled at his sides as he stared at her. "You know why I can't remarry. Why can't you ask for what I can give you? Like my love. Why do you keep putting us through this?"

"News flash! Gordan, I'm not putting you through anything, darlin'. How many times do I have to tell you, I'm not after a reluctant bridegroom?"

"You've made it clear that you don't want things to be as they once were between us. You don't want me in Atlanta or the Caribbean while you're in Oakland. Baby, I don't want those things either." Gordan took her hands in his. "Just listen to me. If you moved in with me, we could be together. Let Sarah run the inn. If you like, I'd be happy to buy you out and send staff to handle the day-to-day operations in order to free you up. We want the same thing—to be together, always."

Cassy almost screamed as she said, "No!" It took all her

self-control not to slap him. She yanked her hands free. How was it possible that one man could be so stubborn?

Gordan cupped her face in his wide palms, when he said, "I could not love you more. You mean more to me than any corporation—more to me than anything else in the world. In fact, I would give you the world if I could."

Even though he held her close, she could not look at him. It hurt too much. She had been wrong to come to Martinique. Finally, she had no choice but to accept that in their case love was not the answer. The hurt of losing him would go on and on. But somehow, she would get past it. She had to.

"There is no other solution for us. I won't give up being a wife and mother, even for you."

Gordan closed his eyes against the pain. Resisting the urge to shake some sense into her, he said, "You're willing to throw what we have away as if it has no meaning?"

"I can't be happy your way. We've been lovers for over four and a half years. It hasn't worked. Stop worrying. And I don't want you to marry me. How could I when I know it isn't what you want? Gordan, we've grown apart. It's something we have no control over, and it's something we both have to accept. It's over."

A muscle jumped in his cheek beneath his bearded jaw when he asked, "What about what happened in that bed? Does that also have no meaning for you, Cassy?"

If only she could shut out the anguish she heard in his voice, but it resonated throughout her system and deep into her heart. She had hurt him, but she was also hurting. It was the last thing she wanted but she could not go back. She could not. Because she believed in the end it would eventually destroy them. It would take all her courage, but she had to say it. She had to.

"It means what it has always meant. You're a wonderful lover." She watched the way his body stiffened as if she had slapped him, then she made herself say, "It feels good to have you inside my body, Gordan. But it won't ever be enough." Her voice nearly broke around a sob when she said, "We've always wanted two different things from life, baby. Always."

"And I'm supposed to do what?"

"I know you've tried to show me that you care for me. And that you've taken valuable time away from business for me. It's not that I don't appreciate it, because I do. But, Gordan," she sighed heavily, "next week or the week after that, you'll be caught up in some new business challenge. That's your world. And things are bound to go back to the way they've always been with you—you moving from hotel to hotel, one business deal to the next, while I'll be cooking and helping my sister manage the inn. We live separate, completely independent lives."

"It doesn't have to be that way!"

"But it does. I'm looking forward to watching my niece and nephew grow up. And, with God's blessing, I'll have a baby of my own to nurture and watch grow."

"I can give you a child."

"No!" Cassy, shaking violently, screamed the word at him.

"You prefer to have some other man's baby inside of you?"

She had grown a measure of control over herself when she said, "It has to be that way. I won't drag you or any man kicking and screaming to the preacher man. I'll get what I want."

"Only, without me."

"Exactly. I would like to return to the hotel. Please."

He swore bitterly before he faced her with eyes cold as ice crystals. "It's your way or the highway. No compromises—no consideration for how we feel about each other!"

"None. We are done here. Take me back," she insisted.

Gordan did not say another word. He turned and walked out.

Cassy listened to his feet on the stairs, then waited until she heard the motor hum. It was then that she collapsed into the chair, dissolving into tears. She stayed where she was until the boat docked.

The trip back to the hotel was an uncomfortably silent one. Before Cassy could reach the elevators, Gordan caught her hand and held it.

She shook her head and then whispered, "We've said it all. Please, let me go." Unable to hide lids swollen from tears, she held her breath, not knowing what he would do.

Gordan stared into her eyes, his body ramrod straight. He caressed the inside of her wrist with his thumb, then abruptly let go and walked away.

Cassy told herself that she should feel relief. She walked away, knowing there were no options left for them—knowing the pain she had seen in his eyes matched the wound in her heart. She did not look around nor did she hesitate as she walked inside the elevator and pushed the button for her floor. Finally, it was over.

With rigid control, she closed the door to her room and hurried over to the telephone. Her first call was to the airlines to arrange for a seat on the afternoon flight leaving for California the following day.

It was going to be a very long day. Her flight would be leaving Martinique for San Juan, then she was scheduled to change planes in San Juan to go on to Dallas/Fort Worth. She would not arrive in San Francisco International until 11:46 PM, nearly twelve and a half hours later.

Her next call was to her sister to let her know her change in plans. Cassy did not go into the details. She could not

talk about it, not yet, not even with her sister. Her last call
was to Adam, canceling their tennis plans in the afternoon
and to say her good-byes.

It was very late before Cassy finally fell asleep, her eyes
burning from unshed tears. As badly as she hurt, she would
not let herself cry again. What good would it do? She had
gotten what she wanted. She had won, but the last thing
she felt like doing was celebrating.

Chapter Fifteen

Oakland, CA

Cassy did not feel as if she could breathe easily until she was in the air on her way home. She had convinced him to let it go. The crushing pressure of that acceptance weighed heavy on her heart. She had done what she had to do. And yet, she hurt more than she ever thought possible.

She was exhausted when her plane finally touched down in San Francisco. But, at least she was home.

"Auntie!" Her niece, Mandy, spotted her first and ran to embrace her.

"Hi, baby girl," Cassy said, returning her niece's hug and kiss. "Have you grown another inch while I've been away?"

Mandy giggled. "I'm glad you're home. Please, Auntie, don't ever go away again."

Sarah laughed. "She's trying to say we missed you,"

Sarah said, as she kissed her sister. "You have to be
exhausted. How was the flight?"

"Long. Where is the baby?"

"We left him with Della," Kurt said, with a welcoming
hug, and referring to their housekeeper. "He's cutting his
first tooth and isn't pleased about it. This everything?" he
asked, indicating the luggage she had brought from the
plane.

"Yes. Let's get out of here." Cassy linked her arms with
Mandy. "I have something for you."

"What?"

"You'll have to wait until later. But I think you're going
to like it."

Mandy beamed. "You give the best gifts, Auntie."

"Thanks." Cassy smiled, really glad to be with her family.
She could see the concern in Sarah's eyes and was grateful that she did not voice them. Just the mention of Gordan's name would be enough right now to send her into
a fit of weeping. Her emotions were just that frayed.

Cassy also knew it was only a matter of time until her
sister found out what she wanted to know. Sarah would
not rest until she was certain that Cassy was all right.

When they reached the inn, Sarah volunteered to help
her get settled despite the late hour, telling her husband
go on ahead. She would call when she was ready to go
home to their ranch. Although sleepy Mandy was not
pleased about being left behind, but Cassy's promise to
make chocolate ice cream with her the next day soothed
her.

Inside, Cassy was greeted by Edna Wagner, Sarah's assistant. "Hey, Cassy. Good to have you back." She stood at
the door of the small business office just off the foyer.
"Did you have a nice time?"

"Wonderful, Edna," she said. "I missed the old place.
Are there any messages for me?"

"I put all your correspondence on the desk in your apartment." Sarah assured her, "I tried to leave everything just the way we found it." Sarah and her family had been using Cassy's apartment while she was away. Following Cassy down the central hallway and into her private apartment near the back of the inn, she said, "I had Gina clean in here this morning, but you still might find one of the kid's toys."

Cassy sank down into the sofa in the lavender-and-cream-colored sitting room. "Doesn't matter. I'm just glad you were able to move back into the inn while I was away. It had to be crammed with the kids and Kurt with only two small bedrooms."

"It wasn't a problem. Kurt and Mandy preferred to stay here rather than the ranch. Well?"

Cassy settled back wearily. "Can't it wait until morning?"

"Not when you're this upset. Are you okay?"

"Not really, but I will be someday soon." She dropped her head, biting her lips, determined not to cry. "When it stops hurting."

Cassy wept against her sister's shoulder. "Oh, Sis. What am I going to do? What if I can't make myself stop loving him?"

Sarah held her, letting her cry it out.

"I'm sorry." Cassy eventually collected herself enough to mop her damp face with the tissues on the side table. She tried to laugh, "You're all wet," but failed miserably.

"Feel better?" The two were seated side by side on the sofa.

Cassy shook her head, sniffing "I had no choice but to come home early. I needed things to get back to normal." She sighed tiredly. "It's over, Sarah. Really over."

Sarah hugged her. "Give it some time, honey. Little by little, you will feel better."

Suddenly restless, Cassy walked to the French doors and

opened them. They led into the garden. She stood inhaling the fragrant roses, their grandmother's favorite. There were many varieties that she had cared for and tended over the years before she had turned the property over to her granddaughters.

"I messed up big time," Cassy revealed.

"What did you do?"

Cassy's laughter lacked humor. "I was so sure of myself. So sure I had made the right decision and nothing Gordan could say or do could make me change my mind. I actually thought I could be fair—spend time with him and show him that I no longer loved for him." She turned to face her sister before she said quietly, "I ended up not only in his arms, but worse—in bed with him. I made love with him." Fresh tears spilled from her eyes before she could wipe them away. "How could I do that, feeling as I do?"

"It's not that hard to understand, Sis. You're still very much in love with the guy. You have been for a long time. When the Mosley women fall in love, they fall hard." She grinned, "You know how many times Granny told us about Granddaddy. Why do you think a good church woman like Granny married a pool shark like Granddaddy? The man owned a pool hall for heaven's sakes." Sarah laughed, reminding Cassy, "She loved that man until the day he died."

"You aren't helping." Cassy couldn't help smiling.

"It's the truth." Sarah's thoughts flew back to her own tremulous relationship with her husband. She had been in love with him since they were teenagers. Even a disastrous marriage to another man and the loss of their child had not lessened what they felt for one another.

"I know. What is wrong with us? Is it some terrible character flaw that we really only love once?" she said, in apparent frustration. "Remember how deeply Daddy loved Mama? They were so happy together. It took years after her death for him to recover enough to go on with his life. His grief nearly destroyed him.''

"Yes, and it was why he couldn't take care of us and sent us to live with Granny. Sis, give yourself some time to think about you and Gordan. I'm sure after you calm down, in a few weeks you'll see . . .''

"No. We're not talking about you and Kurt. Gordan and I don't have a romantic connection that can withstand the test of time. There is nothing left but empty promises and broken dreams,'' Cassy ended, bitterly. "Two months— five years; it makes no difference. Gordan doesn't want to marry me and have babies. He has already been married and has a child.'' Wiping at tears, she whispered, "I can't give that up. It means too much to me. And the worst part of all this, is that I met Adam. I told you about him. He's someone who actually wants to marry.'' She threw her hands up in exasperation. "I didn't have any problems telling him no. I didn't even want him kissing me.''

"He's not Gordan Kramer,'' her sister said.

"No, he's not. He can never be Gordan. I kept telling myself that if I had just met him first or a year from now, then maybe . . .'' Her voice trailed away.

"Why? He's not right for you.''

"No. Seriously, I keep telling myself that someday I can make myself care for someone else. I know I'm sounding a little confused, but it's late and I'm tired. I think I'll turn in.''

"Good idea. Are you sure you don't want me to help you unpack before I leave?''

She shook her head. "It's late. Time for you to go home.'' She walked over to her desk and opened a small, glass, velvet-lined box. "Here, take my car.'' Handing the keys to her sister, she gave her a hug. "I'm certainly not going anywhere tonight.''

"Okay." Sarah did not look convinced. "Are you sure you're all right?"

"I'm fine. See you in the morning."

" 'Night."

Cassy knew she was a long way from all right. Flicking off the lights in the sitting room, she went tiredly into her bedroom. Tomorrow, she would unpack and get back to work, focusing on only the million and one things that needed to be done to keep the inn running smoothly.

At the end of each new day, Cassy congratulated herself on making it through. Even as she smiled for the benefit of those around her, she cried herself to sleep each night. Yet, she kept right on trying not to dwell on what she could not change.

She was surprised a few weeks later when Sarah looked in on her as she checked the cooking supplies in the kitchen's roomy back pantry.

"There's someone in the foyer waiting to see you."

"Who is it?" Cassy asked.

"I don't know. He said he's a friend of yours."

Cassy's heart skipped a beat for a second. "He?"

Sarah teased, "Tall, brown, and gorgeous."

Her hands were unsteady as she untied her apron and hung it on a hook.

"Nothing to say?" Sarah grinned.

"Nope," Cassy called, as she walked past her sister and took a short cut through the dining room. As she stopped to smooth her hair in the mirror, she realized she was wearing her chef cap. She snatched it off her head and handed it to one of the maids in the hallway. "Gina, would you please take this back to the kitchen for me?"

"Sure." The girl was one of the college students they'd hired to help out.

Suddenly, Cassy realized what she'd been thinking. "It can't be Gordan," she mumbled to herself. Continuing, she reassured herself that Sarah would have told her. She paused to speak to a guest. He stood near the office door talking to Edna.

"Adam!" she smiled, berating herself for being disappointed. "What a surprise."

"It's so good to see you, pretty lady." He grinned.

"What are you doing here?" she asked, as he took her hands and kissed her cheek.

He quirked a brow. "I'm here on business, but I might be swayed to stay the weekend."

"Wonderful," she laughed.

"How have you been?"

"I'm well. Have you checked in?"

"Yes, Mrs. Rogers took care of it before she went to find you."

"That's my sister, Sarah."

"I saw the family resemblance. You're both very beautiful."

"Thank you. Which room do you have?"

"The Blue Room," he said, glancing at the tag on his key.

Cassy smiled. "I'll show you. Do you need help with your luggage?"

He grinned, holding a leather duffel bag. "I think I can handle it. I've started going back to the gym. I'm working off the extra pounds I gained in Martinique."

Cassy laughed with him. "I know what you mean. Your room is upstairs."

They climbed the wide central staircase, which was carpeted in rich burgundy and complimented the pale pinks, cream, and deep-rose floral-patterned wallpaper.

"My sister and I grew up in this house. Of course, in those days it was a rooming house. Our grandmother took in boarders to help with the upkeep." She chatted, telling him a little family history, as well as about the inn. She paused at the second door, letting him inside. "Your room overlooks the side garden and Lakeside Park. We're within walking distance of the park."

His gaze had not moved to encompass the large feather-bed, deep, cushioned armchairs with ottomans, and plush carpet underfoot. He looked at Cassy when he said, "You and your sister have quite a nice place here. Everything is very elegant, yet it has all the comforts of home."

"I'm glad you like it. Our grandmother left some lovely pieces, but we used to spend our weekends hunting estate sales and yard sales to furnish most of the place. Your bathroom is here."

She glanced quickly around to make certain nothing had been overlooked, from the flowers on the side table, or the complimentary basket of fresh fruit, cheese, and wine.

Moving to the hall door, she asked, "Do you have everything you need?"

"Almost." Before she could take another step, he said, "I'm not here to tour Oakland, or San Francisco, for that matter. I came because of you. May I take you out to dinner this evening?"

"I'm sorry, but I'm cooking tonight. If you plan to eat here, I'll be your chef."

Adam laughed. "I'm looking forward to it. What time are you free? Can we have a drink later?"

"Yes, I'd like that." she smiled at him. "We serve cock-tails in the Garden Room until one. I can meet you there around eleven."

"Wonderful." His warm gaze caressed her face.

* * *

"Have you been waiting long?" Cassy was out of breath. She had stopped in her apartment to freshen up and change into wide-leg crinkled deep-mauve evening slacks and a cream, lace-edged blouse.

"No problem," he said, rising from a deep armchair.

He had selected a set of dark green chairs, positioned on the far side of the room, away from the large, plush sofas that faced each other in front of the fireplace, and the various coupling of armchairs around the room.

"You, pretty lady, are worth waiting for. What will you have to drink?" He was nursing a brandy.

"Wine, please," she said, settling back and tucking her legs beneath her. Her eyes moved over to the table tucked beneath the archways where their guests were free to help themselves to liquid refreshments as well as assortments of homemade shortbreads, pastries, and desserts.

She admired Adam's long, lean good looks as he filled a crystal wine glass before he joined her. He was not only a nice man, but he was also easy on a woman's eyes, Cassy decided.

"Here you go."

"Thank you. Did you enjoy your meal? What did you select?"

"The marinated chicken in rosemary and wine sauce." He grinned. "My compliments to the chef."

She nodded her thanks. "Glad you enjoyed yourself."

"It's funny, but after a week back at work, I feel as if I'm ready for another trip back to Martinique. It's a place I will never forget."

"It's a magical place. Unfortunately, we have to go home and get back to our real jobs."

"You once lived and worked there."

Cassy stared down into her untouched wine, before she said, "Lucky me."

"Was there a reason you left in such a hurry? I hope there wasn't a problem with your family."

"My family had nothing to do with my decision to leave early." She hesitated, then said, "It was time for me to come home. I would not be surprised if you told me your desk was piled high with work when you returned."

"I'm a lawyer, Cassy. I know a diversion when I hear it. But, yes, it has been hectic." He touched her hand, where it rested on the arm of her chair. "Should I assume by your hasty departure that you did not enjoy your stay this time?"

She shifted in her chair while letting him play with her fingers. "Martinique is always fabulous. What's not to like?"

"My thoughts exactly. We didn't spend as much time together as I would have liked."

Her eyes widened, but she made no response, merely taking a sip from her glass.

"Did you enjoy my company as much as I enjoyed yours?"

"Yes, I did. But . . ." She stopped abruptly.

"No buts. I'm here for some answers, Cassy. You're the first woman I can really talk to and whom I've cared about in some time. I decided long ago that once I found that special lady, I would not hesitate to let her know how I feel. Cassy, I hope that you . . ."

"Surely, you are not asking . . ." Her voice failed her.

His eyes were intent on hers. "You've had time away from the island. Away from distractions."

She knew what he meant by distractions. He was referring to Gordan. And he was making her very uncomfortable. Cassy repositioned her legs.

"Would you consider . . ."

"Marrying you?" she gasped.

"Eventually. But, for now, I was asking if you would

consider seeing me on a regular basis. Oakland is not that far from San Diego." He began to caress the palm of her hand with long, blunt fingertips. He smiled as he said very quietly, "I care for you, Cassy. I would like to get to know you very well. I'd like you to get to know me. Who knows? Maybe eventually you would like to come down and visit with me. I'd love to show you my city."

"Adam, you're a very special man" she said, briefly squeezing his hand. She went on to say, "I'm glad that we met while on the island. You helped to make it easier for me. But . . ."

"But you're still in love with Kramer. I know that, Cassy. Given time . . ."

She shook her head. "Adam, what I'm saying is that I'm glad you and I are friends. It's enough for me."

Adam heard the sorrow in her voice. "It isn't going away, is it?"

"My feelings for him? I don't know. Yes, I'm in love with him and I can't change that. You have no idea how I wish I could."

Cassy was horrified by the tears that suddenly filled her eyes. She swung her legs down, then whispered, "Excuse me."

"No, Cassy. Don't go." He held on to her hand.

"I'm not going to sit here in front of our staff and guests and make a fool of myself," she sniffed.

"Never that." He reached into his suit coat and gave her a handkerchief.

"Thank you." She blotted her tears. "I'm sorry."

"Kramer and I talked after you left."

Her head shot up. "Why?"

Adam chuckled. "As surprising as this might sound, he's a good man. I probably will kick my own butt in the morning for saying this, but the brother was really torn up after you left."

"I don't believe this." She stared at him. "Are you telling me that you and Gordan are now friends?'

"I wouldn't go that far. We ran into each other in one of the hotel's bars. It seemed we both lost. So we sat down and had a couple of drinks." He laughed. "You might say we tied one on. Cassy, Kramer was really hurting. He's in love with you."

"Not enough to change," she hissed, trying not to care one way or the other. "Why are you telling me this mess? Are you on the brother's payroll?"

Adam grinned, roguishly. "As a matter of fact, I'm considering it. He made me a hell of an offer. It certainly would be a big step up for my firm."

"So that's why you're here?" She glared at him.

"Believe me, I'm not here because of him. I care about you, girl. I had to know if I had a chance."

Cassy looked into his eyes when she said, "And I care about you, Adam. But our timing stinks."

"Yeah. I'm almost five years too late," he said, somewhat dryly. "I hate to see you so unhappy. Is there any way I can help?"

"I wish."

"I can wait."

"For what, to pick up the pieces?" she said, unhappily.

He squeezed her hand. "Kramer is a man I can't help but respect. But, the brother is out of his mind if he turned his back on a life with an exceptional woman like you."

"Is there anything he hasn't told you?"

"Not one intimate detail. You, pretty lady, deserve the best life has to offer."

"Enough. I'm trying to be mad at you."

He chuckled. "Let's remain friends. Do you have another sister? That gorgeous lady I met earlier had a huge rock on her finger."

Cassy giggled. "Sorry. My niece, Mandy, is available. But you'll have to wait a few years. She'll be eight this summer."

They both laughed before they settled back to talk about anything and everything, except what stood between them: Gordan Kramer.

It wasn't until the next afternoon, after Cassy had seen Adam off, that her sister cornered her in the walk-in linen closet on the third floor.

"Well?"

"What?" Cassy was busy folding towels.

"Don't play with me, Sis."

Cassy laughed. "I told you all there was to tell."

"Except why he was here?" she asked, as she began folding pillowcases and sheets.

Cassy rolled her eyes at her sister. "Did it ever occur to you that it's none of your business?"

"You might as well tell me, because I'm not leaving until you do."

"That may become a problem. Baby Kurt won't take kindly to missing his lunch," Cassy teased, well aware of the fact that her sister was breast-feeding her son.

"He's had his lunch and having his nap. Now start talking."

"Adam says he cares for me and wants to get to know me better. Suggested we start spending time together."

"Evidently the brother does not ring your chimes."

"I don't believe you said something that corny," Cassy giggled.

"Am I right?'

She nodded. "Adam can only be a friend, no matter how much I wish it were different."

Sarah gave her a reassuring hug. "It will work itself out."

"Not this time, Sis. I don't want to care about Gordan, but I still do. Why can't I make myself stop?"

"I wish I knew. Maybe, if you called him and really told him how you feel . . ."

"No way!" Cassy yelled, leaving Sarah staring behind her.

Chapter Sixteen

"Sarah!" Gina rushed into the office where Sarah was working on the computer. "Come quick! It's Cassy!"

"What is it?"

"She fainted in the Rose Room."

"Oh, no." Sarah only paused long enough to check on the sleeping baby in his portable crib. "Watch him for me, please," she said, before running into the sitting room, which they had dubbed the Rose Room because it opened onto the section of the garden that featured their grandmother's prize-winning roses.

Cassy was stretched out on one of the sofas, trying to catch her breath and sobbing uncontrollably. One of their guests had placed a damp cloth on her forehead.

"Sis, what's wrong?" Sarah asked, dropping down beside her.

Struggling to catch her breath, she pointed to the large-screen television in the corner of the room. She was crying so hard that she could not make herself understood.

Sarah saw nothing unusual about the afternoon soap opera showing on the set. Her bewildered gaze moved to the other guests, who stood watching in stunned dismay. "What happened?"

Janet Washington, a regular guest at the inn, explained, "We were watching when the announcer broke in, saying something about an airplane crash. Then she screamed and passed out on the floor." The others began talking at once, which added to the confusion.

Sarah's troubled eyes searched her sister's face, looking for some explanation. "Honey, what was it?"

Swinging her legs down, Cassy managed to sit up, but failed to slow the flow of tears.

Sitting beside her, she squeezed her hand. "Tell me."

"It's Gordan . . ." Cassy sobbed, collapsing against her sister's shoulder. "His plane went down!"

"No!" Sarah held her and rocked her, her own eyes also swimming with tears. "Oh, no. Not that."

"Sarah, can I do something to help?" Edna, her assistant, had just entered in time to hear the explanation.

"Yes," Sarah said, brushing at her own tears. "Help me get her into her apartment. And would you please call Susan, Cassy's assistant, and see if she can take over the kitchen tonight?"

Together they were able to get Cassy into her private sitting room and onto the sofa. Cassy had insisted that they turn the small television, mounted on the bookcase, onto the all-news cable channel.

Once she had her sobs somewhat under control, Cassy looked at her sister. She had a death grip on Sarah's hand. "What if he's d . . ." She could not say the word and went into a fresh bout of tears.

"Hush now. We won't think like that."

Sarah was so upset that she dialed her own home to talk to their housekeeper. "Hi, Della. Would you please get

Kurt for me at the school? Have him call me. I'm with Cassy in her apartment. Thanks."

It wasn't until she hung up that she realized she had told their housekeeper absolutely nothing, but she was too rattled to sort it out or even try to remember the elementary school number, where her husband worked and Mandy attended. All she knew was that she needed him.

Cassy was hiccupping from crying so hard. She could barely speak past the constriction in her throat. "I—I—I—I can't bear it . . . if—if—if . . ." she could not go on.

"I know, honey. Shall I call his brother?"

Cassy moaned, holding her head, which was now throbbing from the beginnings of a headache. "I doubt he would tell me anything. I'm the ex-girlfriend, remember?"

Just then, the telephone ran. Sarah grabbed it. "Hello? Oh, Kurt. Honey, thanks for calling so quickly. There has been a plane crash. It's Gordan." She wiped her own tears. "No, we don't know anything. I need you. Okay. 'Bye."

When she looked over at Cassy, she saw that her sister was drying her face while staring at the television screen, fists clenched in her lap. She reached out, took her hand. "Come on. Let's pray for him and the others on the plane. Were there others?"

"I don't know."

The two sisters did what they had always done—they called on their faith to get them through. They were both calmer when they finished.

"What about the baby? Who's watching him?"

"Gina," Sarah answered. "He should still be napping. Sis, I think we should call his secretary or Jillian. We can't just sit here until the next news reports. We'll go nuts."

"I can just see Jillian giving me news about Gordan. She can't stand me. She has been after him for years. I just had a terrible thought. Jillian could be on the plane with him. Or even Wil or his son Gordy. Please, not them, too."

Cassy jumped to her feet and began pacing. "I have no idea why I said those awful things about Jillian. Jillian isn't my problem. Sarah, I just need to know he's all right."

"Then let me call."

Cassy shook her head. "No. I have to wait." Mopping her face, Cassy felt as if her entire world had splintered into a billion pieces. She hurt from deep inside. "I know that Gordan and I aren't involved anymore, but I couldn't bear it if he was not all right. I just need to know he isn't out there somewhere in pain—hurting . . . injured. I've got to know he's at least alive!" she said, wringing her hands in agitation.

"It's going to be all right. He's a . . ."

"Shush . . ." Cassy ran to raise the volume on the television, forgetting all about the remote control.

"The head of Kramer Corporation, which includes the Kramer Hotel and Resort complexes around the world, Gordan Kramer's private jet went down this morning off the coast of Venezuela. According to weather reports in the area, the plane may have gone down due to sudden hurricane-force winds. It is believed that the plane crashed into one of the volcanic mountains near the cone of Monte Pelee, an active volcano more than 4,500 feet high, on the island of Martinique. His Atlanta office reported that only Mr. Kramer and his pilot, John Wingate, were on board at the time. Because of the mountainous area, rain-forest slopes, and the weather, it will take time before the search-and-rescue crews can go in to locate the plane."

Sarah was the first to speak. "Well, we know that Jillian and his family were not on the plane. She has to know something by now."

When Cassy realized she had been holding her sister's hand so tightly that she was crushing her fingers, she immediately let go. "Sorry. Do you think Jillian will tell me anything?"

"You have to try."

Cassy reached for the telephone but her hands were shaking so badly she dropped it. "I'm a wreck! I have to get myself under control. I can't function like this."

"You're doing better than I would be doing if it were Kurt."

Cassy looked at her then, in stunned disbelief.

"What?"

Nibbling on her bottom lip, she could hardly get the words out of her mouth. She dropped her head into her hands, moaning pitifully.

"Cassy! Tell me."

"I finally realized what has been staring me right between my eyes. Sarah, I feel for Gordan what you must feel for Kurt. I love him so very much. I've been fooling myself all this time. That love is not going away. It's a part of me." She sighed wearily. "In spite of everything that has happened, I love him just as much, if not more, than when we first fell in love."

She moved back and forth as if she were in a rocker, as she struggled to come to terms with the depth of her emotions. Pressing her hands against her throbbing temple, she whispered, "All I want is for him to be alive and whole." She prayed softly, "Dear God, please let him live—let him live."

Sarah went into the small kitchen on the opposite side of the sitting area and soaked a dish towel with hot water before wringing it as dry as she could. Sarah said, "Here, put this over your eyes and forehead. It will soothe your eyes, take down some of the swelling, and ease that headache."

Cassy didn't have the energy to argue. She leaned back and covered her closed lids with the hot compress. She was weak from worry and grief over what might be, and she was nearly paralyzed with fear.

"He has to be safe. He just has to be," she chanted over and over to herself.

No matter how badly things had gone between them, or how upset she had been with him when they parted, she could not stop loving him. And she had tried. She had clung to what she wanted and flung it in his face as often as she could. She ended by hurting both of them in the process of proving that she could indeed live without him. Suddenly, Cassy knew that she did not want to live without Gordan. He was her world and had been so for almost five years.

She remembered every hurtful thing she had said to him—things she might not be given an opportunity to take back. At the time, it had been so important to make her point. That point provided little comfort right now. Their parting had been devastating. And it would haunt her until the day she died.

Both sisters jumped when the telephone rang. Cassy got to it first.

"Hello?" she whispered, her stomach filled with tension.

"Cassy?"

"Yes. Wil?"

"Yes. Have you heard about . . ."

"Yes. It was on the news that his plane went down. Wil, what happened? How is he?"

"We don't know. The problem could have been due to a sudden storm or there could have been a mechanical problem with the plane. There was a hurricane threat. It's possible it could have blown them off course. They were scheduled to land at Le Lamentin airport. They went . . ." His voice broke as he fought to control his emotions. "I'm sorry." He took a deep breath before he went on. "The tower lost them on radar. They don't know if they crashed into the sea or if they went into the side of one of the mountains. They're looking. All we can do now is wait."

"Oh, Wil. He has to be all right. He just has to be . . . ," she sobbed.

"I keep telling myself that. But it's hard. How are you doing?"

Cassy wiped away a fresh swell of tears. "Not much better than you. Wil, I so appreciate your calling me. I wanted to call you right away, but, considering how Gordan and I parted," she sighed, "I didn't think you wanted to hear from me. He was furious with me the last time we talked."

"Cassy, you have no reason to thank me. I'm sorry I waited so long, but I've been waiting for news."

"How's Gordy? Has he heard?"

"He's here with me. And he is holding up. We're thankful that no one else was on the plane other than John."

"Yes, that was a blessing. Where was he going?"

"To Martinique. The last couple of weeks have been difficult for all of us. He's been impossible to deal with since he got back to Atlanta. Spending time with Gordy helped. But he's been restless. He decided late last night to fly back to the island."

Cassy did not need to be told why Gordan had been upset. She swallowed a moan of anguish and barely managed to get out, "I see."

"I'm not blaming you, Cassy. Gordan was just as much to blame. I want you to know that even if things ended badly for the two of you, Gordan loves you, Cassy."

Cassy broke down in earnest, so upset that she had to give the telephone to her sister.

"Hello, Wil This is Sarah, Cassy's sister. Yes, I know you didn't mean to upset her. Yes, I'll tell her. Please, call us as soon as you hear anything. Thank you."

Cassy had curled up on the sofa into a small, tight ball of misery. Sarah consoled her as best she could. It was a while before she quieted. She apologized for losing control.

Sarah smoothed her hair away from her face. "Stop it. You have no reason to apologize. I couldn't have gotten over Emily's loss without you. So you know I understand. Not that I think for one second that Gordan isn't going to be all right. It looks as if it's going to take time to get to him. Wil promised to call as soon as he has news."

Cassy nodded, dropping her head tiredly onto her upraised knees. "You'd better go check on the baby. I'll be all right."

"Okay. I won't be long. It's time for his feeding. I will be back as soon as I can."

"Okay."

Cassy was numb to everything going on around her. All she could think about was the last day she had spent with Gordan. There was no longer any doubt in her mind why she'd made love with him.

Her feelings for him went so deep. She had been fooling herself by imagining that she could ever stop loving him and marry someone else. It was why she hadn't been able to take a wonderful man like Adam Foster seriously. There simply hadn't been room in her heart for another man.

Gordan filled her heart to the point of overflow. Her reasons for leaving no longer seemed important. None of it mattered. The only thing that was important to her now was that they find Gordan's plane and get him the help that he needed.

She wouldn't think of the tragic loss of the Kennedy plane crash. She couldn't! Gordan was alive. He had to be. The thought of him being out on the mountain, possibly exposed to the elements and injured, terrified her enough. She would not let herself think of him in the water. She shuddered, holding herself and rocking.

The hours passed excruciatingly slowly. Sarah sent her family home, deciding to stay on with Cassy. It was a long, stressful evening and an even longer night. Sarah tried to get Cassy to eat something but failed.

"You haven't eaten since this morning," Sarah fussed, motioning to the covered tray that had been left on the kitchen table.

Cassy, busy staring between the telephone and the television screen, said distantly, "Maybe later."

"Well, at least go lie on the bed. Try to get some rest."

"Sis, you really don't have to stay with me. Kurt, Mandy, and the baby need you."

"You're part of my family. We Mosley girls stick together. Now eat or shut up."

Cassy smiled for the first time in hours. "Thanks. I really missed you when you moved back to Washington to live with Daddy."

"I missed you too. Those were certainly painful years for me. Even though we couldn't be together, I'm glad you stayed on with Grandma. She really needed you. It would have been terrible if both of us left at the same time."

"Yeah," Cassy said. "Gordan never had the closeness that was so common for our family. His father died while he was young. His mother died just days before he graduated from high school. He always had his younger brother to consider. Even as a young man, he had too many responsibilities—college, a full time job, and a child to raise."

"Gordan is a strong man. He has never been afraid of responsibility. He'll come out of this on his feet. Just keep the faith."

Although she was tired, Cassy could not sit still. She wandered the room, touching an African figurine, straightening a photograph that didn't need it.

She grumbled, "Why is it taking so long? Who knows how badly he might be hurt waiting to be rescued? I just hope . . ."

The telephone rang, causing Cassy to forget everything. Sarah was right beside her when Cassy reached for it. Her arm went around Cassy's waist to support her.

"Hello?"

"Cassy?"

"Yes, Wil. Tell me, please." She was trembling so badly she would have fallen if her sister had not been holding on to her.

"They've found them. Cassy, he's in pretty bad shape, but he's alive."

"Thank God!" Her eyes were swimming with tears. She hugged Sarah, saying "He's alive!"

Sarah squeezed her hard, her own eyes watery. "What a blessing!"

"Cassy? Are you still there?"

"Yes, Wil. I'm sorry. I'm so happy. He's alive. For now, that is enough."

"Yeah, it's great." Wil laughed, throatily.

"And John?"

"Yes, him too."

"Where are you?" she asked.

"Gordy and I are in the limousine on our way to the airport. We don't have much news on his condition. He was unconscious when they found him and was having trouble breathing. Dr. Hines, our family doctor, is flying out with us. He thinks Gordan will need surgery, but nothing is certain yet."

"Oh!"

"We don't know any more. They are both being taken to the private hospital on the island. When Gordan had it built and contracted for some of the best doctors in the world, we had no idea he would be the one in need of them. Not like this, anyway. Will you come?"

"Yes," she whispered. There was no doubt about that. She had to be with him. She had to assure herself that he was indeed alive. "I'll take the first plane out in the morning."

"Good. Call me when you land. I'll have a car waiting at the airport." He gave her his cellular phone number. "And, Cassy, thank you."

" 'Bye."

Her sister asked, "How bad is he?"

"They don't know yet. All they know is that he was unconscious when they found him and having trouble breathing. They don't know how much internal damage he has. His pilot, John, is also alive. I've got to pack."

"Of course. Would you like me to call the airport?"

"Yes, please. Will you be able to manage without me for . . ."

Sarah cut her off. "Don't worry about us. I can handle the inn. I have a feeling that I'm going to have to get used to the idea of you being away."

"I won't be long. But I have to make sure he's going to be all right. Maybe a week, at the most."

"I think you're wrong."

"Sis, he may not want to even see me," she said, wearily. "I just have to deal with it when it happens. But for now, I have to go to him."

"Don't worry about the other. I'll get on the telephone and you pack. Wouldn't it be great if you can get a flight out first thing in the morning?"

"I hope so," Cassy said, crossing her fingers.

The two worked together and Cassy was relieved when her case was packed and she knew she would be on the eight o'clock flight the next morning.

"He's going to be all right," Sarah assured, as she prepared to leave for the night.

"I hope so. I really hope so."

"You have to stop worrying, so you can get a little sleep

tonight. It's nearly two now. And tomorrow is going to be a very long day.''

"You're right. Good night. Are you sure you're up to driving home?''

"I'm fine. I'll see you in the morning. Try to get some rest.''

"Good night,'' Cassy said, kissing her cheek. "Keep him in your prayers.''

"I will,'' she promised, with a wave.

Martinique

It was the longest flight on record. As tired as Cassy was when her plane touched down, she did not consider going to the hotel to freshen up. She wanted to go straight to the hospital, without delay.

It was a relief to see a familiar face waiting for her to ease her way through customs.

"Bradford.'' She gave him a hug. "Any news?''

He shook his head. "It's too soon.'' He took her luggage before he ushered her through the airport and to the waiting limousine. After opening her door, he quickly put her things in the trunk. "Where would you like me to take you first—the hotel or the hospital?''

"The hospital, please.''

Cassy leaned back against the cool leather seat with her eyes closed. She had wanted to ask more questions about Gordan, but decided to wait and talk to Wil. She hadn't asked because she was scared.

What if his injuries were more extensive than first thought? Wil had said he was in bad shape. Did that mean he was still having difficulty breathing? Or that they had to do surgery?

Her anxiety mounted as the car sped through Fort de France. The hospital was located on the outskirts of the city, several miles from Kramer House. Her head was throbbing by the time they stopped in front of the modern, white-brick hospital, but she ignored it. The hospital was positioned on a hillside, overlooking a breathtaking view of the ocean. Cassy hurried along the flower-lined walkway toward wide, French-styled double doors. Bradford was at her side.

He guided her down a side corridor to where the family was waiting in a comfortably furnished private lounge.

"Cassy." Wilham Kramer greeted her with a kiss on the cheek. He was every bit as tall and muscular as his older brother. There, the resemblance ended. He had a rough, craggy look about him. His mouth was a shade wider, and he lacked the beard and mustache. It was his dark, intense gaze that captured a woman's attention.

She hugged him, before she stepped back, asking, "How is he?" She was unaware of the way she bit her lip. Even her voice trembled as she waited anxiously for his answer.

"He came through the first surgery fine. They repaired the damage to his right lung. But there was quite a bit of damage to his right shoulder and arm. He has to undergo at least one more surgery, possibly two, depending on how he does. No other internal damage other than the lung. He's going to be on a respirator until that lung is working again."

"Oh!" Cassy clung to Wil, tears running down her cheeks.

"Honey, he's going to be fine."

She nodded, but she could not stop crying. "I'm so glad they got to him in time." Using the handkerchief he handed her, she dried her face and forced herself to smile for his benefit. "I'm sorry. I was so worried."

"Hi, Cassy," Gordan's handsome son greeted her. He had stepped from behind his uncle. He was tall and slim, but, at fifteen, he had promise of developing the Kramer men's broad shoulders and good looks.

"Gordy. I didn't realize you were here." Cassy smiled, giving him a reassuring hug. "How are you?"

"Better, now that I know Dad's going to be okay." He was clearly worried.

"Yes," she agreed, giving his hand a quick squeeze. "Have you seen him?"

Wil answered, "Not yet. He's still in recovery. Shouldn't be much longer."

She sank into a chair, grateful for the solid support. All of a sudden she felt the fatigue from a sleepless night, the long flight, and the stress of not knowing. She was tired and she couldn't remember the last time she had eaten. But none of that mattered. Gordan was her single concern.

"Can I get you anything?" Gordy offered.

"Thanks, no. Come talk to me. Tell me what you've been doing with yourself. It has been a while since we've seen each other."

Gordy and Cassy were old friends. The three of them had vacationed together during many of the boy's school breaks. Cassy would often swim and relax while father and son would fish and dive together. The three of them liked to picnic, as well as bike. Cassy left the hiking to the two of them.

During those times, Cassy had often fantasized that they were a family. And that was all those daydreams had amounted to—fantasy. No. She must not concern herself with the past. Gordan's recovery was all that was important.

Chapter Seventeen

Cassy sat between Gordy and Bradford, while watching Wil pace from his deep-cushioned rattan armchair to the bay windows overlooking the ocean and back again. Ceiling fans hummed quietly overhead, and no one had much to do but glance repeatedly at the seemingly slow-moving wall clock.

When a nurse appeared, all eyes went to her and everyone came to their feet as if choreographed.

"*Monsieur* Kramer has been taken to his room. You may see him now. But, please, only two visitors at one time, *s'il vous plait.*"

Wil cupped Cassy's elbow and began urging her forward, but she hung back. Her slender frame was shaking with a combination of relief and fear.

"What is it?"

"Wil, you go on in with Gordy. You two need to see him first."

"Are you sure?"

"Yes. Hurry, he needs to know he isn't alone," she urged, softly.

Wil didn't argue but went ahead with his nephew, a supporting arm around the boy's shoulders.

Cassy stood staring after them, anxiously biting her lower lip.

"He's going to want to see you, Miss Cassy," Bradford assured her.

Her anxious gaze went to the older man, who had been with Gordan for more than a dozen years. He and his wife had proven invaluable to Gordan, taking care of him as well as helping to care for his brother and his son through the years.

"Maybe," was all she could manage. Her emotions were still so close to the surface that she had to fight back tears as she wandered aimlessly about the room. Eventually, she reached the windows. She glimpsed in the waning light a lush garden and the sea beyond. It was a beautiful spot, both tranquil and captivating. Patients would definitely have something to keep their minds off themselves.

"This hospital is not only beautiful but very modern. Did Gordan oversee the project?" she asked.

"Yes, it was his thank-you gift to the island. It's only been open a year, but he spared no expense in acquiring the state-of-the-art equipment, as well as attracting the best trained doctors and nurses he could find. He was thrilled when Dr. Mandel agreed to relocate to the island."

Cassy nodded, aware that this Dr. Mandel was the highly skilled surgeon who had operated on Gordan.

"He never expected to require Dr. Mandel's skill."

It was so like Gordan. She had never found fault with his generosity. He believed in looking after his own. Even though he owned hotels in other parts of the world, Martinique was special to him, maybe because it was the first.

The more she tried to relax, the tighter her shoulders

seemed to become. She could not ease her fears. Could she handle it if Gordan refused to see her? How could she bear it?

She had to face the very real possibility that she might leave the island without ever seeing him. But how? How could she go home without seeing for herself that he was alive and going to recover? She cringed at the mere thought of his rejection.

Their parting had been anything but pleasant. When she left the island a few weeks ago, they never expected to see each other ever again. Wasn't this his chance to turn his back on her? She had hurt him badly and she knew it. But she had to at least see him. Enough! There was no point in going over it again, especially with Gordan so desperately ill.

Bradford cleared his throat, before he said, "Miss Cassy, I know the two of you have had problems of late, but . . ."

She interrupted, "I have good reason to have doubts about my welcome. But my feelings are not important, now. Gordan getting better is all that matters. As long as I know he can get through this, I'll be fine."

Bradford looked as if he might say more but instead nodded his understanding.

Gordan had certainly been furious with her the last time they were together. She had made love with him, then callously pushed him out of her life. Then he had done what she asked—gone on with his life without her.

For all she knew he could be seeing someone new. Perhaps even Jillian. There was no doubt in her mind that he had never had any problems capturing the female eye. Quite often, Cassy recalled women who would have gladly pushed her aside, in order to get close to him. His wealth alone was like a gigantic magnet.

But it had always been his blatant masculinity that she had found so dangerously appealing. Even from the first, she had been drawn to him. She had been helpless to resist his dark eyes and strong African features.

She smiled to herself, thankful that she had not been brazen enough to chase after him the way so many women were inclined to do. But wasn't that what she was doing now? They had agreed that what they had was over.

Nervously, she ran a hand up and down her arms, as if the gentle breeze of the ceiling fans were doing more than providing a comfortable flow of air. She had come because she had to be there.

"Gordan will be devastated when he learns that John Wingate is in a coma. John has been his pilot for close to seven years now."

"You're right. Does John have any family?"

Cassy felt guilty that she had not thought about asking before. Whenever she had flown on Gordan's plane, she had always been so absorbed in him or thoughts of him that everything else paled in comparison.

"Yes. His wife, Carrie, is flying in tonight. Her plane should touch down in another hour," he said, after consulting his watch. "I should be leaving soon."

"Dad's awake," Gordy said, bounding into the lounge ahead of his uncle. His young face displayed enthusiasm. "He knew me and Uncle Wil."

"That's wonderful." Cassy, weak with relief, dropped into the closest chair. Hugging her arms to herself in an unconsciously protective manner, she had no idea how she was going to get past her fear.

"Bradford, why don't you go on ahead and see him while I talk to Cassy," Wil suggested. The older man nodded, while Wil came over to Cassy and urged her toward the windows, where they would not be overheard.

"What is it?" she whispered, urgently.

"He's awake, but he's in a lot of pain and heavily medicated. Cassy . . ." He took her hand before saying close to her ear, ". . . Gordan knows you're here. He asked for you."

Cassy's eyes went wide with disbelief. Finally, she was able to whisper, "Do you think it's a good idea? I don't want to upset him." She bit her bottom lip anxiously as she waited for his answer.

"He's weak, but he is going to be fine." Wil's voice was even when he insisted, "He wants to see you, Cassy."

She shook her head. "Somehow I doubt that."

"Why?" Wil seemed genuinely puzzled. "My brother cares for you. That hasn't changed."

"Wil, you don't really have to say those things. I'm just so thankful that he has made it through the surgery and that he's going to get better."

"Go to him. He needs you."

She hastily wiped away a single tear that slipped past her lashes. "Seeing me will only bring back painful memories."

Bradford re-entered the room. "Marian will be pleased that he's awake. I must get going. I have to pick up Mrs. Wingate at the airport." He said to Cassy, "He's expecting you."

Cassy knew when she was outnumbered. She gave in gracefully. "Which way?"

Wil said, "Here, I will show you. I want to look in on John."

Gordy stopped his uncle. "Can I ride along with Bradford?"

After receiving Bradford's okay, Wil said, "Sure. You can see your dad later. He needs to rest."

Her heart was drumming loudly in her ears. Although her head was high, she did not look into Wil's eyes. She could not bear to see the pity that she was certain was there. He cupped her arm as he led her into a private wing of the hospital. They had passed the nurses' station before they stopped in front of the third door on the left.

"Would you like me to go in with you?"

"No. I'm fine. I won't stay long. I will try not to upset him."

Wil nodded, before he continued down the corridor.

Cassy took a deep breath before she slowly pushed the door open. Gordan was in a private room. He was hooked up to machines and monitors. He was so still that she assumed he was sleeping. A private-duty nurse sat in the chair at the foot of the bed. She smiled when she saw Cassy and motioned her forward toward the bedside chair.

"Monsieur is resting. *S'il vous plaît,* sit," she said, before she left Cassy alone with him.

He looked so drawn, and his dark skin had an almost pale-grayish cast to it. His chest was bare, a thick bandage covering his right shoulder and arm and another bandage covering the right side of his chest. His breathing was labored, and he was on oxygen. His cheekbones seemed more pronounced, as if he had lost weight, and his mouth was taut as if he were in pain.

Cassy longed to caress his face, ease the tension she saw there, but instead, she sank quietly into the bedside chair. Although she wanted to take his uninjured left hand where it rested against the pristine white sheets, she did nothing more than look at him.

It was enough that they had been able to reach him and that he lived. Despite his injuries and the bruises on his face and upper body, she knew that he'd always been healthy and strong. He would be so again.

Gordan's thick lashes fluttered before he lifted heavy lids. His dark, intense gaze touched her face. "Cassy . . ." he murmured, his voice even deeper, almost gravely so, than normal. "You came."

"Yes. Please don't talk. Just rest." Cassy didn't remember it happening, but her hand was in his.

Gordan squeezed her fingers. "I wish ..." He trailed off, his speech slurred as he struggled to catch his breath.

"Hush. No serious discussions today. Just rest. Concentrate on nothing but getting better. And you will get better. One day soon this will only be a bad memory."

"Stay ... with ... me. Please."

"Yes ... I'll stay," she agreed. "Now, sleep," she urged, softly. It hurt to see him like this. He was heavily medicated and in pain. She knew that no matter what had happened between them, she wanted to stay with him.

Gordan groaned in discomfort, and then he slept. He slept through the private-duty nurse's periodic visits. He was sleeping when both his personal physician and the surgeon checked in on him later. He was also sleeping during his son and brother's visit later that night.

It was only when Cassy tried to free her hand that had gone numb sometime ago that he opened his eyes. The blinds had been closed and the bedside lamp had been switched on.

"Are—you—leaving?" he asked, as he opened his eyes.

Cassy smiled at him, flexing her fingers to restore her circulation. "It's very late. You need to rest. Can I get you something before I leave? Would you care for some ice chips?"

His gaze moved around the room, taking in every detail. When his eyes finally returned to her, he murmured, "Please."

Cassy went to the small pitcher of crushed ice on the bedside table. With the aid of a spoon, she fed him the ice. "Better?"

"Yes. Thanks." He held out his left hand to her. She took it.

Just then the nurses came to care for him. Cassy was asked to leave, but Gordan refused to co-operate unless she stayed. Cassy stayed on.

They had to move him in order to care for him. Gordan grunted from the pain. Cassy blinked away tears, her hands clenched at her sides, but she stayed until he was medicated and settled for the night.

It was near midnight when Wil appeared at her side. He whispered, "How is he?"

"The same. He's sleeping again."

"Has Dr. Hines been in?"

"Several times, and Dr. Mandel. Gordy didn't come with you this time?"

"He's at the penthouse with the Bradfords. Poor kid, he was beat. I don't think any of us got any sleep on the plane last night. Are you ready to go? You have to be exhausted."

"I am, but I'm not sure I should leave. He becomes agitated when I try to leave."

"Come on. You won't be any good to anyone if you don't get some rest yourself."

Cassy shook her head. "I want to stay with him, just for tonight. I don't want him to wake up alone. Will they let me?"

"I'll clear it with the nursing staff. I'll see if I can get you a blanket and pillow." He kissed her cheek. "Thanks." And then he was gone.

Gordan was restless through the night. His nurse was young and pretty and very efficient. He didn't quiet unless Cassy was touching him. It was near dawn before he dropped off into a deep sleep. While he slept, she slept, her hand on his uninjured arm, her head on the bed.

That was how Wil and Gordy found them the next morning. Cassy did not protest at leaving. She was just so glad that Gordan was with family and finally resting comfortably.

Bradford was there to drive her back to the hotel. Nor did she offer a word of opposition when she learned that Wil had had her things taken to Gordan's bedroom. She curled up in the center of his king-size bed and went to sleep. It was late in the afternoon when her empty stomach woke her.

After showering and changing into a plum form-fitting dress embroidered with white violets, Cassy found both the Bradfords in the kitchen. Marian Bradford was a tiny woman, with warm brown skin. She was busy chopping vegetables at the counter, while her husband sat at the round table, sipping coffee and reading the newspaper.

"Hello. Marian, it's good to see you." Cassy went over and gave her a hug. "Has there been any news from the hospital?"

Bradford beamed. "Spoke to Wil. Gordan's doing as well as can be expected. John is better. Showing signs of coming around. Sit," he said, indicating the chair across from him. "Marian has a meal ready."

"You're right. I'm hungry. I haven't eaten since the meal served on the plane. And I can't tell you what it was to save my life."

"Well, darlin', you just enjoy," Marian placed a plate of fruit salad and crab cakes in front of her.

"Looks wonderful. Won't you join me?" she asked, looking from one to the other.

"No, dear, you go ahead. We've both eaten. Besides, I have the laundry to see to. Do you have anything that you'd like me to take care of for you?"

Cassy smiled. "You two always take such good care of me when I'm with you."

"As it should be. I just hope Gordan is feeling better today. Excuse me; I'll check Wil and Gordy's rooms," she said, patting her husband's shoulder as she walked by.

"More?" Bradford indicated the pitcher of chilled, fresh squeezed lemonade on the table.

"No, thanks," Cassy said, enjoying her meal. "Is Mrs. Wingate staying here at the hotel?"

"Yes, Wil arranged a suite for her on this floor, as well as a car and driver to take her back and forth to the hospital."

"That was thoughtful of him."

"There is a little something for you also," Bradford said, before disappearing for a few moments. When he returned, he was carrying a crystal vase filled with two dozen pink roses.

"Oh! There're beautiful. But they couldn't be from . . ." Her voice trailed away with embarrassment.

Bradford handed her the card. She smiled when she saw they were from Wil and Gordy, thanking her for coming.

"They didn't have to do that. I would have come regardless."

Bradford grinned. "Wil knows that. Shall I put them in your room?"

"Yes, please." Cassy returned her attention to her meal. When he returned, he asked, "All done?"

"Yes. I better freshen up and go get my purse."

"I'll be waiting in the foyer."

"You don't have to take me. I can take a taxi." Cassy laughed at his look of outrage.

"Gordan would expect it."

She nodded. "Be right back."

As Cassy applied her lipstick, her glance lingered on Gordan's things—the brush he used to groom his beard, the onyx cuff links he preferred—the cologne and aftershave he liked. She lovingly fingered each item.

She admitted how much she enjoyed sleeping in his bed, surrounded by his things. She had been frightened to see him again, but so glad he had let her. She told herself not to read anything into his behavior. He was still very ill, with more surgery in front of him. Plus, he had been heavily medicated.

There would be time later to sort out whether they did

or did not have a relationship—once Gordan was better. Right now, he was still in critical condition. His health was all that concerned her. For now, he wanted her with him. It was enough.

She collected her purse and paused to examine the book on his bedside table. *"Juneteenth* by Ralph Ellison," she read aloud. She remembered hearing that Ellison's unfinished novel had been completed after his death in 1994.

It was a change from the biographies Gordan generally read in his spare time. Judging by the placement of the leather bookmark, she saw that he was well into the book. Deciding he might want her to read it to him, Cassy picked up the book, then went to meet Bradford.

Cassy knew she should not have been surprised when her heart started to race as she entered Gordan's room, but, nonetheless, it did and she was. She was also a bit uneasy, not certain what to expect. She reminded herself on the way that just because he had wanted her to stay with him yesterday, did not mean today would not be different.

Her eyes went instantly to Gordan. She smiled at him before she greeted both Gordy and Wil, then thanked them for the flowers.

"What's wrong?" she asked, smoothing Gordan's creased brow.

"Nothing," he grumbled.

"Someone has been taking good care of you, I see." She smiled at Wil, who had apparently shaved his brother and groomed his beard and hair. She also noted that the bruises on his face were fading a little, but his breathing was harsh.

"Gordan?" she said. But his mouth was drawn. He was clearly in pain. Cassy's concerned gaze swung back to Wil.

"Can't they give him something for the pain? Where is his private nurse, Mrs. Neville?"

"He refused the medication, the stubborn mule," Wil said, impatiently, his own concern evident.

Gordy stood at the foot of his father's bed. His face was also pinched with worry. His eyes pleaded with her to help.

"Stop ... talking ... about ... me ... as ... if ... I'm ... not ... here." He was winded when he finished.

"Honey?" The endearment slipped out without conscious thought. Cassy took the hand he offered her. "Why aren't you co-operating?"

He let out an involuntary moan. "It ... puts ... me ... to ... sleep."

"Good. That's exactly what you need. We want you well and out of here." Cassy pressed the call button to summon the nurse. She smiled at his scowl. When the intercom clicked on, she said, "Mr. Kramer is in pain. May he have something for it, please?"

"Oui, un moment," was the ready response.

"Stop frowning. Did you eat anything today?"

"Not much," Gordy complained.

"Enough," Gordan shrugged, but the movement caused him to moan from the pain.

"It's time I get Gordy some dinner and settled for the night. I'll check in on you later tonight, big bro. You listen to the lady. We want you outta here."

Gordan looked exhausted, as if he'd used up what little strength he had. "Okay. Son?"

Cassy moved aside so that Gordy could come to his bedside.

"Yes, Dad?"

"See ... you ... tomorrow. Don't ... worry." He was forced to pause often to catch his breath. "I'm ... getting ... better."

Gordy nodded. "You cooperate, okay?"

"Yeah. Give . . . your . . . old . . . man a . . . hug."

Gordy tried hard not to hurt his father, but his eyes were wet with tears when he whispered, "Behave."

Gordan nodded. "Love . . . you."

"Love you, too."

"Ready?" Wil asked his nephew. He squeezed his brother's hand before he left. "Get some rest."

Cassy was touched by the love the three shared. They were a close-knit family.

When they were alone, Gordan motioned her forward, even though he was gaunt from a combination of fatigue and pain. He let out a weary breath when she rested her hand on his arm.

"I'm glad . . . ," he paused between breaths, ". . . you're . . . here. Kiss . . . me . . . baby."

Cassy swallowed a surprised gasp, but she did not even consider refusing the request. Perhaps she needed to taste him to assure herself he was still among the living. She leaned forward, taking care not to put any pressure on his chest, and brushed her lips against his.

"Thank . . . you."

They looked into each other's eyes for a long moment.

"*Excusez-moi.* I have your shot, *Monsieur* Kramer," Mrs. Neville, his private-duty nurse, said. She was accompanied by a male nurse. "Let me help you roll on your left side, sir. *Mademoiselle* Mosley, would you step out *un moment?*"

"*Mademoiselle* . . . stays. Or there . . . won't . . . be . . . a shot," Gordan managed to say, in spite of the fact that his mouth was taut from tension, and he was holding his chest.

"*Oui, Monsieur.* We are going to roll you now onto your left side."

Cassy could see the agony in his eyes and instinctively placed her hand in his. She forced herself to smile, even though his pain was tearing at her heart. She had never seen him like this. But it didn't matter; nothing mattered but getting him well again.

She whispered, "It will be over in a moment. Then you can relax and get some rest. The rest is what is going to get you out of here."

Cassy held on to him until he was resettled on his back and his eyes were closed. His breathing gradually evened out. She used a wash towel to blot perspiration from his brow, then gently smoothed his thick brows with feather-light strokes of her fingertips.

"Rest. Don't worry about anything or anyone. Just rest."

"You'll . . . stay?"

"I'll be right here when you wake. I promise," she soothed, as she stroked his face.

Cassy could see that he was fighting the medication, trying to stay awake. "Let yourself relax, honey. You need the sleep."

"I . . . don't . . . ," he mumbled, tiredly.

Continuously moving her soft hand over his dark skin, she whispered, "Hush. If I have to go to the restroom, I'll tell you before I leave. Okay?"

He nodded, before he dropped off into what she hoped was restorative sleep.

As Cassy settled into the chair at his bedside for the duration of the evening, she tried to read his book, but she could not concentrate. She did not want to think about herself. She was determined to take each moment as it came. Gordan needed her here, and she needed to be here. For once, the future would have to take care of itself.

Gordan was strong enough to have surgery the following day to repair the damage to his right shoulder and arm. Even though Ralph and Renee Halley were also there with the family to offer their support, Cassy could not breathe easily until she knew Gordan was back in his room and resting comfortably. She stayed with him through the

night, not leaving until Wil and Gordy returned the following day.

As the days passed, they developed a routine with Gordy
and Wil spending the mornings and part of the afternoon
with Gordan and Cassy spending the late afternoon and
evenings with him. Kenneth Kittman came to visit with his
wife, as well as friends and staff from the hotel. There
was even an unexpected visit from wheelchair-bound John
Wingate and his wife.

It was often well after visiting hours before Cassy had
any time alone with him. Most important, Gordan was
growing stronger and more impatient with each new day.

It was the third day after his second surgery that Gordan
said, "Come here," with a degree of huskiness she had
not heard in a while.

Cassy knew what he wanted, because it was what she'd
been secretly longing for. She'd given up trying to resist
her feelings for him. It was hopeless because she did not
have the energy to fight him and her tender emotions for
him.

She rose to lean close to him. This kiss was different
from the others they had shared while he was in the
hospital. It was made intimate by the brush of his tongue
over hers.

Her eyes collided with his. He looked so much better.
He was without doubt stronger. His doctor assured them
that he was doing well. Like his family, Cassy was thrilled.
Yet, at the same time, she knew they would eventually have
to talk, something they had not done.

"Have you . . . heard anything . . . about Wil or Gordy?"

"Bradford called while you were sleeping. They got off
safely."

His brother was accompanying his son home, since Gordan was out of danger.

"You should be hearing from them soon."

He nodded, studying her.

She went back to the novel she'd been reading aloud to him.

"Cassy . . ."

She glanced up from the page. "Yes."

"When are . . . you . . . leaving? How soon . . . do you . . . have to . . . get back?"

She blinked, surprised by the question and that she had not given her return home a thought. Her total focus had been on him and his recovery.

When she hesitated, he said, "I've accepted . . . that you're . . . only with me . . . until I'm . . . out of the . . . hospital." He paused to catch his breath. "They're releasing . . . me as soon . . . as I'm . . . off . . . the respirator. Every day . . . I'm breathing . . . more on . . . my own."

"That's wonderful, Gordan."

"Yeah," he said. He took her hand, brushing a kiss on her knuckles. "I glad . . . that you . . . came and stayed . . . as long . . . as you . . . have. It . . . means a . . . lot to . . . me." He stopped to breathe deeply, then said, "So tell . . . me. When do . . . you have . . . to go . . . back to . . . California?" His face was taut as if he were bracing himself for her answer.

Chapter Eighteen

"If I did not know better, I'd suspect you're trying to get rid of me." She forced a laugh, hoping to lighten the mood thus hiding her own uneasiness.

Gordan did not smile. He found nothing humorous about the situation. Clearly impatient by her delay in answering, he said, "You don't . . . have to . . . sugar-coat anything . . . for me, Cassy. I've . . . been out of . . . intensive care for sometime. I've even cut back . . . the pain medication . . . so I'm clear . . . headed enough to . . . deal with . . . the truth. Well?"

Cassy could not withstand his intense scrutiny, yet she did not attempt to pull free from his grip on her hand. Her eyes moved over his bearded cheeks, his firm, square-cut jaw, hesitating on his beautifully formed mouth.

Although he still needed oxygen, all the other machines, including the IV had been removed. He looked good, more in control each day. Yes, he was right, he was healing.

But was he as brokenhearted as she'd been since their breakup? Or had he moved on emotionally?

Suddenly recognizing she had no alternative but to be open, she said, "I'm not," with her voice barely above a whisper.

She could not do it anymore. She had lost the ability to fight what was in her heart, what had always been there. His plane crash had forced her to acknowledge the truth. Cassy had needed to be with him more than he had needed her there.

He stared at her, his confusion evident. Tilting her chin so that he could look into her eyes, he asked, "You can't . . . mean that you're . . . willing to stay . . . with me?"

"If you still want me, then here I am," she said, trying to smile but failing.

"Baby . . . ," he breathed heavily, ". . . still want you?" He chuckled, then gasped in pain.

"Are you okay?" She rose and leaned over him, her hand on his cheek.

"Yeah. I could not . . . want you . . . more."

Using his good arm, he pulled her against him, up onto the bed beside him, until she was practically in his lap, her breasts on his bare chest. He winced from the pain the maneuver caused him.

"Will you behave?"

"Cassy," he said, once he was able to regulate his breathing. He touched her mouth with his. The kiss was sweet, ripe with promise. "Talk to me . . . baby. Tell me . . . what has changed."

Shaking her head, she kissed his bearded cheek. "It's simple. I love you."

"Nothing . . . is simple," he said, stroking her spine. "But I'm not . . . about to . . . question it." He paused to catch his breath before he said, "Do you have . . . any idea . . . how happy you . . . have made me?" He pressed his mouth against her throat, breathing heavily. "I don't want . . . there to be . . . any regrets . . . on your part." He paused, then said, "We both . . . know why . . . you left . . ."

She pressed her fingertips against his mouth in hopes of stopping the flow of words. "It's not what's important now." Her dark eyes shone from her tears. "I did what felt right at the time."

What she could not give voice to was how much she still wanted to be his wife and have his child. But what was the use? That was the one thing that had not changed. She could not help wanting what he could not give her, only she wanted to be with him more.

"Don't." He shook his head, kissing her eyes, licking her tears away. "You did . . . what you . . . had to do . . . to get my . . . attention." He grinned. "My mother . . . used to say . . . I had one . . . hard head."

Cassy giggled. "I wish I could have known her."

"Me, too." He stroked her hair. "You two . . . would have . . . liked each other." He hesitated, before he said, "You two . . . have a lot . . . in common. Big . . . loving hearts . . . and steely . . . determination to . . . hold fast to . . . your beliefs."

"Thank you," she whispered, touched by the comparison. "Don't you think you've talked enough? You're getting winded."

"Not finished. Have to . . . say this." His eyes locked with hers before he said softly, "Cassy, I . . . love you. And . . . promise never . . . to do . . . anything to . . . cause you . . . to regret . . . placing your . . . trust in me." He paused. "I won't . . . hurt you."

"I know. And I love you, " she whispered.

Gordan brushed her lips again and again, his mustache and beard sending shivers of pleasure along her nerve endings. The kiss deepened until they were both struggling to catch their breath, which was not good in Gordan's case.

"Oh, no!" Cassy watched in horror as he collapsed against the pillows and closed his eyes, laboring to breathe. "Should I call Mrs. Neville?"

He shook his head as he struggled to regain control of his breathing. "Just . . . winded," he managed to say, pausing to take deep, slow breaths.

"Are you sure?"

He managed to pat her hand. "I'm . . . fine . . . now."

"Gordan, you scared the life out of me! We can't do this. You're still healing."

Once he regained his breath, he smiled, "I'm not . . . dead yet." He took her hand, placing it against his semi-arousal.

"Shame on you," Cassy laughed, caressing him briefly before she moved her hand away. "You can forget that, Gordan Kramer, at least until you're better."

"I'm looking . . . forward . . . to it," he teased. Moving a caressing hand down her arm, he said, "I've missed . . . you."

"Me, too." She kissed the base of his throat.

He slid a hand beneath her hair to stroke her nape, enjoying their closeness. "I hated . . . doing without . . . you. I've been . . . difficult to . . . be around . . . especially after . . . you left . . . the island."

"I wasn't doing very well myself. I nearly went out of my mind when I heard your jet went down." She buried her face against the base of his throat. "I thought I'd lost you."

He brushed her damp cheeks with his lips. "You can't . . . lose me. You're . . . my heart."

They rested like that for a time, with her against his left side, neither interested in moving. They didn't really talk, more concerned with enjoying their closeness. The sound of the late-night-duty nurses starting their shift caused Cassy to move back to the armchair beside the bed.

"Baby . . ."

"I think it's time I let you get some rest."

"We need . . . to talk. There . . . are things . . . I can't . . ."

She brushed his lips with her own. "Later, you need to get some sleep."

"I feel better . . . when you're . . . with me." He brushed a finger beneath her eyes. "You're exhausted. You been . . . here night . . . after night . . . with me." Pausing for a moment, he said, "Why don't . . . you sleep in . . . tomorrow. Rest . . . all day. Hear?"

Cassy laughed. "I'm fine, or I will be, once you're out of here."

"Soon," he smiled, his eyes locked with hers. "If all goes . . . well, only a . . . few more days."

She pressed her mouth ever-so-briefly over his after glancing at her watch. "Bradford is waiting."

"You can do . . . better than . . . that," he complained.

She shook her finger at him, then giggled at his fierce frown. She leaned close to kiss the very corner of his lips.

"Night, baby."

"Good night," she waved.

Bradford was waiting in the limousine to drive her back to the hotel. "You've got a lovely smile on your face. How's the boss?" he asked, coming around to open the door for her.

"Much better." Cassy's laugh was filled with pleasure as she gazed up at the older man. "He's doing well. He's coming home in a few more days, that is, if he's off the oxygen."

"That's good news. I know he's going to be glad to be out of that place." He motioned to the hospital as he waited for her to climb inside. "Do you know what we need to get ready to take care of him?"

"No, but I'm sure I can get a list from his doctors and Mrs. Neville. She will be coming with us until he's back on his feet."

"Is he staying on the island? Or does he plan on flying back to Atlanta to recuperate?"

Cassy was forced to admit, "I have no idea. I'll make a point to get to the hospital early tomorrow so that I can speak to his doctor. Then we'll decide what is best."

Bradford's face split into a warm smile. "Don't make no difference. Once he is home, we're going to take good care of him. Wil wouldn't have left if there were problems. That boy has turned into a fine man."

Cassy smiled at the pride she detected in his voice. "Has he called?"

"Yes, from his condo. Gordy is back with his mother. He should be back in school tomorrow."

Cassy settled back, as Bradford moved around to the driver seat. Yes, Gordy was with the lovely Evie. Cassy lost her smile. Well, Evie should be thrilled. That woman had certainly ruined Gordan for any other woman. She was responsible for his steadfast refusal to remarry.

Sighing, Cassy realized she wanted him so much, she had no alternative but to deal with it. She had been wrong when she thought that she could change him by issuing that ultimatum. Although she had not realized at the time, that was what she was trying to do. Cassy had known all along that she loved the man. There had never been any doubt about that. No matter what she told herself, she knew now that she could never become seriously involved with Adam or any other man. Just how in the world had she thought she could someday marry another man when she could not bear the man's kisses? All Gordan had to do was touch her and she was his.

Bradford was grinning when he opened her door in front of the hotel. "I think we will all sleep a bit easier this night."

"You're right about that."

Yet, Cassy knew she could not sleep well until Gordan was out of the hospital and beside her. Home had suddenly taken on new dimensions. It was not brick or mortar—or even a place. It was wherever the two of them were together. Her home from now on would be with him.

Cassy was not looking forward to explaining all this to her sister. She had no idea how she was going to explain the unexplainable. Nevertheless, she fully intended to live with Gordan without the benefits of marriage.

The minute she was alone, Cassy put the call through, even though it was late.

"How is he?" Sarah asked.

"He's much better. They're talking about letting him go home in a few days. I'm hoping by the end of the week, if he's off the oxygen. And, eventually, he's going to have to have physical therapy for the shoulder and arm, once he is out of the cast. But at least he'll be out of that hospital soon."

"That's wonderful news. So, when are you going to be able to come home?"

It took her so long to answer that Sarah prompted, "Sis?"

"I'm not coming home. I've decided to live with Gordan. I can't leave him, especially after what happened."

"Surely, you're not blaming yourself for the plane crash?"

"Oh no. I know I'm not responsible for that. Just both our unhappiness since I left him."

"You've told him that you're still in love with him?"

"Yes."

"And?"

"He still loves me, too."

Sarah laughed. "Tell me something I don't know."

"You're not disappointed in me?"

"For what, following your heart? I never thought you had any other choice. You two belong together."

"Thanks, Sis. The crash proved to me, as nothing else could, just how deep my feelings are for him," Cassy confessed.

"Are you sure you're going to be able to deal with living with him?"

"I have to. I can't leave him again." Cassy purposefully changed the subject. "About the inn . . ."

"Don't worry about that. We can work that out. Your happiness is more important to me. You are happy, aren't you?"

"Yes. My future is with him." She was unable to tell her sister that there was a small place in her heart that still ached for a child—his child.

"Cassy," Sarah sighed, as if she heard her sister's thoughts. "You don't know what the future will bring. Who knows? Maybe he will change his mind about marriage."

"I don't want to even think about it. I can't think about it," she whispered. "He's on the mend, that's enough." Cassy went on to say, "I've been thinking about the inn. I have a few suggestions that might solve our problem of personnel, at least for a time."

"What are they? Kurt wants me to sell my part in the inn and become a full-time homemaker."

"What? Are you?"

"No! I have my family, but I enjoy my work. So what's this idea? I need all the suggestions I can get before I tell Kurt about this. He can be so stubborn sometimes."

"Tell me about it," Cassy mumbled, only she was referring to Gordan Kramer. "Sis, why are we so drawn to such mule-headed men?"

"Good question. Ask me in about twenty-five years, then I might know the answer. Better yet, ask Grandma. She can tell you about the Mosley women going back to Great-Great-Granny Atkins."

Cassy laughed. "Okay, okay, let's get back to business. My suggestion is that you start interviewing for a live-in housekeeper. And promote Susan to head chef. She did a wonderful job filling in for me while I was on vacation. What do you think?"

"I think you are a genius. Any time you need a job, call me."

They both laughed.

"Cassy, do you remember Margaret Maxwell? She's a retired schoolteacher. She has stayed several times at the inn. She's from Los Angeles."

"Yes, I do. Sweet, but bossy. Didn't she say she was having a difficult time adjusting to being retired?"

"That's her. She never married and only has her garden these days to keep her busy. Wouldn't it be wonderful if she were willing to become our live-in housekeeper?"

"Fantastic!" Cassy said.

The sisters talked for some time, making plans for the inn, before they hung up. Both were excited about the possibility of hiring Margaret Maxwell or someone like her. Sarah had also made it clear that she was not interested in buying Cassy out. They would continue to share the inn. And Cassy would continue to help out in whatever way she could.

She was thoughtful as she prepared for bed. Her life was suddenly taking on some very drastic changes. But one thing had not changed, and that was Gordan's view on marriage. Cassy quickly pushed the thought away, reminding herself that in this life, no one had everything they wanted.

She had what was important to her. She had Gordan's love. He was the man she loved and respected. Even though they would probably never agree about his hectic schedule, once he was recovered, she could trust him with her heart.

A few day later, she found Gordan in the hospital garden. He was seated in a comfortable lounger, talking to John Wingate and his wife.

"Good morning," she said. She squeezed Gordan's silk-covered left shoulder. He was wearing navy, silk pajama bottoms and a matching robe. "It looks like everyone is enjoying the sunshine. How are you, John? It's good to see that you're looking so well."

"Thanks. It looks like they're going to let me out of here next week," John smiled. Unlike Gordan, he was seated in a wheelchair.

His wife, Carrie, added with a smile, "They want to do more tests. Unfortunately, he's still having headaches."

"Hopefully, it won't be much longer. Are you planning to recuperate on the island or go back home?"

"Home," both Wingates said at the same time, then smiled fondly at each other.

Carrie said, "We will stay on at the hotel until John is ready to travel. But we both want to get back to our kids as soon as possible. We have two little boys at home—six and ten."

Cassy smiled, unaware of the yearning in her eyes or Gordan watching her. "How fortunate. Who's caring for them?"

"My mother," Carrie explained. Glancing at her watch, she said, "Well, if you'll excuse us, John is due back inside."

"See you two later," Cassy said, with a smile.

Gordan waited until they were alone, before he said, "Come here."

Cassy leaned down to briefly press her lips against his. "Hi."

"That's better," he said, holding on to her hand until she gave him another kiss.

Cassy smiled, refusing to prolong the kiss, even though he frowned at her. She made sure it was no more than a brush of their lips. Although he was not on oxygen, but breathing on his own, she was not taking any risks. "I hear you haven't been co-operative this morning, Mr. Kramer."

"You talked . . . to Nurse . . . Neville."

"Your doctor. I ran into him in the hall. What's your problem? You know they aren't going to let you out of here unless you go home with the nurse." She sat down in the chair beside his.

"You look . . . pretty today." He took in the red sleeveless sheath that was belted at the waist and skimmed her soft curves. "I like you . . . in red. How . . . come you . . . don't wear . . . more of it?"

She arched a brow. "My color choice is not what's important. Your health is. What is your problem? Must you be stubborn about everything?"

Gordan grinned. "I'm going . . . home . . . in two days if I . . . have to check . . . myself out." He paused before he said, "What are . . . you doing . . . here so early?" He hesitated, then said, "I thought . . . I told you . . . to rest."

"I thought I told you to behave. We're talking about your health here. Did you actually think you could bully the doctors into doing things your way?"

"Why not?"

Cassy shook her finger at him. "I want you home, as soon as possible. I've made arrangements with Mrs. Neville to accompany us." She glared at him, not about to back down.

"Don't be angry," he said, reaching for her hand. He rubbed her knuckles against his face.

"Then co-operate. I want you well." Her dark eyes filled. "Please?"

Gordan brushed at the tear. "Okay. I'll be . . . good."
Then he said huskily, his gaze on her soft crimson-lined
mouth. "Now you be . . . good and come . . . here and
sit . . . on my lap . . . so I can kiss . . . you properly."

Cassy giggled. "No way. I intend to get you well if it kills
us both."

They both laughed. And Gordan was forced to be content with holding her hand.

"How long have you been off the oxygen?"

"All morning. If I make . . . it another . . . day without . . . they will let . . . me out of . . . here . . . Friday."

"That's wonderful. How long have you been out of
bed?"

"Couple of hours." He paused to breathe deeply.
"Don't worry, Neville . . . will be here . . . with that wheelchair . . . to take me . . . back to bed." He stopped for a
moment, then said, "I don't . . . like being sick."

"I know you don't, love. But it's not forever."

On Friday, one of the young nurses said from the doorway, "Ready to go, *Monsieur* Kramer?"

Although impatient to leave, Gordan grumbled when
she came into the room with the wheelchair.

Cassy quirked a questioning brow at him, waiting to see
how difficult he was planning to be. Bradford had gone
ahead, with the flowers, baskets of fruit, and other gifts of
well-wishes Gordan had received, to bring the car around.

"Problem?" Cassy asked, in all innocence, a smile teasing her lips.

"No, not a . . . one." Gordan swallowed his protest. His
dark eyes met her twinkling ones. A smile tugged at the
corner of his mouth in spite of the fact that the joke was
on him. After settling himself in the wheelchair, he said,
"Let's go."

Cassy laughed, his black leather duffel bag in her hand, the doctor's instructions in her purse.

"Coming?" he called, from over his shoulder. He wore black jeans and a short-sleeve shirt over his cast, the sling around his neck helping to support his right shoulder and arm.

To Cassy, he had never looked better. "I'm right behind you."

Touched by the number of medical staff that came out to see him off, Gordan curbed his impatience long enough to thank everyone and say good-bye. Bradford had passed out individual boxes of imported chocolates and the home-made fruit tarts that Cassy had made as tokens of Gordan's appreciation.

"Finally," Gordan sighed, leaning back against the plush leather of the limousine. "Did I tell you how . . . pretty you look today?" he asked. Cassy was seated on his left, taking care not to jar him.

"No, but feel free," she teased, aware that her white, slim skirt and pristine, white, silk blouse were hardly eye-catching. She caressed his cheek. "You look so much better than the night I arrived. I was so scared."

"I know." He kissed the center of her palm. "The worst is behind us, baby. Isn't it?" he asked softly, studying her eyes.

Cassy could see the question in his gaze and assumed he was not referring to his injury. He was talking about their painful estrangement.

"Yes." She outlined the shape of his mouth with a pink lacquered nail. "I've missed you, so much."

He closed his eyes as if he were savoring her touch, her words. "I've missed you more." He didn't bother to glance at the passing scenery. His focus was on her. "Are you happy?"

"Yes!" she laughed. "My love, you're finally out of that hospital. How about you?"

"I will be tonight," he said, softly, then paused, ". . . when you're beside me, in my arms."

"Now Gordan, you know what the doctor said. I won't do anything that might slow your recovery."

He smiled. "Believe me, I know my limitations." He chuckled, then paused to catch his breath before he went on to say, "I'm talking about holding you. I want you in bed . . . with me tonight . . . every night."

"Yes," she said, around a tender sigh. "I want that, also. It has been so long since we held each other. But, I don't want you to overdo it. We've got to get you well. I'm glad Mrs. Neville agreed to come back to the suite with us." Cassy giggled at the face he made when she mentioned the nurse.

She continued, "This may make you angry with me, but I had a talk with Kenneth Kittman. I asked that all problems pertaining to the hotel be directed to the home office and Wil's attention." Cassy was not sure what she expected, but certainly not the cocky grin that appeared on his face.

"Good. I meant it when I said I plan to follow doctor's orders." He paused, caressing her hand. "But, Cassy, there is still so much left unsaid between us. I want to know if . . ."

Cassy pressed her lips against his, stopping the flow of his words. "No, baby. No serious discussions, at least, not until you are better." She purposefully switched the subject by asking about his son. He had mentioned earlier that he'd talked to both Gordy and Wil the night before.

Cassy had avoided serious discussions since she told him she would live with him. What good would they do? His mind was made up and she could not go on wishing for what she could not have. She loved this man. And she felt so blessed that he was alive and getting stronger each day. Finally they were together.

No. Talking about the past would solve nothing. It was best left alone. She had promised herself that if they had a second chance, she would not let anything destroy their happiness.

Lifting her chin so that he could see her face, he asked, "How long do you think avoiding talking is going to work?"

"Until you're better. Today, all we have to concentrate on is getting you settled. I'm glad you decided to recuperate here on the island. Hopefully, nothing will detract you from getting well, quickly. Isn't that what we both want?"

"Okay." He laced his left hand with hers. "When I built that hospital, I didn't expect to need it so badly."

Suppressing a shudder, she said, "I'm grateful for it. I think it was a wonderful gift from you to the people of Martinique. And you've managed to attract first-class medical personnel. Of course, the sea air, fabulous golf course, beautiful sunsets, and Caribbean had a little something to do with it."

He chuckled. "You have a point."

"Promise me that you won't consider going back to work until the doctor gives his approval. Give Wil a chance to show what he can do. You trained him, didn't you?"

"You won't get any arguments out of me, baby." He touched his mouth to hers.

When the car stopped in front of the hotel drive, Gordan was determined to walk unaided, despite the fact that Mrs. Neville was waiting in the lobby with a wheelchair. Cassy did not say a word when he announced that there was not a thing wrong with his legs. He smiled down at her, squeezing her hand.

They were quickly surrounded by friends and the hotel staff. He accepted the get-well wishes with a smile. He did not protest when Cassy insisted that he rest in the armchair once they reached the penthouse suite.

The foyer and living room were filled with plants and flowers, and stacks of get well cards from friends, business associates, and employees from around the world waited for his attention.

Cassy knew he was winded and exhausted by the way he let both Mrs. Neville and Marian Bradford fuss over him. Mrs. Neville had his medication set up for him in the master bedroom. She had also arranged for a portable oxygen machine to be on hand if needed. It was not until after lunch that Gordan agreed to nap during the afternoon.

"Stop . . . scowling at . . . me."

"You're having trouble breathing."

He caught her hand. "I'm just . . . tired."

"Should I get Mrs. Neville?"

"What I need . . . is you. Come here . . . and curl up . . . beside me." ·

She moved to his left side and carefully rested beside him. She sighed softly when he held her close, listening to the sound of his breathing. When she realized that he was not having difficulty, she was able to relax.

He brushed his lips against her temple. "You feel good." He smoothed his thumb along her nape.

"Glad you think so," she murmured.

"You should be . . . exhausted. You've spent . . . so much time at the . . . hospital with me."

"I'm fine, now that you're here."

"This is the best . . . medicine, baby . . . being able to hold you . . . like this."

Cassy's breath caught in her throat, and her heart raced with pleasure from the wealth of love she heard in his voice. When she tilted her head back in order to see his face, she smiled. His breathing was deep as he slept.

Cassy knew she was lucky. She had turned her back on his love and, as a result, had destroyed both their happiness. Never again. She was not willing to risk losing what they had—it was too important.

As she drifted off, she realized she had learned something about herself. Gordan had claimed her heart. And she would rather be with him and unmarried, than married to any other man.

Chapter Nineteen

Gordan released his private nurse after his first week home. His checkup during his third week out of the hospital went so well, that he began taking walks in the garden with Cassy during the early evening hours.

It was later the following week when Gordan surprised Cassy by suggesting a ride into the countryside.

"Stop worrying," he teased. "I'm fine."

"I didn't say a word. You've been out of the hospital a little over a month, and already you're restless. Next week you will be telling me you're ready to go back to work."

He arched a brow in mock indignation. "You've hurt my feelings. I've been a model patient. I've taken my medication, rested as much as I can. Even my appetite has improved. I've made no complaints, and I'm not outraged that you won't make love with me. And now, look what you accuse me of. Baby, I'm crushed. What's wrong with a simple drive into the countryside?" He gestured toward the chauffeur. "Bradford's at the wheel."

"Do you expect me to believe that you didn't talk business last weekend while your brother and Gordy were here?"

"I made you a promise and I'm keeping it. Stop worrying." He leaned down to press a brief kiss to her cheek. His breathing was still not what he hoped, but he was much better than he had been on the day he was released.

"Poor Mr. Misunderstood." Cassy laughed at his wounded expression, and Gordan couldn't help joining in.

He gasped, pressing a hand to the incision on his chest. "Stop making me laugh; it hurts."

Cassy pressed her lips to his cheek, before she said, "Sorry, baby. Does that make it better?"

He grinned roguishly. "A bit. Now if you climb on my lap and give me a little tongue . . ."

Cassy put her hand over his mouth. "Hush. Bradford might hear you."

"Through the glass partition?" He chuckled. "I've got news for you, baby. He knows all about sex. Unlike me, he probably had some sweet loving last night," he said close to her ear, before he placed a lingering kiss on the side of her throat. "I want you."

Cassy shivered from the heat of his hot gaze, as well as the warmth of his hand moving under her wide-leg shorts to caress her inner thigh. He did not stop until he reached her lace-edged panties. She let out a gasp as he fingered the leg opening, before he gently squeezed her mound.

"Gordan!" She let out a soft moan.

"I might not be able to do anything about it. But that doesn't mean I'm not still a man who adores his woman."

"I want you, too," she whispered. "Now behave yourself." She held his hand in hers. Studying his twinkling dark eyes, she smiled. "You're in an extremely good mood today, Mr. Kramer. What are you up to?"

"Now she wants to know all my secrets."

"Absolutely. Tell me," she urged.

He shook his head. "You'll find out soon enough."

"When?"

He glanced out the window, then he said, "Not long." Gordan cradled her hand in his large, dark one. "Baby, I know these past couple of weeks have not been fun for you. I can't tell you how much I appreciate you being with me." He paused for breath, then said, "The plane crash has taught me to appreciate life in a new way. If nothing else, the crash, along with our separation, has given me a lot to think about. I've learned to cherish every moment we have together."

"Gordan," she said. Although warmed by his confession, she shook her finger playfully at him. "Now don't get too serious on me."

His forehead creased in a frown, but he said nothing more.

Cassy worried her bottom lip, suddenly fearful that she had hurt him, which was the last thing she wanted. But, she also knew she was not prepared to get into an in-depth discussion about their relationship.

She knew him. He would not be satisfied until she told him she no longer wanted to be married and have his baby. She could not lie to him. Why couldn't he accept that she was with him because she loved him and leave it there?

It was not necessary to go over and over what could not be changed. She couldn't help what she wanted, but she was wise enough, now, not to let it keep them apart.

Eventually, things were bound to change. He would go back to his work at the helm of Kramer Corporation. And she . . . She was not sure what she wanted to do. Perhaps she would open a pastry business that supplied his hotels. That was something to consider. Cassy assured herself that this time it would be different for them. She would be at his side. There would be no lengthy separations—no bitterness nor resentment.

If only he would leave the past in the past. Cassy suppressed a moan of frustration, resting her head on his left shoulder. It would work—it had to.

Bradford turned off onto a secondary road, and then onto another even smaller one, which finally turned into little more than a track that wound its way past a grove of coconut and palm trees, past a lovely meadow of wild flowers, then came to a dead end. They were forced to stop at the base of a gently rolling, tree-lined hill.

"Where are we? Why are we stopping?" She had certainly not expected this beautifully serene place. "Are we having a picnic lunch?"

"You'll see." He got out and held his left hand out to her. "Come on, let's take a look around."

Cassy slid out and stood beside him. "I don't understand."

What was he planning? Had he bought this property? Was he considering building here? It would be perfect for an apartment building or condominium complex. Judging from the sounds and the smell, the sea had to be close by. It was just the place that would appeal to his wealthy, high-profile clientele.

"Up ahead." He took her hand and guided her up the hill. "Careful," he said, cupping her elbow when her sandal slipped. Like him, she was dressed in navy cargo shorts and a sleeveless T-shirt, hers lavender, his white.

"What are you planning to build here—condos?"

Gordan smiled, but he did not answer. He continued on.

"Isn't Bradford coming?" she asked, looking back to where the older man was lounging against the hood of the car.

"Nope, just you and me." He gripped her waist when she slipped. "Did you hurt yourself?"

"I'm fine. But you're out of breath. We should not be climbing hills." She stopped to glare at him. "Must we go to the top of the hill? Why can't you tell me here?"

"Only a few . . . more yards."

"But, honey, you're winded."

After a few moments of slow, concentrated, deep breaths, he urged her forward. "It's not much further."

Cassy did not like it. But she could see by the set of his jaw that it was useless to argue with the man. He had something to show her and show her he would.

"What do you think?" he asked, once they had crested the hill.

"What a spectacular view! I can see the hotel and the pier from here."

She was gazing out over the water, deep blue meeting the azure sky. "I love it! How did you find it? It certainly will be a wonderful place to build apartments or a condominium complex."

As Gordan labored to catch his breath, he swallowed with difficulty. After a few moments, he said, "Do you love it enough to consider living here with me?"

She whirled around to face him. "In a condo? Of course."

"Cassy, I'm not talking about condos. I want to build a house here. I want it to be our home." He cupped her face. "A home where we can live and raise our child."

Cassy's eyes went wide. "What are you saying to me?"

"I'm asking you to marry me, Cassandra Mosley. I love you. And I'm not willing to risk losing you—not ever again."

She could not find her voice in that instant if her life depended on it. She stared up at him in total shock. He could not have surprised her more if he'd said he was selling his hotels and moving to China.

"Baby, I want you. I want to make a life here on this island with you. If not here, then anywhere in the world you choose." He paused to catch his breath before he went on to say, "Nothing is more important than your happiness and our being together—always. If you want to live in Oakland near your sister, then that can be arranged."

"Gordan . . ." She stopped abruptly. She did not trust her own ears—could not believe what she'd just heard. "Say that again . . . please."

"I'm asking you to be my wife."

"I don't understand. Are you saying you've suddenly changed your mind?" she whispered, not bothering to conceal her bewilderment, her doubts.

She had waited so long to hear those words. She's prayed for them. Now, suddenly, he was saying everything she wanted to hear. But, why? When she left the island she had given up all hope of marriage. Not until that horrible plane crash . . . The plane crash!

She nearly cried out in misery. This was not about love! It was about deep gratitude. How many times had he told her how much he appreciated her coming to him and seeing him through this ordeal?

Moving away, she turned her back so that he could not see her disappointment—her hurt. Could anything hurt her more?

"You've changed your mind." It was all she could manage to get past the tears lodged in her throat.

"Yes. I've been trying to tell you for a while—even before I left the hospital. But you always stopped me," he said, then stopped for a moment before he went on to say, "I was beginning to wonder if you've . . . decided against marriage?"

She should have seen it coming—expected it. The terrible accident had completely changed the course of their lives. She had given up all hope of more, while he had spent weeks in bed unable to do anything but think. But it was not about love. Cassy took a deep breath, desperately trying to clear her thoughts of emotions in order to make sense of all this.

"What caused you to change your mind?" she finally managed to ask.

"You did," he said, tightly, his left hand moving beneath the sling to his plastered arm, which had suddenly started to ache.

The pain was nothing compared to his growing fears. He had expected surprise, but not the hurt and disappointment he'd seen on her pretty face. He went to stand behind her.

"I had plenty of time to think while I waited near the wreckage of the plane. I tried not to think of the pain as I struggled to breathe or my inability to get help. I couldn't help John. I couldn't help myself. He had me worried. He was unconscious. Although we both were flung clear, I could still feel the heat of the fire. We were there for what seemed like an eternity. There was nothing to do but wait, pray, and think—reflect on my mistakes."

He hesitated a few moments before he went on to say, "There was that overwhelming sense of loss, pain, and emptiness deep inside that had been there since you left Martinique. I finally faced the truth." He hesitated for breath, then said, "You were gone from my life and there was nothing I could do about it. I knew that if I survived, I had to get you back." He took a deep breath, then added, "When I woke in the hospital, you were there. You had come to me—despite everything that had gone wrong between us. Your coming meant . . . everything to me."

Oh, she knew it meant everything to him—so much so,

that he was willing to give up his precious freedom to keep her. Cassy bit down hard on her bottom lip to hold back a sob as she struggled for control. She could have said she wanted him any way she could get him, but she did not. Suddenly she realized that wasn't true. She needed to know he wanted her to marry him because he loved her just as much as she loved him—not simply to bind her to him due to a misplaced sense of gratitude. It had to be about love or he would someday come to resent her and that she could not bear.

He said, "There is something about a man facing his own mortality that makes him realize what really matters. You're what matters to me." His arm went around her waist and he eased her back against him. Gordan's voice deepened when he said, "Baby, do you love me enough to be my wife—enough to give me that daughter I've been longing for, with your beautiful face and soft curls?" He kissed her nape. "Please."

Cassy sobbed, shaking with anguish. She had waited so long—so long. It had never occurred to her that those precious words could hurt her this way.

"Cassy?" Gordan gently clasped her shoulders.

"I can't," she whimpered. "Gratitude may be enough for you, but it's not enough for me. I don't want that kind of marriage."

He moved around her until he could look at her. Finally, he said in a hoarse whisper, "How can you say that? You know how I feel about you. How I have always felt about you."

"I thought I did," she said, wiping at her damp cheeks. She laughed, only the sound was filled with equal amounts of pain and bitterness. "Well, I got what I wanted. Only, I don't want it this badly. You don't have to marry me to keep me with you." She would have walked back down the hill if he had not caught her arm. "Let me go."

Gordan's face was taut with frustration when he said through his teeth, "Never again."

Looking down at the hand wrapped around her arm, she asked, "Do you plan on making me stay here?"

"I'm planning on doing whatever it takes to keep you in my life."

There was a prolonged silence as they stared at each other.

Cassy was the first to speak, "That was clear by that marriage proposal you didn't mean." She flung the angry words at him while trying to divert her face. She was furious about the tears that would not stop trickling down her face.

"Look at me!" When she refused, Gordan whispered throatily, "Please, baby. Just listen to me." The hand that held her arm began caressing her soft brown skin. Taking a deep breath, he said, "I meant every single word. I asked you to marry me for one reason and one reason alone. I am in love with you, Cassandra Mosley," he paused for breath, "and I won't stop asking you to be my wife, until you say yes."

Cassy looked at him then, but her eyes were so full of tears that she couldn't see him. "Gordan . . ." She nearly strangled on the word.

His left arm slid to her waist and he pulled her as close to his chest as his cast would allow. He gently kissed her temple.

"How can you doubt it? I started falling in love with you the first moment . . . I looked into your eyes that night you prepared that fabulous meal for my dinner guests." Gordan stopped, taking a breath, then said, "I fell a little more each time I saw you after that. It hasn't stopped, baby."

His lips brushed against her hair before he said, "I didn't

think I could love you more . . . then on your birthday you throw your gift back in my face. But I was wrong.''

"Gordan . . .''

"Let me finish. Why do you think it hurt so much when you made love with me on the boat and then demanded I let you go? It was as if what we did didn't mean to you what it meant to me.''

He didn't give her time to respond, but then, even if he had, he would not have received one because her face was buried against the base of his throat.

He whispered, "I'm grateful that you came to me after the crash and stayed, despite our estrangement. Even though you . . . thought I would never remarry, you still came. And you've . . . agreed to remain without marriage.''

Gordan tightened his arm even more around her. He said, huskily, "And it made me love you more—something that I did not believe possible.'' He stopped to catch his breath. "You're nothing like Evie. I have no idea why I treated you as if you were. I didn't even realize . . . that that was what I was doing until you pointed it out to . . . me on the terrace outside the jazz club. Do you remember that night, Cassy? You . . . were with Foster and I was furious.''

"Yes, I remember,'' she murmured, leaning into him, needing his support.

"It was wrong of me to compare the two of you, and I regret it. Evie has never understood . . . what love means. I let my experience . . . with her blind me for years. You changed all that for me, baby.'' He stopped, then said, after taking a deep breath, "You showed me what it means to love and be loved. I must have been . . . out of my mind to let you leave Atlanta without . . . talking this through. Maybe then I could have dealt with my fears about marriage. But, like a fool . . . I let you go, believing that you needed time to come around to my way of thinking.''

"It wasn't all your fault. I was also to blame. I should have been straightforward about wanting to get married someday. But, for years, I was caught up in establishing my career. By then, years had passed. And I was afraid to bring it up, because I knew how you felt. On my birthday I realized I had no choice but to tell you."

He chuckled. "I'm glad you didn't tell me early on. I would probably . . . still be running from the best thing that has ever come into my life."

Cassy pressed her mouth to his throat. "Gordan, I love you so much. But I want you to be sure this is what you want. I don't want you to ever be sorry."

"How could I be? I'll have you."

"Kiss me . . ."

He groaned, but eased back enough to look into her eyes. "No! I'm not letting you distract me this time. Will you marry me?"

"Yes, my love."

His deep sigh of relief resonated through his chest. "Thank you," he said, as he pressed his mouth against hers. "You'll never regret it. I promise."

Holding her close, he blinked back tears of profound joy. She had no idea how much her faith in him and willingness to forgive meant to him. But he intended to devote his life to making her happy.

Cassy could only hang on. She felt like a little girl on the merry-go-around. The knowledge that she loved and was loved in return made her so happy—more so than she could contain. When he first asked, all she could think of was that he had said nothing about love. How could she have forgotten, even for a second, how deeply they loved each other? It was what made all that they had been through worthwhile.

"If this property doesn't please you, then we can keep right on looking until we find it."

"No! I love it here. I can hardly wait!"

"Neither can I." He laughed heartily, then moaned in pain.

Cassy pulled back to study his face. "You're in pain. Why didn't you say something? Let's go back. We've been out too long as it is."

Gordan grumbled halfheartedly in protest, but she was right. He was quickly losing his strength, his shoulder and arm were throbbing, and he was tired. As they made their way down the hill at a much slower pace, it was Cassy's arms around his waist supporting him. When she realized that he was slipping, she yelled for Bradford to help.

Gordan didn't like it, but he didn't complain when Bradford helped him the rest of the way down and into the car.

"You okay?" Cassy was breathless as she scrambled in beside him. "Should we call the doctor."

"Sorry. I'm ... just ... a little tired ... Did ... too ... much," Gordan managed to get out, breathing with difficulty.

"Hush," she insisted. "Don't talk." She squeezed his hand, worry apparent on her small African features.

When he had caught his breath somewhat, he smiled at her. "No, doctor. I'm better. Come here." Once she was rested along his left side with his arm around her, he let out a sigh, "That's better." For a time, he simply held her close. Then he said, "Baby, we can be ... married just as ... soon as I can ... arrange it. I have dual ... citizenship, so there should be ... no problem with us getting married here ... on the island. How about next week ... in the hotel garden?"

"Next week?"

He grinned, glad to see that the fear had left her pretty face. "Too much time? Gee, I thought it would ... take your sister a week to close ... down the inn and ... get the family here." He stopped to breathe, then said, "Hmm, you think she can do it in a couple of days? That's even better. Then there's your . . . grandmother and aunt." He grinned. "And your dad and stepmother . . . and twin brothers."

Gordan barely managed to suppress a laugh at her outrage. He didn't have to wait long for her to erupt.

"A few days! Close the inn! Gordan, I can't plan a wedding in a week. A month isn't enough time."

"Okay, I just thought you would want your family here." He paused, "But, I can make arrangements for . . . a special license tomorrow. I'm sure we can . . . be married by Wednesday, at the latest."

"At least a month," she insisted.

He grinned, then gave her a brief kiss. He was more than a little frustrated because he could not deepen the kiss the way he craved. "It's not fast enough to suit me. But . . . I've waited four and a half years to . . . make you mine. One month is my limit."

"Oh, Gordan." Cassy tenderly placed a kiss on his lips before she said, "We've waited a long time to marry. But I'm not going to get married without both my family and yours being there. We're going to do this the right way."

He nodded. "We'll call them after dinner."

Cassy dropped her head. Her voice was filled with tears when she said, "My dad and my stepmother might be able to come. And my twin brothers. Maybe even Grandma and Aunt Rose." Her voice broke. It was a moment before she could go on. "Sarah won't be able to come. She can't just close down the inn. We have guests with upcoming reservations, as well as staff to consider. It's impossible."

"Nothing is impossible." He kissed her temple. "Call her. Tell her to cancel all . . . reservations for the next month. And re-book for . . . the following month. I'll send her a check . . . to cover the cost of the lost reservations and employee vacation . . . expenses. I'll also send a plane . . . to pick up your family and mine. I'll have Kenneth . . . start making the arrangements with the desk . . . for the rooms in the hotel for our guests."

Cassy gazed at him with a mixture of wonder and love. "You're willing to do all that to make me happy, aren't you?"

"That and so much more. You're my heart."

Her mouth was too warm and inviting for Gordan to resist. He took a kiss, only this time, he slid his tongue inside her mouth to sample her sweetness. Cassy was as breathless as he was when he stopped.

"Thank you, my love," she whispered, knowing she should be angry with him because of the kiss. But she didn't have the heart to scold.

When he could breathe evenly enough to speak, he said, "If you're happy, Cassy, then so am I. I'm not . . . going to give you reasons to regret this decision . . . not ever."

Chapter Twenty

It wasn't until later that evening that they were able to complete the calls to both sets of family members.

"Isn't this the most beautiful night you've ever seen?" Cassy asked, from where she stood on the balcony. Thick scented candles were on every available surface.

"That depends," Gordan said, from behind her. His left arm was around her waist, his hand spread against her midsection just below the fullness of her breasts. Her curvy bottom was nestled against his thighs.

Cassy tilted her head back so she could look at him from over her shoulder. "Depends on what?"

"How one defines beauty. I find you a lot more appealing than a few stars."

She laughed. "Tell me more, *Monsieur* Kramer."

Turning her until her breasts were pillowed on the left side of his chest, Gordan said, seductively, "I'd rather show you, *Mademoiselle*."

His mouth was hot and insistent on hers, his tongue

stroking hers as deeply and intimately as he would like to stroke her feminine center. When he eased back, he was out of breath.

"Oh, honey!"

"I'm fine," he whispered breathlessly, pressing her against the long, hard length of his shaft. There was no mistaking what he wanted. Judging by her husky feminine moan, nor was there any doubt what she also wanted. He moved her against his arousal.

"Gordan . . ." she whispered, breathlessly. "We should not be doing this."

"We should be doing more," he insisted, once he could breathe evenly. "Or haven't you noticed how much we need each other?" He paused, then said, "And don't tell me you don't want me. I can feel your pointy little nipples even through my shirt. Besides, you were making that sexy sound you make deep in your throat when you're fully aroused. Stop telling me no."

She stroked her fingertips over his bearded cheek, closing her eyes as she tried to shut out the erotic memories of his soft beard on her breasts, moving down her stomach to her . . .

"Cassy?"

"I know that you are—" she searched for the right word while easing her hips away from his "—ready. Please, try to be patient. We have no choice but to wait until your lung has healed."

"The problem area is a lot lower," he complained.

Cassy could not help laughing. At his scowl, she brushed his lips with hers. "I'm not laughing at you, but, my love, you know I want to make love with you, also. That has not changed—nor will it."

"It's been too long since I've been inside of you." His frustration was evident as he pressed his mouth against her throat, loving her feminine scent. He dropped his arm and took a long moment to slow his heart rate. "I like waking every morning and looking into your pretty eyes." He surprised her when he asked, "Have you been happy here with me these past few weeks, baby?"

"Oh, yes."

The pleasure he found reflected in the warm sparkle of her dark eyes satisfied him. She looked as if the stars were captured in her gaze.

"Have you been?"

"Without question."

"Gordan," she said, unable to hide the sudden anxiety in her voice.

He smoothed the soft crease in her brow. "What is it?"

"I want you to be sure. I don't want you to feel trapped or feel as if you have lost your freedom."

Gordan shook his head. "What I regret is the anguish and unhappiness I put us both through all these months. I get furious with myself when I remember how I let what happened between me and Evie affect what was happening between the two of us. That mistake nearly destroyed what we have."

"It's over," she soothed.

"It should have never happened. Your leaving showed me, as nothing else could, how deeply I valued you. I never want to go through it again."

"It was devastating trying to make you change when I realized I couldn't. I did what I felt I had to do," she said, quietly. "It hurt us both."

"I know, but it was never your fault. It was mine. The blame was never yours. And I hated when you started seeing Foster. You hit me where I was most vulnerable."

"But I didn't do it to hurt you. Besides, Adam was never more than a good friend."

He stroked her nape. "You didn't have to tell me that.

But I'm glad you did. I had no right to be jealous—but it didn't stop me."

"Adam came to see me—a week or so before the crash."

Gordan's mouth tightened. "I can't fault the man's taste in women. What did you tell him?"

Cassy smiled. "Thank you, but no. I had enough problems. I had no room in my heart for another man. Only you, my love."

He grinned. "Good." He dropped his head until he could touch her lips to his. "Sweet . . . so sweet."

Cassy fought the urge to deepen the kiss. "We can't . . ."

He frowned, saying, "I hate this."

Cassy studied him.

"What?"

"We should postpone the wedding," she said.

"No!"

"You can't tell me you won't be upset on our wedding night if we can't make love."

"Of course, I will—if that should happen. But it won't happen. Come with me and I'll show you." There was no mistaking the determined glint in his eyes.

"Will you be serious? What if we can't make love for another two or three months, like the doctor warned us. You know as well as I do that he said it could take as long as six months before your lung is completely healed. Look what happened today." She caressed his face. "We should consider putting the wedding off until you're completely better."

"Hell no!" he scowled. "We are going to . . ."

"I don't mind waiting until you are better. But you're . . ." She let her voice trail away.

"I'm what?"

"Stubborn! And I think you will be furious with yourself if we have to wait a while. It might be easier if I go home for a few months."

"Absolutely not!"

She glared up at him while he glared down at her.

"Why are you being so unreasonable about this?" she demanded.

"If you must go back to California for a few months, I'll be sitting next to you on the plane. We're done with being apart. Got that?"

Cassy nodded. "But I only thought. . . ."

He brushed his lips against hers again and again. When he groaned and would have deepened the kiss, she pulled back, dropping her head on his shoulder.

"The wedding has been set for the twenty-fifth. I will be there. Will you?"

"I will. Oh, Gordan. I'm not trying to make you angry. It's just that I don't want you disappointed in any way on that day—our wedding day."

"You didn't have to explain. Baby, I know you're concerned about me."

Cassy watched as Gordan began blowing out all the candles. Then, he grasped her hand and pulled her along with him. She didn't bother to ask where they were going. She knew by the time they'd reached the living room.

She considered pulling away from him but quickly dismissed the thought, not wanting to put any strain on his injuries. Gordan did not slow down until they were in the bedroom with the door closed.

"Gor. . . ."

Cassy could not say more because her lips were crushed beneath his. He licked them before his tongue slid between their cushiony softness, inside to her sweet bounty, and lightly caressed her.

Cassy moaned, feeling her knees weaken, but she did nothing to resist him. His hot caress was intensely provocative before he pulled back. Although her heart was racing in sweet anticipation, when she looked at him, worry immediately replaced desire.

His lungs had suffered because of a few moments' loss of control. He was fighting for each new breath.

Her arms immediately went around him, even though she was furious with him. She wanted to shake some sense into him while hot tears raced down her cheeks.

"You know better. Weren't we just talking about this?"

"I'm ... fine. Give ... me ... a ... second."

When he had caught his breath somewhat, she helped him to the side of the bed.

"Sit here." He indicated his lap. When she shook her head no, he persisted, "Please."

"Behave," she scolded him. "Do you need help?"

Her hands went to the small buttons lining the dress shirt that had been bought several sizes larger to accommodate the cast. When her fingers reached his waist, his hand went behind her and unzipped her purple dress, then pushed it off each shoulder in turn.

He watched with satisfaction as it clung to her shapely hips. A gentle tug sent the garment to the floor. She stood in lavender, lace-edged panties and bra.

"Please," he whispered, indicating the bra.

Cassy hesitated, studying his eyes. It was the first time she had actually undressed in front of him since his return from the hospital. Although they slept together, she took care to dress and undress in the privacy of his dressing room.

"I want to ... look at you. Hold you ... against me, tonight ... baby." He paused for breath. "Nothing more."

"Promise?"

"Yes."

Their eyes locked in understanding. He was seated with his muscular thighs apart. His arousal was unmistakable.

She slowly unhooked the clasp and let the garment drop to the carpet.

"Don't stop there," he said, throatily.

Cassy's hands were unsteady as they dropped to her hips. She eased her fingers beneath the lace and eased the panties down until she could step free of them.

She could feel the heat of his gaze moving over her. He lingered on her breasts, caressing their fullness, then he practically scorched her skin with a hot path down her ribcage to her waist, then lower. She closed her eyes, yet felt the heat of his eyes on her feminine mound.

"You're so beautiful," he whispered. "Thank you. It's so good . . . to see you like this. Nothing concealed . . . no secrets." He caressed her with the deep tone of his voice. "Baby, I wish I . . . could show you how important you are to me . . . how much I love you," he said, quietly.

Cassy smiled at him, her eyes brimming with love. "I know, but not tonight, soon." She went to him, pressing her lips against his throat. "I love you."

He groaned, and would have pulled her onto his lap, but she eluded him. She removed the sling carefully to support his arm and let it rest in his lap before she worked his shirt off.

"I will be so glad to get . . . this thing is off."

Holding his injured arm, he rose to his feet so that she could unhook and unzip his slacks. After he had stepped out of them and his briefs, Cassy eyed his tall, dark frame. She smiled at him.

"Only a few more weeks." She briefly stroked his chest and pressed her lips to the puckered scar were he'd had surgery, but she did not linger.

"Cassy . . ." he moaned. Then Gordan laid back against the pillows.

"Need this?" she asked, holding up the sling.

He nodded and accepted her help. She smoothed his

frown by kissing his bearded cheek and brushing her mouth briefly with his.

"I can't wait to be your wife."

"I can't either," he said, curling a strong left arm around her waist and pulling her down beside him. Pressing his open mouth against her throat, he said, "I'll never give you a reason . . . to regret marrying me." Stroking a hand down her spine, he murmured throatily, "I want you to look in the top drawer of the dresser . . . on the right-hand side."

"Now?"

"Now."

As she crossed the room, she was aware of his eyes on her back. She decided then and there that she adored the feel of his warm gaze on her bare skin.

"The velvet case. Bring it to me, please."

"Honey, what have you done?"

He chuckled. "You'll never know until you bring it here."

Once she was settled against his side, he flipped the lid open.

Cassy gasped. Inside the satin-lined box were the brilliant amethyst and diamond lever-back earrings he had given her for her birthday. There was also a matching bracelet and two rings.

He lifted the rings and held them on his wide palm. "Do you like them?" he asked, softly. "The engagement ring has exactly . . . four and a half carats to symbolize each year we have loved each other."

The center princess-cut amethyst was surrounded by a double tiered row of marquise-shaped diamonds. The wedding band was channel set with alternating rows of amethysts and diamonds. Like the earrings and the bracelet, they were set in platinum.

"Oh!" she whispered, blinking back tears. Cassy watched

as Gordan slid the engagement ring on her left hand before he placed a kiss in the center of her palm.

She threw her arms around his neck and kissed him. "I've never seen anything so lovely. Thank you."

He quirked a dark brow. "The earrings should look familiar. They're the ones you threw at me on your birthday."

Flirting with him through the thickness of her lashes, she asked, "Should I apologize?"

He chuckled. "I deserved it. Put them on. I've waited a long time to see you in them." But, before she could move, he snapped the matching bracelet around her wrist. "Now, model for me."

Cassy complied, jumping up and walking around the foot of the bed, turning her head from side to side while holding out her hand. "What do you think, my love?"

"I think I'm lucky to have you. You are breathtaking."

They pulled the comforter back and cuddled together beneath it. Cassy snuggled with her head on his left shoulder, her legs between his. The room was plunged into darkness, the only light coming from the moonlight through the sheer curtains at the wide window.

"Tired?" he asked, close to her ear.

"Too excited to sleep. How about you?"

"I'm excited all right. I just can't do a thing about it." His long-fingered hand caressed down her back to her soft bottom. "Cassy . . ."

He kissed his way down her throat to the swells of her breasts. He laved her cleavage, then he stopped and just held her. His heart raced and his breath was quick.

"I have nerve enough to have an erection . . . but I can't do a thing about it." Then he whispered into her ear, and told her in vivid details how he would like to make love to her.

"Soon," she moaned. "It will be more than worth the wait, don't you think?"

"As long as you're wearing my rings and have my name . . . I can wait. The loving is not just the lovemaking." He paused for breath. "You're all that matters to me. If I lost everything . . . tomorrow it would be okay, as long as I have you. I need you, Cassy."

"I need you, too, my love. In spite of what we had to go through to find each other again, it's wonderful. I'm glad it happened the way it did. It makes our love so special—worth holding on to."

"There was never a time when I didn't want you . . . with me, baby. It was why I first suggested . . . we live together. I was fed up with those lengthy separations."

"I hated them, too."

"Are you going to miss your work at the inn?"

"Yes, but not nearly as much as I would miss being with you. If I get bored with being a housewife, I can always open a pastry shop in one of the hotels."

"Mmm. Or you can always take over Jillian's job. It's available."

"What do you mean? Surely, you haven't fired the multi-talented Jillian?"

"I'm going to offer her a promotion. We'll need a hotel manager for the South African resort. Jillian is more than qualified."

"South Africa, hmm. You think it's far enough away?" She laughed.

"I hope so. She made the mistake of making a play for me. She won't . . . get another opportunity to come between us."

"I appreciate that. Although, how can I blame another woman for being attracted to you?" Cassy caressed his mid-section. "You're so wonderfully sexy."

He chuckled. "I'm glad you think so."

Then she said, seriously, "Are you sure you have time for a wife? I don't want to have to make an appointment to see my own husband."

"If I've learned nothing else through all of this, I've learned that life is too short to waste. It's Wil's turn to travel. That way . . . we can divide our time between Atlanta and Martinique. And, if it's absolutely necessary . . . for me to travel, I'd like you to be with me."

"And a baby?" she whispered.

He laughed, giving her a squeeze. "As soon as we can . . . manage it. I love you, Cassy."

"I love you, Gordan."

They talked late into the night, making plans for their future filled with love.

Epilogue

Cassy and Gordan were married in a sunrise ceremony on the hill where he had proposed to her and where they planned to build their home. They were surrounded by their families and friends. Wil and Gordy stood up with Gordan. Cassy wore a flowing, long, white chiffon dress, edged with lace, and violets in her hair. Her niece, Mandy, was the flower girl, in a frilly lavender dress, and her sister, Sarah, in a lavender chiffon dress with baby Kurt in her arms, was her matron of honor.

And when the minister asked who gives this woman, her entire family, including her grandmother, aunt, father, stepmother, twin brothers, and brother-in-law gave her to Gordan with declarations of love. They all cheered when Gordan kissed his new wife.

They had planned a candlelit wedding reception at the hotel's ballroom that evening, complete with a local band and steel drums, for their guests enjoyment. It was after midnight before the bride and groom managed to slip away.

Although Gordan's cast had been removed, he was still in physical therapy, so they decided to postpone their honeymoon until he was fully recovered.

Cassy woke in her husband's arms to the most incredible daybreak. They had spent what was left of their first night as man and wife cuddled in a cozy sleeping bag on their hill. They had talked and kissed until dawn.

Two months later, they traveled to New Orleans while their house was being built. Eight and a half months later, their twin daughters put in an early appearance while their parents were visiting with family at the Parkside Garden Inn in Oakland, California.

Dear Reader,

I would like to thank you for all your kind letters and cards, as well as your support over the years.

When I first wrote "Mama's Pearl" which was a part of the anthology A MOTHER'S LOVE, I was deeply affected by the close and loving bond the two sisters (Sarah Mosley-Dean and Cassandra Mosley) shared. It was a difficult story to write because I lost my own sister, Mary Alice Suggs. I knew that I would eventually tell Cassy's story. ISLAND MAGIC is that story. I hope you enjoy it.

I have recently moved back to my hometown, please take note of the new address: P.O. Box 944, Saginaw, MI 48606. If you would like a response, please include a self-addressed legal-size stamped envelope. Or check out my web site: *www.tlt.com/authors/bford.htm*

Best Wishes
Bette Ford

ABOUT THE AUTHOR

Bette Ford grew up in Saginaw, Michigan, and graduated from Saginaw High School. She obtained her bachelor's degree from Central State University in Wilberforce, Ohio. Bette began her teaching career in Detroit and completed her master's degree from Wayne State University. She has taught for the Detroit Public Schools HeadStart program for many years. She is currently writing full time.

Her books are FOR ALWAYS, FOREVER AFTER, ALL THE LOVE, novella MAMA'S PEARL a part of anthology A MOTHER'S LOVE, AFTER DARK, ONE OF A KIND and ISLAND MAGIC.

Coming in August from Arabesque Books . . .

__THE BUSINESS OF LOVE by Angela Winters
1-58314-150-2 $5.99US/$7.99CAN

The heir to a hotel chain, Maya Woodson is determined to make her plan to go public a success—even is she *is* at odds with handsome Trajan Matthews, the investment expert who's overseeing the deal. But when a crime endangers the chain's future—and their careers—Maya and Trajan must discover what they cherish most . . . if they are to find a love-filled future.

__FIRST LOVE by Cheryl Faye
1-58314-117-0 $5.99US/$7.99CAN

When shy Lena Caldwell and Quincy Taylor strike up a friendship, it isn't long before a sweetly sensual fire is sparked. But as their attraction grows, Quincy's past mistakes inject doubt into their newfound romance and the two must confront their insecurities to find a love worth fighting for.

__SOULFUL SERENADE by Linda Hudson-Smith
1-58314-140-5 $5.99US/$7.99CAN

Hillary Houston has it all—personality, looks, talent, and now, sexy engineer Brandon Blair. But when Hillary is offered the chance to become a recording superstar, Brandon's threatened with the possibility of losing the woman of his dreams . . . unless he can find a way to keep her forever.

__ADMISSION OF LOVE by Niobia Bryant
1-58314-164-2 $5.99US/$7.99CAN

When supermodel Chloe Bolton settles down in her mother's rural South Carolina town, she is at instant odds with handsome, reserved Devon Jamison. But amid hidden hurt and unexpected romantic rivals, Devon and Chloe begin to discover what they both really desire—to gain the dream they want most and have always waited for . . .

THESE ARABESQUE ROMANCES
ARE NOW MOVIES FROM BET!

__*Incognito* by Francis Ray
   1-58314-055-7   **$5.99**US/**$7.99**CAN

__*A Private Affair* by Donna Hill
   1-58314-078-6   **$5.99**US/**$7.99**CAN

__*Intimate Betrayal* by Donna Hill
   0-58314-060-3   **$5.99**US/**$7.99**CAN

__*Rhapsody* by Felicia Mason
   0-58314-063-8   **$5.99**US/**$7.99**CAN

__*After All* by Lynn Emery
   0-58314-062-X   **$5.99**US/**$7.99**CAN

__*Rendezvous* by Bridget Anderson
   0-58314-061-1   **$5.99**US/**$7.99**CAN

__*Midnight Blue* by Monica Jackson
   0-58314-079-4   **$5.99**US/**$7.99**CAN

__*Playing with Fire* by Dianne Mayhew
   0-58314-080-8   **$5.99**US/**$7.99**CAN

__*Hidden Blessings* by Jacquelin Thomas
   0-58314-081-6   **$5.99**US/**$7.99**CAN

__*Masquerade* (in *Love Letters*) by Donna Hill
   0-7860-0366-9   **$5.99**US/**$7.99**CAN

More Arabesque Romances by
Monica Jackson

__HEARTS DESIRE

0-7860-0532-7 $4.99US/$6.50CAN

When Kara Kincaid realizes a prominent Senator is her deadbeat dad, she swears revenge. But her goal is sidelined when an unexpected passion with his assistant, Brent Stevens, draws her into a brutal game of desperate secrets, lies, schemes . . . and love.

__LOVE'S CELEBRATION

0-7860-0603-X $4.99US/$6.50CAN

Teddi Henderson was devastated when her husband J.T. walked out on her and their child with no explanation. Two years later, he returns with a story straight out of the movies—he's a government agent and they are all in danger. But can Teddi trust him again with her life . . . and her heart?

__A MAGICAL MOMENT

1-58314-021-2 $4.99US/$6.50CAN

Atlanta lawyer Taylor Cates is so fiercely dedicated to her work at a battered women's shelter that she'll even risk her life for it. Private Detective Stone Emerson must uncover the truth in order to save her, but first he must convince her to believe in him—and to believe in their smoldering heat.

__THE LOOK OF LOVE

1-58314-069-7 $4.99US/$6.50CAN

When busy single mother Carmel Matthews meets handsome plastic surgeon Steve Reynolds, he sets her pulse racing like never before. But he and Carmel will have to confront their deepest doubts and fears, if they are to have a love that promises all they've ever desired . . .